BARNES COUNTY

BARNES COUNTY

A Novel

Damon Garr

SATORIWORKS

DEDICATION

To the memory of Chief Deputy Sheriff Joann Barnes, killed in the line of duty on December 10, 2002.

Though Terry Stegman did not know that she was about to die, her heart pounded in her chest harder than she wanted to admit. Surely it was due to the speed at which her cruiser traveled the narrow gravel road, gliding just on the surface of the stones. Any animal, a thin little whitetail, a possum, or a mangy dog, that dared to step into the road would die. She would not swerve. If another vehicle approached from the other direction, just over the next blind hill, the outcome was certain. This danger elevated her heart rate but, in her mind, she held the images of two dead bodies.

Deputy Stegman had worked for the Sheriff's Department for nearly ten years and had many occasions to see the dead. Auto accidents were common on the winding blacktop highways of Barnes County, Missouri. The elderly die alone at home. Farm accidents, men gored by bulls. She had never been early on the scene of a double murder. A young couple, meth-addicts most likely, but a young couple just the same, were each shot several times and beaten as well. It did not horrify her, nor did it sadden her. She had her own experience with the sadness of death for perspective. The violence of it left her feeling stunned. Now, here she was, speeding these back roads to the home of the suspect.

At least Bill was right behind her. County Sheriff for what must have been twenty years, he had saved her, given her purpose after her husband's death. He had leaned his long arms across the cattle gate and told her that her sense of justice would make her a natural.

"What makes you say that?" She was lining a trough with sweet grain.

"You want to set things right. You always knew how to keep Bob from going too far."

"He knew how to conduct business."

"A powerful man can lose sight of right and wrong. I expect he had some help keeping hold of how things should be done."

On Sunday mornings, Terry and Bob used to have breakfast at a place called Lou's in the nearest town, the nearest thing that amounted to more than a dot on a map or the crossing of two state highways. It had been a time they set aside to be together, away from the responsibility of the farm, the phone calls from Bob's lawyer or various realtors. All of that could wait.

They could have been going to church. They probably should have. Around every corner, there seemed to be tucked a little white Baptist church, so many in fact that no one likely knew that there wasn't a one they had set foot in since the day they were married. Asking someone what church they went to was a common question when getting to know someone, right up there with 'Do you think we're gonna get some rain?' A question by itself that irritated Terry because next they'd ask when you thought the rain'd let up. She'd usually answer the church question by saying she'd go to any church that had a preacher worth her respect. To the other question, she'd say 'eventually.'

They never were alone at Lou's, but you got a seat and a handful of folks to joke with. It was something that Terry looked forward to. When, on a Sunday morning, Bob turned left out of the driveway instead of the customary right, she spoke up, "Where the hell do you think you're taking me?"

"I wanted to go to the diner in Sheridan."

She stared him down.

"Stop it," he slapped her knee. "We always go to Lou's. I thought we need a change."

"If you want change…," I'll give you change, she thought the rest of the sentence to herself. There was always something more to her husband than what appeared on the surface. She knew him well, knew what to expect of him. Part of what she knew was that she would never fully understand him. He wasn't the sort of person to display himself fully. She could speculate on what kept him from opening up to her, but it didn't concern Terry. He was who he was, and she loved him.

Sheridan was the county seat and the hub of all activity in Barnes

County. The diner was on the main square, across from the county courthouse.

They had no sooner walked into the diner than he stopped at the table of real estate agent Jan Snell, putting his fist calmly but firmly on the table. Terry watched, waiting to intervene as Jan looked up to him, and Bob spoke.

"You're not about to sell that Parker place to some out-of-towner, are you?"

"Now, Bob, that's not up to me."

"Aw, don't tell me that."

"You can always make a higher offer."

"What if I just make a better offer?" There was an emphasis there that Terry didn't know how to take.

"I'll give the Parkers any offer presented."

"Well," he leaned closer to Jan, "maybe this part of the offer won't be on the contract."

Jan stared at Bob for a minute, her already slack jaw agape, a too-thinly plucked eyebrow raised. Terry moved in.

"Alright, that's enough. No business on Sunday. Good to see you, Jan." She pushed Bob to a booth in the back.

Terry watched him as he sat and began looking over the menu, not saying a word. She didn't want to be, but she was mad. Mad that he used their morning together for business, and maybe mad because what he'd been suggesting to the realtor didn't sound right.

"This is bullshit." She kept her voice down.

Bob looked up and around quickly as if he'd missed something.

"We always go to Lou's," she mocked. "You came because you knew she was going to be here."

"We had some things to talk about."

"What are you trying to bully her into?"

"Some guy from Pittsburgh's coming in and gonna buy the Parker place. That's four hundred fifty acres."

"We don't need it. Not on the other side of Sheridan."

"No, but we could lease it out. I know Pfenning's looking for more acres for his cattle."

"Then put in an offer."

"They'll only take the asking price. Besides, who knows what this

Summers guy's gonna do with the place? Maybe he wants to put up another Wal-Mart."

"Summers. Like the Summers that lived down H by the concrete place?"

"I think I heard it might be a relation."

"Bob. We own some of the property used to belong to the Summers. Besides, if he's gonna pay what they're asking, then he wins."

He had a pained look as if she'd struck him. "Don't say it like that."

"You can't try to bribe or extort Jan on some other deal, alright?"

He shook his head.

"Alright."

Bob rubbed his hand over the bald top of his scalp. "Fine."

She nodded at him. "Maybe I'll have some pancakes today."

"That'd be a change." It was what she always ordered.

Remembering this, she made way for the black cows nosing their way into the bin and looked at the sheriff leaning lazily with his chin on his hands, the black cap on his head with its six-pointed star commanding authority. "He didn't need a woman to keep him in line."

"Besides, I see how you handle things."

He was referring to her handling of her husband's death, but he didn't know the full story. He didn't know how she had spent that night. All anyone knew was that she was a hard-working and determined woman who was not going to sit around moping to herself, even if her much-loved and well-respected husband died of a cancer that turned him from a strong, proud man to a thin invalid in six months. Started deep inside, and took him before she could even accept that he had taken ill.

What choice did she have, really? They had a large farm that needed her, though most of the work was handled by an able farmhand. A handsome young farmhand. Still, it had to be managed. There were his affairs to put in order. A million different and suspect business dealings that needed to be settled, a new order to be established.

It had been a year and a half and things were settled, at least Bob's dealings, and what had she to do now?

Bill stood straight, glanced back to the road, his cruiser parked in the shade next to the barn. "And you know these guys I got working for me? The Parker kid? I need someone to show them what working hard really is."

"I'll give it some thought, Bill." She had known it was as good as a yes. It would give her enough time to accept it before consenting.

Over nine years she'd been doing it now. And except for one man, a hell of a man, a deputy she recruited herself, she was still the only deputy worth a damn. Despite that, she loved it. Even loved the adrenaline that came from listening to the engine of the Crown Victoria at high RPMs and the dense trees and shrubs whipping by her in a blur.

The car slid a little as she braked on approaching the Jiles place. She hoped that Bill wasn't too close behind. All that dust would have made him drop back a lot. Otherwise, he wouldn't have been able to see the road. She turned on a narrow drive, a long stripe of green between dirt ruts, scanning the scene as she approached the house.

It was a small, low house that backed against the woods. Shingles were missing from the roof, and the eaves were rotting. Signs of neglect were obvious, though not much worse than most houses in the area. One car sat up close to the house, but it did not belong to the suspect.

"Two-twenty-one," she called on the radio. "Ten-twenty-three. Suspect's vehicle is not here."

"Ten-four, two-twenty-one," the radio barked back.

Terry stepped from the car as Bill pulled up to the house. She saw him speaking into the radio, his voice coming from far away on the radio in her car.

When he approached her, Terry spoke in a whisper. "Looks like somebody's here, at least."

"Let's see what they know."

They turned and walked up to the door.

It was early March, and a ceiling of gray sky hung low overhead. All the snow had melted during a warm spell, the mud season was coming, but now it was turning cold. Just enough now that Terry could see her breath. It was the sort of cold that was unsettling, but not the type to make your bones shake.

Terry was not thin, but somehow the cold managed a way to get under her skin, to make her body shudder. As she had stood at Bob's funeral, her sadness was set aside as she battled the ache in her hip, trying to keep herself from shaking. It seemed like half the county was there, and Terry owed it to Bob's memory that everyone saw her grieving properly. All she wanted was to dash back to the big black car, to the warmth that would soften her skin, where she could cry in peace.

Her mother was there. Her mother, who had probably not stepped further outside than the porch boards of that old house in twenty years or more. She stood close to Terry in the biting cold, often leaning for support. When Terry felt close to passing out from the cold, shuddering, the preacher's voice fading off into the crystallized air, Virginia McIlheny, the matron of the family, took her gloved hand in hers. Terry let out a gasp that sounded like a sob. Heads turned, then bowed.

Her mother was not one for affection. While some of the women in the family were soft, following a womanly instinct, Virginia had taken after or, better said. she adored, worshipped, and prayed in the church of her own mother, a woman widowed early by a man whose actions brought him his just rewards, a woman who saw things go bad and thought the only way to persevere was to lock up her heart in a box and bury it beneath the potatoes in the root cellar.

Terry had taken the gesture, a simple squeezed hand, as affection when it happened. She had been stunned in her grief into thinking that her mother had reached out to her to comfort her. Later, on one of Terry's rare visits to the south of the county, to the house where she had spent her youth, when she was still in a period of sensitivity, of wanting to believe the best of people, she learned the truth.

Her mother was old and stooped, but she could not be called frail. A tree bent and beaten by the wind, but still standing. The gesture, Terry thought, might be a new opening to their relationship. Her grief left her with few places to turn, and a couple of weeks after the funeral, she found herself in her mother's living room.

There was a lack of color about the house and the living room. Virginia operated the house from the room, either from a wingback that looked out the front windows or from a table she used as a desk. Terry watched as Virginia leaned close to the table, making notes in her ledger. They still ran a small farm on the property, maybe thirty head of cattle, and they leased the rest of the acreage. It once had been a great enterprise, legend had it, but now Terry thought it was so meager as to be depressing.

They were having bits of broken conversation while Virginia worked. When they had fallen into another sinkhole of silence, Terry sought their rescue by stammering, "I wanted to thank you."

Virginia held up a finger as she scribbled. When she looked up, she let down the finger, allowing Terry to continue.

"I just thought that was nice of you to take my hand."

"Someone had to help you keep it together."

"I—what do you mean?"

"He may be dead, dear, but you can't let folks see you fallin' apart."

"Wait. You took my hand because you thought I was gonna make a scene? I thought you were being nice." Her voice was raised.

Virginia laughed. "Honey. We are proud women in this family. We don't go acting like it's the end of the world, just because a man dies. People see you falling to pieces, they'll think you've gone soft, and they'll walk on you."

Maybe Virginia was right. Maybe this had set Terry on the course she followed after Bob's death. Maybe this was why she set out to prove she didn't need a man. Or maybe this moment proved to Terry that there was no love in the world without Bob. There was nothing to be gained by allowing emotion into life.

She knocked on the front door. Bill stood behind her. She knew that he'd be watching the sides of the house and listening for movement from inside and out.

A woman opened the door, just enough for her face to be seen. She was mid-to-late twenties, meth-thin, hair dyed blond.

Terry tried to read her, but what appeared as nervousness might easily have been the effects of methamphetamine.

"You seen Jimmy?" She sought to calm her with her tone, with casualness. It was easy to put on an authoritative professional tone. Save that for intimidating speeders or people you're about to arrest. When you want information from someone, be their friend.

The woman shook her head quickly and spoke. "No, I ain't--."

Suddenly, Terry heard the quick ping-ping of a twenty-two being fired, saw the wood splintering the door as the bullets penetrated it, and she felt a thump in her chest. The bullet that went into her vest knocked the wind from her, and she stumbled back from the front steps, pulling the gun from her holster. Before she could raise her gun, she was hit in the head and fell to the ground.

She was still conscious, hearing the faraway sounds of a gunfight. She saw only gray, the low sky like a dirty shirt hanging over her. Dying, there was little doubt. The word wasn't there, though, nor the concept. She saw only the word end, physical like a dead-end alley, like a lizard's tail cut off. She was falling, sinking. Slowing down. It felt to her like nodding off while trying to watch the final minutes of a movie. You just want to keep your eyes open, but sleep keeps taking you. Only it wasn't sleep. It was a precipice from which there would be no return.

She began to lose herself in a high ringing like a whistle. Like the kettle when Bob had wandered off, leaving the water to boil on the stove.

"You want I should get that for you?" She sat at the kitchen table with her coffee, Sheridan Times unfolded in front of her. The whistle rattled in her head. "What the fuck?"

Grudgingly, she got up from her chair, pausing to look out of the kitchen window at the expanse of pasture outside, a handful of black cows milling about in a haze of morning fog. She brewed Bob's tea, dipping the bag in and out of the steaming water, watching it turn dark. She added a bit of honey, refreshed her coffee, and took both cups with her.

"Where are you, you ol' bastard?" Terry saw him standing just outside the long morning shadow of the barn. He stood still, his solid frame, studying the landscape. She took his tea to him, handed it over without a word, and took up the same stance as him. The haze was rising, burning off, making the subtle roll of the pastures shimmer gold, a fancy carpet maybe, or the floating transparency she felt in dreams.

Bob reached, pulled her to his side, and kissed her hand.

2

The old dog circled the back door, claws clacking on the linoleum, a heavy pant with a hint of whine. Sam put on his hat and looked at the golden retriever. "Come on, old man." He opened the door, the dog bursting free and leaping to the ground before lifting his leg on a dead spot in the grass. Sam was younger than the dog, in dog years, but he didn't move with as much energy. His movements were always very deliberate, but today they were slow.

He walked with the dog down the slope from the house, passing through a gate, down to the feed bin. With a work-booted foot, he kicked at the feed, grown heavy and clumped. Two old cows began sauntering up towards the open holding pen. "Here they come, boy." He moved away from the bin to give the ladies some room, and the dog followed.

Just outside the fence for the holding pen was a weathered stump, Sam's vantage point for surveying his pastures. With his dog by his side, he would sit here in the dusk before dawn, thinking about his day to come and, sometimes when the air had the same light at the end of the day, he would reflect on the day's progress. After they first moved here, he took great pleasure in this spot, in these moments. He had retired and was free to live at his own pace. Then things changed. And now they had changed again.

The brisk air made his eyes water and he stood. Bill was going to be released from the hospital today, and Sam had better make sure things were in order in the office. He leaned and grabbed the dog roughly by the scruff. "Enough lollygagging, old man."

The two days since Terry's death had been a challenge for Sam, requiring him to fill in for her as well as Bill. Sam's wife, Natalie, was far from happy, especially after what happened.

"I thought you retired." She had confronted him like this before. The day before, he had been unloading groceries from the car for her. He had just mentioned that he was going to go out in the evening to serve a warrant.

"Come on. Who else is going to do it?"

"We came here to get away from all of that." She talked loudly with her head in the refrigerator.

"And we did. This isn't Pittsburgh, is it?"

"Don't talk down to me." It was only a hint of how mad she probably was about all of this.

"I'm not. I'm just saying we left there, I left the Police Department, and we got away from the situation there. And it's not the same thing here."

"No, Sam. We left Pittsburgh to live a more relaxing life. For you to retire, raise cattle and nap in the afternoon."

He set a handful of bags on the counter. Not sure what he could say next that might appease her, that might move the peace process forward. Basically, she was right. It was supposed to have been a leisurely life that they were moving to. And he did regret it some.

"How long did we live like that, Sam? A year. About one year."

It was only a year, but then it had been alright still because it had been part-time, the deputy thing. But now things were different. He'd practically slept in his uniform the past two days since Terry was killed and Bill, the sheriff, was shot. That uniform had been on since he'd put it on that afternoon, hearing that first call come across the scanner of a possible double murder. No one else knew what to do in their absence. He had to make sure things got done.

Sam went to where Natalie stood in front of the pantry and took her in his arms. "I will be careful. I am not going to get myself killed."

She pounded a fist against his chest as she began to cry. "Don't you say that. She didn't get herself killed. She didn't. You would have done the same thing she did. If it had been you, you'd be dead, too." She pushed away from him and went up the stairs.

He put the rest of the groceries away by himself.

She was still sleeping when he came back in with the dog, but she stirred when he put on the heavy, creaking leather belt. What a beauty, he thought. And he was making her miserable, making her worry. He wanted to believe that she was wrong to worry, but he wasn't so certain of his safety, not so certain that procedure would save his life.

"Don't sleep all day." He kissed her forehead.

"Hmm," she settled into her pillow. "I will if I want to."

And she would. She had taken to this retirement thing wholeheartedly. She'd never been much for holding down a job as it was.

She had been a receptionist at a downtown Pittsburgh high-rise when they met. Sam and his partner had been called in because her company was having some trouble with a terminated employee.

"Lucky bastard. I don't know what he's throwing a fit about," she had said, pointing towards a desk where a man was tossing files and office supplies over his shoulder, cursing people by name.

They stood by as the man gathered his things, and then they escorted him downstairs and out the front door. Sam then volunteered to go back up to the office to tell her what to do if the man returned. When he spoke to her again, Sam asked her out.

It was 1973 and he'd taken the job on the Pittsburgh Police Department after returning from Vietnam. He'd been an MP and it just seemed the natural course. His other option was a bit more terminal.

"Why not the steel mills?" She asked as they sat in a booth in a dingy restaurant in the college district. He had told about his family's preference for employment in the steel mills up the Ohio.

"That would have been the easy thing to do," Sam said. "My brother took the job there because our father worked there. And he got the job because his brother worked there. But it was also a job of last resort." He paused for a moment to consider his talkativeness, then continued. "He only did it because he'd given up on what he wanted to do. It was a fallback for him; why would it be the first thing on my list?"

"What did he do before?" She leaned to him across the booth, apparently interested in what he was saying.

Sam, though, wasn't quite so eager to answer. He felt a little ashamed to admit what he was about to. It seemed so small.

"He was a farmer. We come from Missouri, from a long line of farmers. A big family farm that he lost to the bank. He inherited it from his father, who had inherited it from his. The bank took it away, so we wound up here, living in my uncle's house."

"Farmers? Really? My family, too."

"No kidding?" He was happy to turn the subject away. He realized that he was getting a little angry about the whole thing.

"From here in Pennsylvania. Beaver County. A beautiful place. Big red barn. Horses. Milk cows. The whole thing."

"That's great."

"I go back up there every weekend. It's a good change from being here all the time."

Thinking of his own life, his new life, patrolling the grimy, soot-covered streets of Pittsburgh and returning at night to a crowded house, pushed into a hillside, looking like it was barely hanging on, a house shared with his uncle, his father, his parents, his brother, he responded, "I bet."

"You ever think of going back to Missouri?"

"Maybe someday," he turned to look at the growing crowd standing by the bar. "Maybe someday."

The Jiles place was on his way to Sheridan. His route consisted mostly of the little gravel roads. A mile and a half straight along one until the T, then a right, then the next left, and it went straight until it began to follow a creek, and on like this until he passed the Jiles place. Eventually, he would end up on a two-lane blacktop that would take him to town.

He slowed on the approach, and he began to remember. He had turned the car nearly sideways on the road trying to brake and make the turn that day. But, no. This time, he accelerated. He wasn't going to remember today.

The sheriff's office was in the basement of the county courthouse. It was a red brick building, like an old schoolhouse. It was one of the oldest buildings still standing in Sheridan. He couldn't imagine what it must have cost when it was built, or how on earth they would have raised the money for it. Couldn't have been that much in taxes to assess. Must have been some wealthy folks around.

The office was accessed via a discreet door on the side of the building where the side road sloped off from the main street. A rusted sign with black letters on white. "Police." Though the seven cells that amounted to the county jail were contained inside, there was a distinct lack of security. Sam had been pushing for a redesign since he began work there. There was only the unlocked door, then two chairs that constituted the visitors' waiting room, in front of a window where the dispatcher also acted as a receptionist. A hall to the left led to offices and storage rooms. To the right was a steel door, left open, that gave access to seven small cells and a secure interrogation room that also served as a visiting area. The cell doors were solid, not bars, with a scratched Plexiglas window at eye level and a slit at hip level for meal trays. Sam was thankful for this construction. He never really had to look at whatever deadbeats, waiting for arraignment, trial, or transfer to a state prison, might be residing there.

When Sam entered, a commotion was coming from the cells. His hand went instinctively to his holster as he stepped through the open door. Three deputies stood around a cell door, shouting back and forth, and one of them banged on the door with a nightstick.

"What the hell's going on here?"

The closest deputy turned. "Jiles's freaking out. Parker went in there to pull out the bedding and got hit."

"You didn't cuff him." Sam walked up to Parker, into his personal space, forcing him to stop his banging and back away from the door.

"Naw. He was laying on the floor, pissing himself. I didn't think he'd move." Parker had some redness on his jaw.

"Go write it up. It's another charge."

"Oh, yeah. Great. That's another one, you son of a bitch." Parker shouted the last bit as he walked away. The other two stood at the entrance.

"You, too. We need all accounts. I'll take care of this."

They left and Sam peered through the window. Jiles lay on the concrete floor, shirtless, his hands over his ears, his legs moving like he was running.

"Jiles," Sam's voice turned low, powerful. "Jiles. Smoke break."

The skinny man started shouting nonsense to himself.

Sam went to an empty cell, pulled out the pad and scratchy blanket and even the toilet paper. Heading back to Jiles's cell, Sam saw that a hand had emerged from the slot. "Where's that cigarette, boss?"

"Here." Sam smacked a handcuff on the tattooed wrist. Faded flames.

"Fuck, man."

"Gimme the other."

"Fuck you."

Sam yanked hard on the cuff, pulling the prisoner by the wrist against the cell door.

"Shit." Jiles hit the door. Then the other hand emerged.

Holding onto the handcuffs around Jiles's wrists, Sam opened the door and looked this killer in the eyes.

How does it make you feel to look into the face of someone who has killed someone close to you? For Sam Summers, it wasn't quite as dramatic as you might think. Not as dramatic as Sam would have thought. In these two days that Jiles had been in his cell, Sam had never been alone with him. The opportunities this presented were startling, but Sam didn't see a killer here. He saw another criminal, a perp, another detoxing meth-head.

Jimmy Jiles was gaunt and green. His heavily blemished skin was tinted and his long jaw twitched. He tilted his head so as not to look Sam in the eyes. He was shirtless, and though the temperature was low in the concrete and steel of the small jail, his skin gleamed with sweat. A bandage that had covered a wound just below his shoulder blade swung loose on a hinge of yellow medical tape. The wound itself, the only marker that he had suffered at all from the firefight that followed his ambush of two police officers, was swollen and oozing. Dried blood circled the entrance wound, but the skin edges were puffy and black.

"I'll get someone to come look at that."

Jiles had looked at Sam's face closely, possibly aware of his vulnerability or just in some stage of detox so that he was startled by Sam's words. He took a moment before he seemed to recognize what Sam might be talking about. He didn't seem quite in the same world.

Sam led him hard by the cuffs to the other cell, contact with him making him angry. The fact that he had to interact with this man at all made him violent. He didn't want to hurt Jiles. He was not interested in exacting revenge. Sam knew he would gain nothing from vengeance. Still, he could easily beat down this man, and no one would say a thing about it or question the justice in it. Just to see him made him feel like doing it.

He pushed him into the stripped cell and put his hands through the slot. He pulled hard on the little chain that joined the cuffs at the same time he closed and latched the door. The lanky body slammed against the inside of the door.

"Fuck."

"Yep." Sam uncuffed him and walked away.

"Hey," Jiles called.

"What?"

"That cigarette?"

"Nope. Smoke break's over."

3

It happened very quickly. The can whizzed past his ear, just slow enough for him to recognize the brand. Dr. Pepper. Then the familiar epithet, long and growing in intensity as a vehicle approached and then quieter as the pickup shrank in his sight down the road in front of him. "Fucking faggot."

Logan was walking home from school and he hated it. It was one of his least favorite times of day. High-schoolers let loose into the day while the rest of the more reasonable but entirely soulless world was still working. Most other fifteen-year-olds are excited for the final bell, but Logan was conscious of the tightening in his stomach, the rising feeling of nausea as the clock began its dreadful countdown to the freedom of the hormone-overloaded teenagers that filled the halls of Sheridan High.

The only thing that made this time bearable was Dot Baxter. Dot was a year ahead of him and twice as smart, he thought, but it was what made her stand out to him. To Logan, she was just different, though she wore the same uniform of jeans and t-shirts worn by all others. Even her hair, a streaky brown, was worn in the traditional fashion, and this didn't deter him. Logan knew what it was like. He had gone for a long time trying to maintain a sort of anonymity of dress, trying to blend in to avoid exactly this sort of interaction. It didn't stop anything, though. He had tried to be the respectable son of the county sheriff. Tried to just be normal. He understood why Dot chose to blend in; it was what was necessary in this podunk town.

Logan Wallis did not blend in any longer, and for this reason, he drew drive-by insults and hurled Dr. Pepper cans. He wore his hair dyed black, hanging long into his face and cut shorter and somewhat spiky in the back. His own wardrobe consisted mainly of black jeans, the baggier the better. Nine Inch Nails and Marilyn Manson t-shirts. His winter coat, what he wore on this cold March afternoon, was puffy and tan and felt incongruous and ridiculous. He felt stupid in it, but the cold required it.

He had waited about five minutes after seeing Dot leave the school building before leaving. Logan had been able, through dumb luck or wishful thinking, to sort out that he might catch Dot, if he walked the alley behind her house, up in her bedroom changing out of her school clothes. Might just catch her in some moment of solitary freedom that would reveal something to Logan that he could carry with him as a talisman, a rune stone that told the truth about who Dot Baxter really was.

The insult of others passing, that fact that someone would care enough about his presence to throw a full can of soda at him and to curse and call him a name that they viewed as insulting and hurtful, spoiled Logan's desire to pass slowly down the alley behind the Baxter house, just slowly enough that Dot might in some leisurely luxurious feeling see him there and call to him, invite him in from the cold to spend some time getting to know her. It made him angry. It made him shake with anger. His instinct had been to raise a middle finger to anyone who would treat him in such a way, but after spending a previous long afternoon hiding in a dumpster from a carload who had come after him for such a gesture, he resisted. Instead, he thought of his father's guns.

At home, in a locked cabinet, was enough firepower to solve his problem with these guys forever. He could shoot each one of his top ten with a different gun and still be left with a choice of weapons to use on himself as the police came after him.

He knew it wasn't right to think this way. Columbine wasn't that long ago. He remembered sitting on the floor next to his mother, crying about the TV reports. Whether he was crying over the terror-stricken faces of the students or just because his mother was upset, he didn't know. It was a tragedy, he understood then. Now, as a teenager himself, he understood the urge.

They were farm-boy football stars who ran the school. Hopeless jocks who didn't know that they were destined to live the lives of their fathers over again, or worse. How on earth he merited their ire, Logan didn't know. You would think they'd be too busy with football practice and chasing cheerleader tail when actually they were getting it from fat girls who they thought would never tell. But Logan knew one of those fat girls, and she had told him the details of Bo Newell coming into her house at night when her parents were out and making her do it, even though she wasn't ready. But she had really asked for it, flashing him a soft white boob in the equipment room during gym class. Logan knew. He also knew of their fathers' drunkenness, the domestic violence, speeding tickets, evictions. He knew these things, sure, but never contemplated using these facts against them. These items just filled in the gaps in his understanding. That Ben Murah had been suspected of raping his sister just fit the idea he already had.

Logan spent way too much of his life concerned with people like Bo and Ben. Maybe it was because he'd known them all through his childhood, because Bo had once, in junior high, stolen Logan's clothes in gym class, making him chase him outside in his skivvies. Maybe it was because Ben, once while passing in the halls, punched Logan in the chest, knocking the wind out of him and leaving him on the thinly carpeted floor to be stepped over. That he fantasized about retribution was only logical. He had spent a considerable amount of energy on how he might exact revenge if the opportunity presented itself, but he spent much more energy, an overwhelming amount of concern, trying to avoid these two and their gaggle of hollow heads.

The route home that included the alley behind the Baxters' house was created out of a need for stealth. It kept him off the main streets where someone might hurl insults and objects at him.

In the security of the alley, he slowed as he approached the old house inhabited by the Baxter family. What might she be doing now? Right now, could she be upstairs, slipping out of the tight jeans and sweater she had worn that day, admiring herself naked in front of a mirror? Or could she be now behind that reflection on the kitchen window, seeing him and thinking about how nice it might be to spend time with someone like him.

Logan remembered the scare of the yell out of the truck, the way it felt like a little bolt of lightning through him, leaving little energy behind to stir up anger. Dot could be in there right now sucking off

Bo Newell. He stepped up his pace.

After unlocking the door, he entered the front hall of his house and sent his heavy backpack sliding across the tile, into the kitchen. "Oh, yes. A strike. Oh, thank you, thank you." He turned to blow kisses at appreciative fans. He then made fake muscle poses, then spun on his toes while flipping the bird. No one was home.

He'd been on his own for the past two days since his father was shot, but essentially alone since his mother had left them. Left them. That was how he thought of it. Sure, she'd given him the pitch about things not working out and no-one wanted to hurt anyone and they just had to do what was best for everyone. But the simple fact was that she'd been stepping out, and then she left. She walked out that door and did not come back. Fuck her. Good goddamn riddance. Slut.

And if he ever had a moment alone with the cuckolding carpenter that stole his mother, he might have something for him as well.

His cousin Angie would be coming by later to bring over and heat up some casserole. His aunt had sent her over to check up on Logan, to make sure he wasn't getting into trouble in the house alone. How much trouble could the sheriff's son get into? He lived with a damn detective. But Angie coming by wasn't all bad.

Like most of his cousins, she was quite a few years older than him. Mature. She was also hot. Oh, sure, he felt some guilt about the way he looked at his own cousin, but God didn't give her that body so it would be ignored. Besides, she would sit in the kitchen smoking cigarettes with him, treating him as if he were twenty-one and had the same concerns she did. She wasn't all that smart, and he didn't really care if she quit her job at that little place on J that sold ceramics to go to beauty school. She could be a hairdresser or an astronaut for all he cared, as long as he had these ten minutes smoking cigarettes with that.

It was already dark when they arrived. Logan was seated at the kitchen table, the light pouring down onto his textbooks and notes. He didn't understand why he needed to take biology. There was nothing to be gained, nothing to be retained. He had sketched out his notes and been over them several times, repeating terms and definitions. Humiliating to have to memorize these things. Beyond useless. He drummed his hands on the table and looked around the house, into the dark outside the cone of light over the table. He was sick to death of this house. Sick of the gray walls, the ratty couch with its saggy cushions, not like anyone around here would notice. Logan didn't think one thing had changed in the house in the time he'd been alive. Nothing but age and general degeneration. The kitchen chair he sat in, with gold-colored corduroy fabric, had been out of fashion since he'd wet his first diaper. They wouldn't get rid of a thing. A leg on a side table in the living room had been repaired with a black wood screw drilled through the top, without bothering to countersink. It was how things were done around here. But you can't jerry-rig a marriage, can you Sheriff Wallis?

The sound of a car door outside made him jump. He hadn't seen lights or heard anything. He sat up straight in his chair and looked with determination at his notes, the open textbook. Then he heard another door and remembered. His dad was coming home from the hospital. Logan jumped up and looked around for anything incriminating. Surely, there was something around that would get him in trouble. Not seeing anything and not having time to search the rest of the house, he ran his fingers through his hair to undo any styling that might seem over the top to his super-square father. He went to the door.

"Christ, boy, turn on some lights in here." His aunt Francine, all two-fifty-plus of her pushed through the door, fat hand slapping for the light switch. In her wake was a tall, thin man, straggly hair standing at angles, pale like a zombie and bandaged and sewn like Frankenstein's monster. Logan felt his fingertips, his nose tingle. Shooting blindly, that hillbilly tweaker had shot his father in the neck, missing an artery but severing the band of muscle, sternocleidomastoid, and requiring surgery to repair. Logan had been to see him the day it happened when a pink emergency slip had come to find him and pull him out of class. He'd been so startled and scared that immediate reflection wasn't possible. Standing among nervous and crying family members had a contagious effect. Only the next day, when he went back to the hospital after a fitful night on his aunt's couch and his father asked him, choked and dry, why the hell he wasn't in school, did he begin to put it in a less reactive perspective. Let the women get all fussy about it. He had survived. Move on.

His father wore his coat over his pajamas, his jaw was held tight, and Logan backed away. It was a face that said stay away, it said leave me alone or I'll really let you know what's bothering me. Logan knew that look the way an impala knows what a lion is when he first sets his eyes on one. Logan could think of hundreds of other places to be besides anywhere near his father when he bore that expression. What was on the other side was something he did not care to witness.

When Logan was ten, he had been playing football in front of the house with Pete Cavaricci. It was not so much football as it was two bored skinny kids, who knew nothing about sports and were not at all athletically inclined, throwing a ball back and forth. Actually, Pete would toughen up and eventually threaten some other kid with a knife and end up being sent away to what everyone called a "boys home."

It really couldn't be called catch, either. That would imply that one of them might have the ability to throw in the general vicinity of the other, and that this other might actually be able to get his hands around the ball before it hit the ground. Needless to say, when Logan laid into it, attempting to throw a hard, fast one at Pete, the ball flew hard but sailed over Pete's head and through the front plate-glass window of the house. Logan felt his body go numb as he watched the ball pierce the window, bringing the surrounding glass down slowly like cartoon teeth when someone has been struck in the mouth.

It could not be repaired with scotch tape or a hastily driven wood screw, and maybe this is what had made his father so angry. Logan saw it coming and went to hide behind the garage until his father came home, and when he heard the bellowing voice, low and loud, he knew the sort of trouble he was in for. Grounding, extra chores and a general resentment that lasted to this day. It still came up as something he should still be sorry for, as if letting him live was a challenge for his father. Though it might not have been the expense of replacement that got to his father. The look when he told him that he'd been playing catch and had overthrown Pete was a look of disgust. Or maybe distrust. As if maybe his father thought that he did it on purpose.

Upon seeing his father entering the house Logan had backed himself into a corner, making way for his aunt and trying to escape the view of his father, but then Angie entered. The stark overhead light of the entryway caught her red hair and lit it up, blinding Logan. He was almost grateful to see her, but as she turned to find him, in his corner, he felt humiliation take over. She was seeing his cowardice, seeing his fear. His braggadocio on her previous visits proved to be a show, and here he was proven to be nothing more than the teenage boy he was. Not her equivalent that he'd enjoyed thinking he was in her company.

"Here." She threw a plastic bag at him. "That's his stuff from the hospital."

He held the bag by its string and looked at her. She pulled a pack of cigarettes from the pocket of her parka and stepped out into the cold.

Logan closed the door after her and went up the stairs to ferry the bag to his father's room.

4

"Just awful. Just awful."

"So true."

"I talked to Francine, you know, and he's going back to work today."

"Oh, that's right?"

"I don't know how you do it. See someone killed in front of you and then just go back to work."

"After getting shot yourself."

"Yes, yes."

"Just awful."

"And she was so nice. That mouth, you know, but after all she'd been through losing her husband."

"Oh, yes."

"I can't talk about it. It's just too awful. You know that the Governor is coming down for the funeral. Oh, it's too sad." Annette Headrick put a closed fist to her mouth and, with the other hand, bid farewell to her friend. She walked down Sheridan's main street, holding her lips closed, glancing once to the county courthouse across the street.

The old courthouse was grand with red brick, white stone around its windows and doors. It sat back from the main street, retail shops, and small offices along the state highway. Behind those storefronts, commercial fell away quickly to a sort of haphazard residential. City planners had once tried to impose a grid on what had been a loose gathering of large houses, surrounded then by smaller ones. The resulting effect was a series of stops and starts, with no street going straight through for more than a block or two. Even the main street ended at the cemetery, causing the highway to jog a block and a half to the west before continuing south.

Annette dropped into a store called the Book Stop.

It was a pale-yellow store with white shelves, smelling like spice. The bell above the door rang as she closed the door behind her. She looked warmly around, comforted by the heat, the smell. Her good friend, Sally, appeared from behind a curtain, took position behind the counter, and they exchanged greetings.

"Here," Annette produced a paperback from her thick white purse. "I can't read this."

Sally looked at the dark, dramatic cover of the murder mystery on the glass counter. "No, I bet not."

"Too much of that stuff around as it is. It kept me up last night."

"I got the thing." Sally leaned, with some obvious discomfort, to a box on the floor and retrieved a book, a thick paperback, glossy raised letters, flowers. "This will help."

Annette took the book from her friend and looked over the back-cover blurbs. "I just can't believe it, you know. This is good country, with good people. How does it happen?"

"He wasn't from here."

"That's right. Come up from West Springs. I hear."

"Not from our county."

"Oh, thank the Lord. Burt Simms said they had drugs in that house, a whole lot."

"Is that right? That stuff's all over."

"I guess so. But Terry was such a good girl."

"She was just doing her job."

"Just trying to clean things up around here. So good. Stern, you know. But after all she went through."

"At least she's gone on to be with him now."

"Her family, too. You remember what happened to Dean McIlheny? He would have been her grandfather, right?"

"That's right. Quartered, I heard."

"Four horses. That's right."

"Business deal gone bad."

"So long ago. Things were different."

"His wife held it together best she could."

"Her daughter after her."

"You can't expect things to go well after something like that."

"Hard times."

"At least Terry did well for herself."

"Marrying Bob Stegman."

"And then losing him so early."

"The cancer."

"Awful."

"You know what I can't bear to think of?"

"Yes?"

"It's Frank, their hired man, all by himself out there."

"Been with them since he was a kid."

"And no respectable family to speak of."

"Lot of Indians living in that holler like it's the old west."

"Hard-working, that kid."

"I hear."

"Oh, that reminds me." She tapped her thick, ringed finger on the glass counter, beneath which were some stale packaged shortbread cookies next to some handmade jewelry for sale. "Do you have anything for a teenager?"

"Let's see." Sally walked from behind the counter.

"You know my granddaughter's going to be staying with me for the summer."

"Is that right?"

"Coming down from St. Louis. Be good for her to get away from that city."

"Good for you. She's just a teenager, ain't she?"

"Sixteen years old last November."

They were silent as they looked over the spines. Sally's fingers stopped on the yellow spines of classics. "You can always go with the classics. Dickens."

"Oh yes. Great Expectations. It was good for me. But I don't want her to…."

"I'll let you know if anything comes in."

"Great. Thanks." Annette held up the other book and pulled her long coat tight. At the door, she turned back to Sally. "Don't forget. Garden club on Saturday. Gotta plan our spring trip."

"Bye." Sally waved and turned back to the counter.

Out in the cold, Annette hurried to her Oldsmobile, slamming the door closed behind her as if she had better keep out the cold and whatever else out there might be after her. The big car started, and she cranked all the knobs and levers that might maximize the heat. The blast of warmth hit her face, and she began to cry.

5

The trees leaned over the asphalt, lighted by the truck's headlights. They passed slowly as if he were walking. He was probably driving too fast. He didn't dare take his eyes from the centerline for a second. There was some peace in imagining what might happen if he did. He could release the steering wheel from his hand and, within moments, it all would be over. He would cease feeling all that he felt.

Franklin Redbird was driving his farm truck home from a bar in Jasper. He knew no one there. He talked to no one. He had been able to lean his elbows on the bar, smoke and drink without anyone asking him how he was doing, without some idiot going on about what a tragedy it was, how awful it is that she's gone. Yeah, you look real broken up.

What did they know? They don't know what it's like without her. They barely knew her. Didn't really know her.

It was Hell, pure Hell. If they really wanted to know. It was like getting your hand caught in a thresher, only it wasn't your hand, it was your heart. And it didn't happen for a second; it happened continuously. Not a moment went by without a pain that made him want to collapse and writhe on the floor. Like getting kicked in the balls by a horse, where you feel just sick, like your insides are all in the wrong place.

The bar in Jasper was too far. Frank was tired, and it didn't feel like he was getting any closer to home. Branches like bony fingers stretched out to the car, and he couldn't go fast enough to feel safe, fast enough to push it all away. But it wasn't really like he wanted to go home. What was there to go home to? There would be no light on in the Stegman house. No light that he could see from his bedroom to signal her presence. To let him know whether she was in the living room, the kitchen, or the bedroom. Those lights had been both a godsend and pure torture for the years that he'd been living and working at the Stegman farm.

He had come to the farm eager to work, eager for a chance to do something. He was a boy, really, working odd jobs around the county. He was putting a new roof on a barn up in Cain when the shiny pickup pulled into the yard. You didn't do much in Sheridan without coming to know the name Stegman. Word was that he would be mayor soon. Everyone either worked for him or owed him something, but nobody feared him. He just wasn't the type of guy you were liable to cross. Just too nice.

This didn't mean much to Franklin. Everyone was better off than he was. Everyone deserved the same amount of respect. You needed to be grateful for every opportunity, every door opened, every hand extended. When Bob Stegman stepped from the truck and shouted up to him, Frank had no idea who he was. And who he was didn't matter.

"Redbird?"

"Yes, sir." Frank was extended over an opening, stretching over a twenty-foot drop to the hayloft. He pulled back and crouched near the edge of the roof.

"You got some time to do some work on my farm? Got fifty head that need their shots."

"Yes, sir." He looked down at his gloved hands, his thin bare belly, the plywood sheathing on which he stood. "Suppose I ought to finish here first."

"Sure. You finish Nick's barn. How long you need?"

"If it don't rain, I ought to have it done by tomorrow night."

"Day after tomorrow, then. I'll see you." Stegman headed to the truck.

"Where at?" Frank wanted to step forward so he might not have to shout, but there was no more forward in front of him.

Bob had to look back. "What's that?"

"Sorry. Where's your farm?"

"J, north of 22." He raised a hand, then closed himself in the cab.

Frank came down from the roof that night when he could no longer see the nails he was hitting. Nick met him at the bottom of the ladder.

"Thought Stegman had come to steal you away."

"Sorry, sir?"

"He wanted you for a job, didn't he?"

"Sure. Told him I'd finish here tomorrow and work at his place the day after."

"You told him you'd finish here first?"

"Yes, sir. S'alright, ain't it?"

"Oh, sure."

The next day, the weather held, and he finished the job with a little of dusk left. Nick paid him cash for the work. Frank bought a can of stew at a convenience store and found a quiet farm road off J to park the car and spend the night. He hadn't been home much lately. A converted grain shed, with its low door, circular shape, and cone roof, had served as the bedroom of Franklin and his brother, Washington, for the last three years. It was one of many scattered shelters that lay around the bottom of the hollow his family had settled generations ago, after being pushed from their original homeland.

The Redbird camp, a conglomeration of small buildings, farm animals, crops, and a very extended family, sat in a small hollow that opened on one end to the Verdant River. The only access was a rocky, one-lane, unmaintained road that passed through a washout before a sharp rise and then an equally sharp decline into the hollow.

Frank, if he was working, stayed in his truck, somewhere near where he was to be working the following day. He was only nineteen then but was expected to pull his own weight. Not only did going home mean a return to what wasn't the most comfortable of settings, it also meant either pitching in with the labor required for the survival of the larger family, or at least a contribution of money to help satisfy the needs of the whole. He was nineteen and working on his own, not simply as accompaniment to one of his brothers or many uncles. It also meant that he was earning his own money for the first time. He was not inclined to see it slip from his hands. He'd been taught that hard work was its own reward, but cash in his pocket after a day's work felt like a greater benefit.

The Stegman place was the largest on that stretch of J. It was one of those handsome farms, well-maintained, white barns, cut lawn, mature trees. A newer house set close to the road. Enviable, brick. An older, squat original farmhouse sat further back, next to the barn. An implement garage sat along one of the fences, the noses of tractors and the hitches of bush hogs and tillers poked out of the dark into the morning sun.

Franklin parked his truck next to Bob Stegman's and felt a little funny about it. Next to the handsome Dodge, dualies, all glittering bent metal, he had parked a ten-year-old Chevy that had been given up for dead and left to rust in the Missouri seasons. He was not ashamed of his hard-working phoenix of a pickup, but to put it next to something so ostentatious and proud didn't seem quite right.

He stood behind his truck for a moment, hoping that he might be approached or that he might hear Mr. Stegman already at work. The yard was silent. Not even crowing roosters could be heard in the early morning light. Looking around, he spotted a well pump in the shadow of the small house. From the bed of his truck, he got a water cooler, another roadside find, took it to the pump, and began to fill it.

He was just replacing the lid when he heard footsteps on the dirt and small gravel of the drive. He was expecting the size and heft of Bob Stegman. Instead, it was the figure of a solid woman with strong features but long hair that softened her form. She held out a steaming tin cup.

"I'm sorry." He brushed his hands against his jeans. "I shoulda asked. Just needed some for the jug."

"It's fine. Here. Coffee."

"Thank you." He did not drink coffee, but he would not refuse the offer. "I'm here to do some work for Mr. Stegman."

"He's rustlin' them up to the pen." She motioned to the north of the barn. "You any good with a horse?"

"No, ma'am. I never— "

"'Ma'am?' I am nobody's mother. You can drop the ma'am."

"Yes…I never been on one before."

"Well. Head on over to the pen. They'll be heading this way soon. Stay away from the gate, though. The sight of you will spook 'em."

He nodded and took his leave, afraid he had not made a good impression. Stealing water. No experience with a horse. Calling her a name she didn't appreciate. While Frank was concerned with the impression he had made and how it might affect his prospects, he did not give Terry Stegman much thought. It wasn't that she wasn't something to look at, but she was a woman. She was somebody's wife. She was not one of the girls he'd seen his brothers chase. Not one of the high school girls that they still drooled over.

He had no idea that within five years Bob would die and he would be staring out of the darkened windows of the little house at the glow emitting from behind the drawn shades of the larger. No idea that he would someday, under the new moon in March, be driving home after spending an entire evening sitting in the smallest of bars, one that smelt of sawdust, salt, and Busch, not wanting to go home because going home meant going to that house, meant waking up on that farm and facing another day.

Franklin tightened his eyes to focus on the task at hand.

6

In a trailer among hundred-year-old oaks in the southern part of the county where the land turns hilly and rough, where limestone cliffs rise out of pastures, where sinkholes appear in otherwise solid landscapes, Harlan Lustig stood on top of his coffee table, his toes among ashes and burrito wrappers, his fingers mimicking the actions of a rock guitarist, his head crashing up and down, his hair whipping against his neck and his face, to the sound of Black Sabbath. "Fuck. This is awesome."

Two younger men, one sitting in a low chair, rotating it back and forth while his feet stayed planted on the carpet, the other sitting on the couch, attempted not to watch the spectacle.

The song came crashing to an end, and Harlan leaped from the table, beer cans and bottles falling to the floor. "How come I never heard that before?" He spun to the long-haired one, a NASCAR tank top under his winter coat. "You got more of that with you? Bring it in."

The racing fan looked to the other, wearing his ball cap, a sweat-stained Mariners cap, backward, who motioned him to the door. He hurried out.

"I'll trade you for some Michael Jackson." Harlan laughed. He was excited but almost angry that somehow in his youth he had missed out on the violent joy of "Paranoid." He'd grown up in St. Louis in the seventies and eighties, and he listened to the same things most others in his economic class were subject to. It was not fair that he'd missed the likes of this.

Harlan found an old button-down dress shirt lying on the floor next to the couch and chuckled to himself as he put it on without buttoning it over his pale, thin chest. He'd worn the same shirt back when he worked at a Mitsubishi dealership in Kirksville. It was deemed his lucky shirt because he had worn it when he had made his first and only auto sale.

"So, whatcha looking for?"

"Just a couple grams."

"Shit. That's it?" Harlan threw his hands in the air. "Where you work?"

"Huh?"

"A job. You got a job?"

"At Play-Craft."

"That camper factory? How much you make?"

"Huh?"

"Jesus. How much you take home in a week?"

"About three?"

"Shit, then you need more than a couple grams. What you gonna use that money on?"

"Dunno."

"Girls? You gotta girl? Naw. You pay some rent maybe, you gotta eat, but what else?"

The other man in the dirty coat came in with a stack of CDs. The interrogated one looked pleadingly at the other.

"You take home three hundred a week, and you're gonna come to me for a gram or two today? Then you're gonna use it up and come back to me for another couple? What do I want to do that for? Do I want to strange guys showing up at my door every couple of days? I should just kick your asses out of here right now and tell you to come back when you're ready to spend some of that money you make, but...." He reached for and took the stack of CDs.

Harley loved what he did and had a hard time concealing that from these two redneck kids. If only he'd been this good at selling those little Jap cars. Guy come here for a bindle, and I'm not going to see him again. Guy buys a couple of grams or more, and he'll be back. He'll be back right away. Tweaked and looking for more. It's all about customer retention, baby.

He'd flipped through the CDs twice, not realizing he'd seen them once already, then stacked them one by one neatly on top of the table in a stack that on the first try wasn't quite right. He razed the little tower, and with care, he tried again. Successful, he turned to his audience. "So, what's it gonna be? Taking four today?"

They haggled for some time. Harley tried to strike the right balance between the price and the quantity, along with the Sabbath and other CDs. An agreement was made. He disappeared from the room a moment to fetch the drugs and, when Harley returned, the pair stood nervously by the front door. "Christ, what's wrong?"

"Nothing, man."

"Bullshit."

"It's just that…." The guy in the ball cap spoke, "You're the one that guy was after, ain't you?"

Harlan doubled over in laughter, a compulsive laughter that seized his chest and caught his throat. It had gotten around. He liked the idea that these guys were scared of him. Nearly as much as he liked the fact that a guy was so enraged with him as to want to kill him.

It helped, too, that the man was now behind bars.

"Suppose you're right. Boy, was he mad."

"Dude, he killed those guys." The racing fan.

"Whoa, yeah, too bad for them." They didn't seem relaxed, despite his laughter. He leaned in close, "You know…," dramatic pause, "I was there. No, that's right. I was there when he did it, beat the shit out of them then shot 'em." He looked from one to the other. "Again and again."

He liked the notoriety the event provided, but his heart was pounding as the fresh memories came back. He turned from them and sat on the couch, cutting lines on a CD case. "Come on," he commanded.

"Why didn't he kill you?'

"Dipshit didn't even know I was there. I was in the bathroom when he came in."

He had been doing a private, celebratory bump. He'd just made a major sale. Dale Kelly and Jennifer Somebody-or-other. He'd made some good deals with them before but, this time, it was for $25k. Harlan had known they had been buying from Jimmy before, but he wasn't worried about cutting in on someone else's territory. It wasn't his fault if Jimmy couldn't garner customer loyalty. He had no idea that this sale might set off Jimmy the way it did.

He kept a paper bindle of crystal on him most of the time, either for consumption or spot sales. You just had to offer samples once in a while. The bathroom was a skinny little job, Formica and mildew stains. Harlan had hopped up on the counter after taking a leak and was on to a second line when he heard the pounding at the front door.

Cops. No doubt. He looked out the window, skinny and set high above the bath-shower combo. Mean bastards, these county cops. Always nosing, hoping to find something. They could come up with some reason to hold him, but nothing to send him to jail. He knew they were looking to get him. It was why he'd had Jenny pick him up in town. Why he'd had her put the money in a tire hanging off a fence post a mile down from his house the day before. Took no chances.

The voice, the volume, the booming anger of it clued him in that he was not dealing with the cops. The voice was terribly familiar, especially at that volume. He heard a quick yelp from Jennifer and jumped down from the counter, finishing what remained of the packet. His eyes darted from the door, as if seeing the voices and noises behind it, to the window. The little window would have to do. He then went to the thin horizontal window and turned the crank on it. Listening to things breaking and yelling and violence from the living room, he tried to get himself out the window. His head, his arms, his legs first, then again. It wasn't going to happen without possibly cutting himself in two. Not possible.

Harley, still not quite panicking, frightened some but still amused, was reaching for the knob on the thin bathroom door when he heard the first shot. His hand recoiled as if he'd been shocked by the handle. Then there was a quick series of shots, and Harley slipped into a new sense of urgency. His reflection over the humor and absurdity of the situation disappeared, and his survival became paramount.

He cracked the door. The view was limited to only a sliver of the living room, and he saw Jimmy Jiles, pistol raised in the air, pass quickly from one side of the room to the other and then back again. His view was blocked by the hallway that led to a bedroom. He leaped from the bathroom and down the hall, his sounds hidden by Jimmy's repeated shouts of "Where is he?"

Harley was prepared to leap through the screened open window when his darting eyes spotted a telephone. His fingers fumbled over the buttons and, on the third try, he got through.

"What's your emergency?" The voice was ridiculously calm on the other end. Harley thought he heard the male operator take a drag off a cigarette.

"He's shooting up the place." His voice was a harsh, breathy whisper. "He said he's gonna kill me." He had taken in the words earlier, but only now did he recognize their gravity. "He's probably already killed someone."

"Who, who?" The operator gave away his disbelief. "Who's got the gun?"

"Jimmy. Jimmy Jiles."

"Where are you?"

"Fuck, I don't know. Uh. Dale Kelly's."

"Where? Address."

Harlan heard the operator making the call on the radio. "Kelly's. Fuck. By that stupid fire tower."

Again, the dispatcher called over the radio, coming up with the road number.

The shooting began again. Again and again, each blast punctuated by a guttural, primal shout. Jimmy sounded distinctly like a madman.

Harley dropped the phone on the waterbed and flew with his hands in front of him through the screened window. He landed in the grass with an unrecognized pain and was quickly back to his feet, running like he was on fire towards the tree line at the back of the property. He was prepared for shots to ring out in his direction at any time. The darkness of the forest was not getting closer, not quick enough, while he braced himself for the burning pain of a shot in the back of his thigh, in the shallow of his back, in his head. But nothing happened by the time he came to the fence, three strings of barbed wire that he tried to jump like a hurdle. His lead foot caught, and his momentum sent him tumbling into the damp, decaying leaves on the other side of the fence. He struggled to get to his feet in the dampness, using a tree to right himself. Once upright, he scampered like a jackrabbit through the trees.

The boys, the buyers, looked at Harley where he was still cutting lines, over and over, the razor blade cutting deep lines in the acrylic CD case. He laughed at them.

"Does something for you to have a man looking to kill you."

7

Bill knew pain, but damnit, this hurt. He wasn't going to take those pills. Not again. Jesus, he wanted to be on earth. Not wherever the pills and the shots had left him for the past couple of days. He was aware of the grimace on his face. He couldn't make it go away. Others would see that he was in pain. They would be looking today. Judging. He was lucky to survive. That's what they had all said. Those who came to see him. It could have been him just as easily. He knew that. It wasn't, though. Now, he had to go back. Had to go back to being who he was before what happened, before he saw what he saw. Before he saw her die.

He dressed, careful with his collar around the bandage on his neck. Lucky. He looked about the same. A little paler, maybe. And that grimace. But he was still who he was. He straightened his tan shirt and put the belt around his waist. It felt heavy. Heavy, though it was lighter. The clip in his weapon would be nearly empty. It would smell of gunpowder, that metallic smell, strong like a flavor. He would have to clean the gun. Maybe he would clean it today at the office. But he had reports to write. He was the only witness to an officer's death. He, himself, had shot a suspect. Though the suspect lived.

Downstairs, Logan had already cleared out. His bowl with drops of dried milk around it still sat on the table. Well, at least he put the milk away. Bill paused for a moment, looking at the bowl, the shadow it made on the kitchen table, and he wondered if he should leave it. He was bothered by its sight, and his son had probably left it there to spite him, so why did he really care? What urgency was there today, this morning, to put the bowl in the sink or even in the dishwasher and wipe a wet rag across the table? There was no need. No one besides him would be bothered by it. Just him.

He left the bowl where it was.

It was bright outside. Brighter, really, than it should be. It told him that winter was on its way out and spring would be here with its budding trees and green grass. Not yet. Not time for that yet.

The left side of his car was dotted with a handful of holes. The small, pathetic holes of a .22. A twenty-two didn't always have the strength to go through bone. Here, it had penetrated the sheet metal of the rear fender, and it had penetrated the skull of Terry Stegman.

Bill wanted to slam his hand on the car's trunk. It was his impulse. But he hadn't the strength. It was a sad and pathetic gesture. What room was there for petty violence? How could acting on his anger make him feel better at all? He took a deep breath against the pain and squeezed his tall, thin body into the car. He was going to go back to doing what he always did. People would be looking to him. Not only did he have his team of deputies, a team that lost one of its own, but there was a public that wanted to see that the sheriff was in control.

He loved his job. He loved having the security of the population of the county in his control. He really was looking out for everyone he knew. When he drove the county roads, he was proud of the responsibility placed on him and of the honor that it was to have been elected to his position. For twenty-some years, he had been the sheriff of Barnes County, duly elected to serve. Election, though, comes with its own pressures. He had faced competition for his position, but even when he ran unopposed some sought to remind him that his fate could be changed on Election Day. One of those who reminded him of his mortality had been Bob Stegman.

Bob was respected; not exactly well-respected, but respected none the less. He had been there on the stage when Bill claimed his first victory, along with his other supporters including one of the county commissioners and the Sheridan Police Chief. He had felt pressure then, but he was a shoo-in to replace the retiring sheriff. It hadn't always been that easy.

Bob had once been developing a piece of property just outside the town limits on county road H, but there had been all sorts of complaints. The large machinery had left mud on the road, neighbors complained about the noise of the trucks. The trouble came when it was put on Bill to serve a stop-work order for supposed code violations.

A by-the-book sort of sheriff might have simply gone out to the site and kicked everyone off the job, but Bill called Bob to let him know.

"Why the hell do they keep bothering me?"

He had known Bob would not be pleased, known that he hadn't been terribly pleased by Bill's previous contacts with him over the work being done to the property to put up a strip of stores.

"I'm just doing my job here."

"Bullshit. You're the goddamn sheriff around here. You tell 'em that you make the rules."

"But I don't."

"You're telling me. We could use a more take-charge sort of person as sheriff.

"The commissioners make the laws, Bob. You know that."

"And I know that we got an election every so often to replace them and the county sheriff."

"Now, Bob."

"I'm just saying that you could've made this right without me having to pay people not to work."

"I'm gonna have to go over there now."

"You're kidding me." The phone dropped. "Do you believe this guy? Gonna shut me down. Son of a bitch."

Bill could hear Bob walking away from the phone, shouting, and he was just about to hang up when someone picked up the receiver.

"Bill?" It was Terry.

"Yes. Sorry about that."

"No. I'm sorry. What did he do?"

"I don't know. Something about the work or the scope of the project matching the plan he gave to the county."

"Of course, of course." Cursing could be heard. "Don't worry about him."

"I'm just doing my job, Terry. You know that." He knew she was sympathetic, but he was worried. Having Bob Stegman against him could be a real problem. "I just wouldn't want this to change anything."

"He needs you on his side just as much as you need him, Bill.

Besides, he'll go cuss out one of the commissioners, have a beer and be himself again."

"You're probably right."

Terry had always been right. And if she wasn't right, she'd make it right. He had always known her to be reliable, known to trust her judgment. It was why he wanted to bring her on at the Department. She would be a great help to him, and it just may give her a purpose in the world. After her purpose passed away.

Driving actually felt pretty good to Bill. The warm wheel in his hand. The framed view through the windshield. His way was populated by the familiar sights. He passed the Country Mart, the old Presbyterian church that had since become an antique mall, the cemetery, the abandoned armory, the hardware store. These were the same old places. He'd seen changes, but no one could call it progress. The modern age had bypassed Barnes County, and Bill was fine with that. The bits of the real world that filtered into the twenty-first-century streets, streets that could easily be mistaken for the streets of the previous century, made changes in the world that Bill did not appreciate. The modern age had brought with it dope and people so screwed up on it that they shoot without thinking. The modern age also taught a woman that she was free, that she was liberated, that it was fine for her to sneak around on her husband, to divorce him, and leave him with their only son.

Bill parked his car. Standing up straight and putting his hand to his bandage as a reaction to the pain, he looked across the street to a big house that stood, bright and blue, as a reminder of how things did not go the way he wished. It was a handsome house, big porch, Queen Anne features, and you'd never think of it as out of place unless you knew that it was new. And if your wife had met, innocently enough, the contractor who was building the house when she was really there to bring you lunch. And if she started running around with him, trying to keep it from you, in this small town where you grew up, where your mother was everyone's friend, where everyone had once pinched your cheek as a child and then voted for you as an adult. That house may be handsome and well-built, but it was blight just the same.

Elaine Wallis was attractive, or at least attractive enough when the pickings were slim that she gathered the attraction of men since before she was reasonably old enough to be such an object. As she had grown older, she had compensated for the lines carving their way across her face like concrete cracked by tree roots with the use of creams and makeup. The layers on her face could not conceal the jowls she was inheriting from her mother, and the rouge she thought might make her look younger just made her look flushed as if she'd struggled her way up a long flight of stairs. All of it didn't matter much to Bill. She was his wife, and that burning he'd had for her after she'd stood outside his stall as he groomed his horse was not likely to wane even if she grew a mane and tail herself. Despite her aging, other men still felt her worthy of their attention.

"Seen Elaine yesterday." Annette Headrick spoke to him at the counter at the diner where he was picking up lunch for the prisoners, back when things had the appearance of justice and order.

"Is that right?" Bill was not exceptionally eager to talk to Annette. Though she had been a friend to his mother, his babysitter as a child, she was also a town know-it-all, spreading the word on anything that someone didn't want out there.

Annette leaned close in, so close that he could smell her old-lady smell, medicinal ointments covered up with weak perfume. "Down by The Bend."

The cash fluttered from his hand. Elaine was in Jeff City, taking classes to become a realtor. She had said. Like she had the Friday before. He wasn't going to let Annette know as much.

"My daughter and her little one were down from St. Louis, and we were taking a drive and saw her car sitting—that little blue Toyota— and I didn't think nothing of it. Didn't figure it'd be her. But there she was, sitting there like she was waiting on something. Kinda funny, ain't it?"

"Excuse me." He bent to pick up the bills off the grease-stained tiles. It was Annette, and Lord knows she could be wrong, and she didn't see well anymore. Ran straight into the Douglas' car at a four-way. Didn't see the other car. Could be she saw some other woman sitting in her car down by The Bend, down where the kids from the high school go to get personal, the place where sixteen-year-old girls got pregnant, jealous boyfriends got bloodied by new tougher ones, where some went to buy or sell drugs, where just fifty years before the area had its last lynching. Using the rope that kids used to swing themselves out over the green river, let go and splash with a flash of light caught in the leaping water. No one went down there for anything good. Well, what might be good was likely to be trouble.

"A couple of miles on, we passed a pickup headed that way."

"Well, she made it home okay." He stood now with a stack of to-go containers in his hands.

"Good, good. Well, have a good day." Annette raised her hand to wave and turned, her voice filled with what Bill took for joy.

It was only the first of these reports. His stomach was only beginning to know that unease, his heart only starting to feel the wrenching that would continue, that still tormented him as he looked at that stupid blue monstrosity every goddamn day he went to work.

8

Sam squinted as he drove into the morning sun. Generally, patrols weren't part of his regular function, but Sam liked to take a route that took him through most regions of the county and allowed him to check on the trouble spots. He had already checked on the house of Ben Hornsby, a doctor from St. Louis who had a vacation home in the county. Sam still had trouble with that concept. If people had the money, they'd vacation in Florida. Who in their right mind would have their second house on the edge of the Ozarks? Hornsby was a hunter and a drinker, and Sam's guess was that the house allowed him to do both away from the scornful eyes of a wife.

The house had been broken into three different times in the last year. Guns, liquor, TVs, and stereo equipment found missing when Hornsby came down looking for turkey. When he came back for deer, he brought replacement items. These new items were gone a week after his return to the city. Again after that, the thieves took an emergency generator and stripped the house of copper pipe. There wasn't much left for the scavengers until Hornsby could have someone repair the house, but he had been pretty mad after the second break-in and worse after the third. It made both Hornsby and Sheriff Wallis breathe easier if Sam drove the cruiser through the circular drive and peered in the windows once in a while.

Finding everything in order at Hornsby's, Sam's second task was a drive-by of Harlan Lustig's trailer. Harley, as he had people call him, had made quite a name for himself, at least in the sheriff's office, in the short time he'd been in the county. After pulling that little trailer onto a two-acre lot sometime the previous spring, Lustig had been on the switchboard at dispatch pretty regularly. The first was a call about people snooping in the woods behind his property. He was not calmed by the information that those woods belonged to somebody else, and if someone stood on the other side of the fence line and stared at him from dusk 'til dawn, there wasn't a damn thing the law could do about it. Sam and Terry had to stumble through the poison oak at dusk to set his mind at ease.

The second call was about folks speeding down his road. It wasn't his road to begin with, but then again, it raised a lot of dust, and there was the intersection of two thin dirt roads just a quarter-mile down. Someone could get killed. Lustig wanted someone to come out and set up a speed trap, never mind that none of the deputies were big on writing any moving violations unless you were driving like you might kill someone. Sam, again, had to go out to the Lustig place, every tree on the property line now adorned with a no trespassing sign, and try to calm him down, telling him he'd follow up if he could get a license and description of any offending car. He had to go back out there the next week when the stop signs at that intersection had changed direction. Someone had set it up so folks driving Lustig's road had to stop now. Lustig claimed he knew nothing, had hoped county crews had changed it after his complaint.

There had been talk of Lustig cooking meth, and this was the main reason for Sam to cruise that trailer. At the same time, his calls to the sheriff's office had dwindled. Lustig never invited Sam inside on any occasion, but he didn't believe that he could be doing it there. He could, though, still be cooking somewhere. It was his involvement in the events of a couple of days prior that confirmed it for Sam.

The dispatcher had known Lustig's voice, though it was shaky and scared. And it had been Sam who had to go around on the evening of that horrible day and bring Lustig in for questioning.

It was dark, and Sam's nerves were rattled by what he had seen, by what had happened. Lustig was not known to be violent, and no one had ever seen him with a gun, but there's no reason to think that a man won't take a shot at an officer if he thinks he's got a reason to. Deputy Parker came along as backup.

The two cruisers pulled one after the other down the short driveway that sloped away from the road. They parked, leaving their headlights lighting up the lot, making dark shadows behind the bony trees. The night air burned inside Sam's nose, turning each breath to crystal. The trailer was dark as if it hadn't been occupied in some time. Parker stood behind Sam, waiting for him to go up the steps and knock on the metal door. Sam wasn't ready to do that. If someone was inside and didn't stir with the sound and light of two cars on the lawn, then he wasn't about to startle him to life by banging on the door.

With gestures, he told Parker to stay put, that he was going around the trailer.

It was a small mobile home, barely just a step up from a camper, bought off of Bill Wallis's family. The property came off someone from Kansas City who used it for hunting and was starting to sell off lots near the road to help him pay the tax expense. It was a worthless piece of land unless you wanted to be out where no one was likely to bother you, or you were up to something you didn't want anyone knowing about.

Most folks, when they move a trailer on a piece of land, will doll it up, do the best they can to make it look like a legitimate house. Lustig hadn't even bothered to cover up the hollow underneath the place. When Sam was in the darkness on the lee side of the trailer, the darkness deep, it was from this hollow that he heard a noise.

He had been stepping silently on the wet, dead leaves, remembering playing games with his brother in these woods. He had worked hard at making his steps quiet. The Indians knew how to move through a Fall forest of crisp leaves and dry branches without stirring up a single squirrel. He wanted to do the same and had worked at it, eventually learning how to make his older brother scream like a girl when he jumped him.

Sam's ears caught a hurried breathing, a panting like a wounded animal, and this was pretty much what he expected to find as he drew his weapon and shone his flashlight on the underside of the trailer. A pair of wild and glaring eyes shot back at him, and it took a full beat for him to understand that they were human. He shouted to Parker as he studied the sight, a muddy and panicked Harlan Lustig shivering in the dirt under his trailer.

This morning, there was another car at Lustig's, an eighties Firebird. Sam stopped just long enough to jot down the license plate number. He thought the car looked familiar, but he didn't know it from any case he'd worked.

On his way to his next stop, an abandoned house on J and then down to The Bend for whatever could be found there, he had to pass by the Stegman farm. He was beginning to remember visiting the farm on other occasions when he noticed something in the road ahead. Six or seven heifers were milling about the road, a couple of cows standing on the blacktop, another couple eating the sour, dead grass out of the ditch. They'd come through a hole in the fence, just past the driveway, posts leaning over lazily, barbed wire lying slack on the ground.

Sam flipped on the cruiser's lights, hit the siren with a couple of loud squawks to put some fear into these girls, and maybe also to get Frank's attention, then stepped out of the car. He took his hat in his hand and stretched his arms, trying to slowly work them back to the hole in the fence. They weren't minding, so he turned to the one closest to the downed fence. If he could get one back in, maybe the others would follow.

He'd had to push, but he got one through and turned around to assess the position of the others when he saw Frank emerge from the small house. He was tucking in a work shirt that wasn't completely buttoned, his boots were unlaced, his dark hair stood on one side, the trace of some hard sleeping.

From Sam's perspective, Franklin was still young. The hard work in his life had only kept him fit and had tanned his already dark skin. He was a good-looking guy, but Sam guessed that Frank didn't know it. A monk's life he'd been leading here, working for Terry, and Sam and his wife felt a little bad for him. The guy deserved a woman, or at least a good time once in a while. For all they knew, he never even went out in the evenings when he was free. As he approached Sam, it sure looked like he'd learned how to have a good time and was suffering for it now.

"Sum bitch." The curse came hard and wrong off Frank's tongue.

"Don't sweat it. We'll get 'em."

They worked together to get the cows back on the right side of the fence, and the heavy black cows wandered freely and calmly there as if they hadn't upset anyone's morning.

Sam began attempting to upright the leaning posts while Frank went for the post driver. Frank ran only part of the way to the barn, and a hand went to his chest, then his head. Sam, then, looked over his shoulder. He could make out a pair of skid marks angled on the asphalt, aimed at the gap in the fence. The lines of rubber came off the blacktop and continued in the torn-up grass before disappearing in the hollow of the ditch. At the base of the fence, around Sam's feet, the dirt and grass were disturbed from where a bumper struck and bounced up, sending whatever vehicle into the fence.

This sort of evidence was not uncommon on these roads, and rarely was there ever a car still there, or any attempt made to contact the property owner. Driving the winding blacktop, you could almost spot skid marks extending off the pavement about once a mile. Maybe they should have more patrols at night, try and stop some of the drunks on the way home.

Frank made it back, looking sick, and together they did the best they could to pull the fence tight and drive the posts. Stepping back, Sam could still see some slack.

"I'll have to get that puller out. Damnit. I just did this stretch last spring."

"Put 'em in another pasture 'til then?"

"Suppose."

"You want help with that?"

"Naw. I'll get to it this afternoon."

"Sure. Let me know if you need help." Sam picked his hat up from where he'd had to put it while struggling with the fence. Frank was walking back to the house along the path next to the fence. "Alright. Have a good one."

"You too." Frank waved a hand without looking back.

Sam wished he had an excuse to look at the front of Frank's truck.

9

Harley was looking for a way to burn off the crank he'd snorted that morning. He had stacked and restacked CDs, scratched at a spot on his temple, and even washed his dishes. He still had some to sell, but he didn't like to do it when he was this wound up. His nose burned and his teeth were clenched. And a bit of paranoia was always nagging. He needed to cook another batch, but couldn't do that until dark. He wasn't about to go out and get components, ingredients in this state. They'd make him as a user in a second. He wasn't really a user, no. He did it on occasion, but he figured if he didn't binge, then he wasn't like them. And since he'd learned to cook, he wasn't having to buy it. That was always a rule. Using on occasion was alright, but buying meant you were a user. Not a problem. He was just down here to make a buck off the fucked-up hillbillies. Toothless fucks.

He was pacing the room, the small living area of the trailer, picking up things, putting them in another place, or away. Then he would circle around again to move the thing from its new position to another. No, he hadn't really come down here to get involved with the hillbillies. It was going to be therapeutic. Get him away from other things. A simplification. No one knew him here. No one from St. Louis was going to come down here looking for him. It was a way to shun aspirations in favor of isolation. It hadn't quite worked out like he'd expected.

And then what? What happened? It was like always. Found himself around the wrong people. Maybe they sought him out. Maybe that was where he belonged. He could be in a room full of college graduates, professionals, and he'd be talking to the help. He'd be talking to the busboy, who would offer him a joint. Why did he think it would be any different if he got out of St. Louis? He'd been on his way home from a new job, his new life in the country, stopping at the Country Mart for some ramen, maybe he'd splurge for some brand-name soda. Standing by the door, taking that last drag off a cigarette before going inside, and this scraggly guy says, "Hey, wut's up?"

Harley had been in his own world and the question from a stranger caught him off guard. He answered with a "hey" and a nod.

"You looking for some ice?"

"Ice?" He wondered why the guy would give a shit about what he was going in to buy.

"Crystal, man. Meth." He came closer. He was about Harley's age, but stringy. He had a sparse, light-colored goatee. Long arms hung out of a sleeveless shirt, tattoos reaching up them from his wrists.

"Ha." Harley chuckled. Of course, he looked like a guy that might be looking to score. He thought he was looking to buy some groceries but really, he must have been looking to score because here is the offer. Right in front of him. "No, man. No." His words were infiltrated by his light laughter.

"No?" Red eyes darted back and forth over the landscape behind Harley. "Something else?"

"I'm cool." Harley stamped out his cigarette on the concrete.

"Come here." This guy turned and waved him to follow.

He did.

The guy took him over to a woman who was standing against the building, in the shade. She looked like a boxer. Eyes and the bones around them looked swollen, battered. She, too, wore a sleeveless shirt, with the collar ripped out and low to reveal tanned and wrinkled cleavage. Maybe she was his mother. Harley didn't want to think about this woman as his girlfriend.

The guy snapped his fingers at the woman and held out his hand. With a quickness, she put something in his hand that he pocketed. If he'd have blinked, he would have missed it. The guy continued.

They went around the corner, and he began to get a little scared. Not scared, but concerned. Was he about to get mugged? A guy going into a store probably has cash. The lanky guy was probably going to jump him, and his woman was going to come back and finish the job.

Again, they turned another corner, to the back of the building, and

Harley felt compelled to speak. "Wait a minute."

"Jimmy." He introduced himself, pulling something from his pocket.

"Harlan?"

This guy, Jimmy, backed himself up against the cinder block of the building, next to a green dumpster that reeked of sour milk and spoiled meat sitting in the sun.

"I'm good, man." Harlan waved a hand, trying to tell him he wasn't interested. He really didn't think he was. Pot, sure. He'd had his share of experiences with cocaine, even heroin, with the guys from the north side of St Louis, but crank? Didn't sound like the thing for him. Cocaine has that clean feeling, the powder so white, fluffy, pure. The high so genuine. Meth had a reputation. Sure, rat poison might get you high, but it was still poison.

"Here." Jimmy was drawing on a glass pipe, twisting it back and forth.

He could leave, right? He could walk away right now. But he'd been thinking about that high from cocaine, thinking about getting high, and he had an opportunity right in front of him.

The high was more or less sudden, and extreme. It hit him like he'd had a sudden fright, a shot of adrenaline. Harley felt like he'd just jumped off the building. He felt his fingers expanding, stretching as if he crouched behind this grocery store in Sheridan, Missouri, growing larger, stronger. A pair of horses standing on the ridge on the other side of a fence behind the store stopped in their labor of pulling out the grass with their blunt teeth to raise their long heads and take notice of Harlan Lustig growing larger, bigger, greater.

So, that's how it was. Now he was hanging out with true dope fiends, using and learning to cook from the stretched-out madman. But he'd follow up this with other wrong decisions.

"That's who I am!" He extended his arms as he continued to pace his room.

The sound of a car coming down the drive made him drop to the floor. His nose in the carpet, he listened and shook. The fear was still in him. He could still feel the panic that fueled his sprint through the woods and creeks that finally led him home. The distance he ran made him feel no better. No matter how many fences and streams he put between him and Jimmy Jiles, he felt no safer. He knew this guy. He knew from his bragging that he would shoot a man and not think twice. He'd once told Harley that he'd killed a couple of guys with a fire poker and burned them up in his fireplace. It was why he moved north to Barnes County. It didn't matter if was true because Jimmy was a bad man, and if it wasn't true, he wished it was.

Jimmy carried a shiny little gun. Harley had once come close to telling him that it looked like a woman's gun. That was just before he shot holes in a man's car outside a bar in Hudson. Jimmy ran a lab in a house in a hollow by the river. And when he showed it to Harlan, it wasn't showing off, it wasn't even a matter of educating Harley. He'd pointed out the tanks, the goods, the overall size of the operation as if he'd been telling him to fuck off. It wasn't a matter of pride but some sort of righteousness. Harley had to hide his awe. It was a large operation. He had no idea how much dope it was liable to produce, but it was impressive. What was striking was seeing a drug produced. Sure, he'd known people with pot plants, but it produced shitty weed. The good shit came from far away, a hell of a long supply chain that eventually put it in his pocket. Here, though, was the raw product to finished goods. All in one spot.

In no time, Harley had quit his job at the RV factory in order to cook meth for Jimmy. He used just enough to keep him producing long into the night while Jimmy was out selling and stealing. Harlan had no fantasies about them being a team. He'd spent most of his adult life working in menial jobs for bosses who didn't respect him. Harley sometimes thought himself naturally subordinate.

It was getting near dawn one night and a batch, in its last stages, was reducing while, under the bare bulb of a kitchen, Harlan had slumped over the table and fallen asleep. A fitful sleep with a bit of crystal he'd snorted at dusk the previous evening still running through his veins, but there he was drooling when Jimmy and his girl came bursting through the door. They'd been laughing, but as Harley's eyes flicked open, Jimmy kicked the table. "What the fuck?"

Harley, upright now, wiped his face with the back of his hand.

"You want it all to burn off?" Jimmy cranked down the burner. "Shit, man, what's wrong with you?" He turned back to Harlan, his light green eyes always made Harley look away. "What if we'd been the cops, man? You didn't even hear us coming."

He had no excuses and felt the usual shame that accompanied letting someone down. He'd done it a million times, but it never ceased making him feel like shit. It was the feeling he had sought to escape by leaving St. Louis and here he'd done it again.

Jimmy leaned in close, giving Harlan a chance to study him. He was fair-skinned, his face and arms perpetually sunburned and peeling. He was Harley's age, but living hard isn't good for the skin. The sketchy Colonel Sanders look had been shaved off one night when it prohibited access to an itch on his chin. The meth-fueled grooming had left him without a layer of skin at the bottom edge of his chin. Close to Harley's face, the red chin looked damn sore.

The gun, he noticed then, was pressing into his sternum as if Jimmy was driving a stake into the ground. Harley felt the hollow of the cylinder, the circle from which a bullet could emerge in a split second, the blink of an eye, without a moment to react.

It was then that the idea first struck him of going out on his own. It would be hard to let anyone down if he weren't working for anyone. He knew enough of what he was doing and thought he'd do well without this bastard.

His breath stinking of Busch and rotting teeth, into Harley's face, Jimmy said, "Dumbass," and slapped him in the face with the little shiny gun, then turned away laughing.

Harlan peeked from behind the US flag that served as a curtain over the window of his front room. A low and rusting Pontiac was ticking in the gravel drive. The knock on his door came from CeeCee Dawkins, the car's owner. The name cracked him up. The only CeeCee he'd ever known was an enormous black woman whose son dealt smack. She was as mean as she was warm-hearted. It was said she'd knifed two husbands, but you'd never know it from the way she treated her son's acquaintances.

This CeeCee was a thin white woman with her hair so bleached blonde that it was white. If she ever went in a pool, Harley thought, that hair'd be green for a month. She'd given birth a month or so before to a boy whose father remained unknown. People had guesses, but they were no closer to knowing than CeeCee. And though she'd had this baby only a few weeks prior, you'd never know it to look at her. She wore tight sweat pants that hid nothing.

"Did you send two boys to my house this morning?" Harlan asked as she came up the steps and into the trailer.

She came in with her newborn in an infant carrier and set it down on the floor. She bent over and pulled back a gray blanket to peek at the child, then covered him up again. During this, Harlan was distracted by her pink pants and her bare ankles, one of which revealed a Def Leppard tattoo.

"Those kids said you told 'em where to find me. I don't need everyone knowing where I live."

"D'you sell 'em somethin'?"

"Course."

"Well, then."

"What can I get you?"

"Jimmy really looking to kill you?"

"That's the shit he's talking."

"He's a scary bastard."

"Lucky the county got him before I did." Harlan was enlarging in his new position. He'd become a dealer. In his previous life in St. Louis, Harley had spent enough time in the company of and being ripped off and pushed around by dealers, and it was nice to find himself on the other end of things. He was no longer subordinate. He set his own rules, and everyone else had to play by them. So, he'd taken some customers from Jimmy, and they weren't just small users. He sold to either the major fiend or a downstream supplier. He'd been there that day making a twenty-five-thousand-dollar deal. Already been paid, he was there to deliver and, understandably, Jimmy Jiles didn't like it. Should've been his deal. In the end, Jimmy'll get sent up and put to death for killing three people, and Harley stands here now about to make another deal, his reputation improved. If he was worth trying to kill and worth shooting three others then he was a serious dealer.

10

He failed to see it. It glowed before him, flashing, pulsating colors, fifty inches diagonally and flat. Frank had been sitting in front of it, too close to it, from some time in the day's afternoon to well into the night. The room around him, not his room, lighted by the colors emitted by the television. Not his television.

He was in the living room of Terry's house, seated in a side chair because he wasn't about to sit on the couch. The beer cans piled up on the floor next to him, accumulated through the steady consumption of the case at Frank's feet.

Entering the house was not something he had been willing to do initially. It had not been out of bounds for him for some time, but it was still someone else's house. He had spent time on that couch, in her company. There were phases when Terry wanted to watch movies every night. Frank was not discriminating. Things would change, though, and Frank would have to get used to sleeping in his own bed again. And he would not complain.

How could he, though, bring himself to enter the house when its inhabitant was still newly buried? He had avoided it, until that afternoon came, still feeling like a morning to Frank, and he had been looking for a drink. He had entered through the garage. Extra provisions were stored on the concrete floor. There was a vacancy here that bothered Frank.

A pale blue Crown Victoria usually occupied the center of the garage floor, a cherished rig Terry had named Vicky. The car had traveled in the funeral procession directly behind the hearse, before Terry's family, and well in front of Frank.

The hollowness here resonated, felt to him like a similar

hollowness in his chest.

Frank already felt weak and haggard. It had been a long night and the day was becoming nearly unbearable. It could be and would be fixed by a drink. The consumption of alcohol would dull the pain. It would take the glare off the day. The lines of the door frame, the corners were sharp and painful. A drink would soften the edges.

He knew the source of the pain, of course. He knew a drink was not going to resurrect her, to bring her back so that he might stand in her presence once again. And that made him want the drink all the more. Nothing was going to change things. Nothing was going to set the world right again. It would be, now and forever, this God-awful place where someone like her, someone so kind, so earnest would no longer exist.

There was a case of beer there on the floor of the garage, but it was warm. Inside, though, there would be cold beer in the fridge. He took the beer and went inside.

Bob Stegman had been a big, proud man. Only in his weakest moments had Frank ever despised him. Though, envy him he did. Bob made a lot of money, made hard, though, risky choices that nearly always brought him success. And though it seemed to Frank that the money nearly poured in, Bob was also cheap. The house had been built to look nice for the road, complete brick face, high-arched windows, but inside the cheapest materials were used. The kitchen floor was a thin linoleum that showed wear. The appliances were bought wholesale, intended for furnishing low rent apartments.

In the years after Bob's death, Terry had not been afraid to spend money, steadily upgrading the house. The refrigerator was now a gleaming silver thing, with every button and feature available. What was the money for if not to improve her life, she would always ask.

The television had been a logical choice for upgrading.

It pulled him in. He watched anything, allowing himself to be drawn into the retelling and dramatization of aerial battles, home improvement shows, overly dramatic news magazine programs. He immersed himself in it, drinking the warm beer in greedy swallows.

And still, despite the absurdity or melodrama of the program, Frank remained aware of what it was he was trying to avoid. He wasn't thinking about her, not consciously, but she was there. Or, rather, she was not there.

It was one year after Bob's death when she came to him. He had been awakened, ripped from dreams of being tangled in tall grass and vines along a fence line, by footsteps on the gravel driveway. Frank bounded out of his small bed, the clamor of bedsprings screaming in the night, and looked out his window as he pulled on his jeans. A flashlight bounced in the dark.

Though his mind held doubts, he knew that it was her. She was finally coming to him as he had always imagined. How would she do it? Would she fall into his arms, wanting his strong arms around her? Would she come to him with lust in her eyes, attack him with kisses, and take him straight to bed? He picked up a shirt off the floor and met Terry at the door.

"Goddamn house." She walked in past him. He watched mutely. "Noises all night. Fucking place crawling with spiders or something."

It was never her form that drew Frank to her, but here, standing in the middle of the night in his starkly lighted living room, she was beautiful. Her usually harsh features, the sharply drawn nose, flat cheeks, were softened. Her plain white t-shirt revealed a waist, breasts.

"You'd think it'd be better by now. That house just ain't right sometimes."

"Sit." He pointed to the couch.

"Hate to bother you, Frank. Know you need your sleep."

"S'alright."

"That house. I swear sometimes it just wants to swallow me up. And I got to get out. And if I didn't come here I'd be out wandering on the blacktop."

"It's not a problem, Terry."

"You know you're a good guy." She looked at Frank quickly then leaned her head back on the couch, talking to the ceiling. "You've been here a long time. You never complain."

"You know I love it here." Love was a strong word.

"Do you ever wonder if you've missed something, Frank. I mean, you've been here forever, a million other things could've happened to you."

"If things are this good, why would I question it? It's not good to go around wanting more."

She turned to look at him, her head at an angle to his. Her eyes were open, inviting.

"Things are open to me now in a way they've never been. And it should be exciting, it should be a new life. And all I want is for things to be the way they were." She yawned, looking back at the ceiling. "I'm like a leaf floating on the breeze and still wanting to be clinging to the tree."

"Things are different, now." He was struggling to reassure her, afraid that change would lead her away from him. And wanting for things the way they were was only wanting for Bob again. "You're already making changes. You started working for the sheriff's department. But it doesn't mean things have to change too much."

Terry was silent. It looked like her eyes were open, slits at least. Frank waited, watching her.

"I'm tired, Frank."

"Come on." He stood. "Use my bed."

"No, no."

"Come on." He held out his hand and she took it. Frank was aware of how limited their opportunity for touch had been. She didn't really seem to him like someone who needed touching. Yet, it was what he wanted to do.

"I'll go back home," she said after she stood, her hand still passively in his.

He pulled her to his room and, with the sight of it, she collapsed on top of the covers, pressing her head into the pillow.

Frank went around to the other side of the bed and lay down on top of the covers as well. And he watched her sleep until he, too, faded from consciousness.

11

High, thin clouds were beginning to line the blue ceiling of sky, while underneath flew a formation of geese. A checkmark. They flew rhythmically northward, but Annette thought she'd seen them, this same group, flying south only minutes before. Maybe she was confused. She would be expected at her desk at the Barnes County Historical Society today, but she stood at the back door of her house, looking at the sky.

She was dressed. She was ready to leave. Something compelled her to stay and keep her eye on the day. Was it Winter or Spring? It was a day in between. It was a day without season or a bridge between seasons. Spring would allow her to work in her garden which lay bare and dead behind the house, picked over and neglected. Spring would crowd the scratchy trees with leaves. They would color the stripe of Lloyd's Creek that she looked down on from her house. The leaved trees would hide from view her old house and barn that sat down a side road by the creek.

The house she lived in had been built for her mother. A modest house situated on the paved road to ensure easy access, allowing a newly married couple privacy in the old family home a half-mile away. The old house was only a young couple's home for a short time, though, because her mother took ill. Annette's presence and care would be needed continuously, and she would only be a half-mile away. She moved just up the hill.

It may have been her absence that put her husband into a particular state, but a look at family history would show that a propensity towards this sort of thing had always been there. And maybe it had spurred Annette's decision to move up the hill. A violent and self-destructive drunk, Ralph shot the engine of his truck in a rage. For others, though, it would be blamed on high-schoolers stirring up trouble. She'd seen him smash bottles over his head, crush the knuckles of his hand pounding the barn door.

No one drinks that much and goes hunting, she knew. It had been October and he was found with his thirty-ought-six in the rocks of the dry creek bed. She could smell him when they brought him up to the house but for others, it had been a tragic accident. Even though it had been deer season, he had no license.

The death of Annette's mother soon followed and she was left alone in the widow's house on the hill, with a view of the creek bed and the house that still contained her marriage bed. Occasionally, at night, she thought she could still hear him banging around in the vacant house.

Annette turned from the window to think about her day. She needed to write some text for the county's website. She didn't really know how it all worked, though others had tried to show her. They could simply use the text contained in the tri-fold brochure they handed out at the office and local shops. She had protested. They wanted not only to explain some of the county's history, modest though it was, they wanted to encourage visitors.

On the counter huddled apples and a five-pound bag of sugar. The table was adorned with a glass milk jug stocked with fake flowers brighter than the day outside. Where would they get fresh flowers for her grave? The Governor's coming. They can't use those plastic flowers. Maybe she should call the Hampstead man at the parlor and make sure he knew to get real flowers. She tried to imagine a mahogany casket, flowers resting across the top. Annette felt something fluid in her nose and she went for a tissue. "A shame."

And he would have seen it happen. How can he go on? How can he stand over her casket tomorrow? Little Billy Wallis. While his mother was nurse to the ill and infirm at the hospital, Annette had watched over Billy. Five days a week since he barely knew better not to use his own drawers as an outhouse up until the time he got too big for his britches. Seems like he was barely a boy at all. Always tall, thin and quiet. Like he grew up knowing he would go to war, that he would be sheriff for this damn county as it falls to ruin.

She pressed the tissue to her nose.

12

Friday nights are particularly tortuous to a boy of fifteen. Especially so when he has no girl with whom to spend his time. And worse when one has a particular hold on his heart with a grip that would tighten as Friday became Saturday, then Sunday eventually. It put Logan in a notably anxious state. His last chance to glimpse Dot Baxter before the weekend came at the end of the school day.

As he watched the laboriously slow swing of the minute hand to the arbitrary release time of 3:05, Logan settled on a new course of action. His usual tactic of delay and pursue would not grant him contact, would not put them face to face. It only led to an excess of hope that deflated to disappointment.

World Geography was for idiots. What does it matter what the gross domestic product of India is? And what did it matter if they were fighting with another country about land so rough that no one in their right mind would live there anyway? Logan sat in the back, right corner of the class, his feet on the back of the vacant chair in front of him. He stared at the cheerleader in front of that, counting the seconds until she touched her hair again.

Before he could say five in his head, she flipped her blond hair over her shoulder, letting her hand drop only to bring it right back to twirl a lightened strand between long fingers. Give her five years and she'll have swollen up with a baby, have cellulite on her thighs and cry when she sees her stretch marks and drooping tits. Imagining what her breasts might look like after a child made him think about what they might look like now. In his mind, he cut and paste images he'd seen through the privacy filter at the library over the cheerleader in her uniform. He couldn't imagine anything that would satisfy the parameters of age and form but still, he had to shift in his chair.

He was thinking about what it must have been like for Skip Nelson to slip his hand under that yellow and black cheerleading sweater, slide it up over her ribs, over-tanned skin, to where it goes soft and pliable, when the final bell rang. Shit. He put a hand in his pocket to adjust, then held his backpack in front of himself as he pushed his way to the door.

After rushing to his locker in the noisy halls, doing his best not to bump too many shoulders and invite trouble on himself, he then found his way to the wide concrete walk in front of the building and stood there fiddling with his backpack.

The building was late fifties construction, one-story, wide walks and overhangs, long strands of symmetrical windows with many small panes. It was likely meant to be less intimidating than the traditional, multi-floor high schools but to Logan, the style of the structure was reminiscent of a yawn.

A feature of the construction and design of the building that Logan usually found frustrating, and today was grateful for, was the way all the students were squeezed out of one of two sets of doors. The doors in the back, which led only to the ball fields, or these front doors were the major egresses. So, Dot Baxter would have to walk out those doors to get home.

He stood at the edge of the concrete, trying not to step into the soggy winter grass while not getting in the way of the escaping students. He had his winter coat thrown over one shoulder and he held his backpack in one hand while the other rummaged through it. He wasn't looking for anything. The position was meant to make him look like he was doing something, not like he was waiting for anything.

Dot emerged. She was the picture of ease and casualness. Her coat was squeezed at the end of one swinging arm and the other hand held only a textbook and a notebook. She was mercifully alone. She was not with anyone of her usual group, those she could usually be seen with and who usually did not give Logan the time of day. She had her head tilted as if she were saying goodbye to someone, wishing them a good weekend, and when she turned to face the front, her eyes caught Logan's.

He returned a quickly calculated smile that would project a similarly casual attitude. It should show his pleasure at seeing her but not betray any eagerness. By the time she raised her hand in a wave, Dot was near to him. He quickly zipped his pack to turn and walk parallel to her.

"That Biology quiz was brutal, huh?"

"Not as bad as last week's."

He was walking next to Dot Baxter and having a conversation. The idea of what was occurring nearly made him smile giddily. She had spoken to him before, a few brief conversations, always in the company of others. One of the conversations was actually the spark that ignited his infatuation. In the fall, they had been sent to the hall to work on a group project. Their other two partners were cheerleaders who couldn't stop their gossiping to do any work. The two blondes' ignorance of the project inspired the same in Logan and Dot.

In the hall, the light from the doors came shining down the waxed floor, and lighted, in silhouette, Dot's bare legs. She sat leaned against the brick wall, one leg flat on the floor and the other arched in the reflected light. Her calf was slender and as smooth as the waxed floor, but the light on her thigh revealed glowing hairs. Normally invisible, the light hairs revealed a rejection of the normal beauty codes. It may be required that women shave their legs, but Dot was only willing to give in as high as the knee. The partial rejection was admirable, and the revelation came with an intimacy. He was in on a secret, he felt, on decisions made in the shower or tub. In moments of nudity.

They walked up a slight hill towards the town's center, past a church that was now an antique shop. In the shadow of the white building, the air grew cold and Logan seized a moment of silence to ask, "You going tomorrow?"

She turned to him. "Suppose."

Maybe it was an inappropriate question. Inappropriate because he was really looking for a way for them to be together during the funeral. Can you take a date to a funeral? And maybe he was only asking because he could either be alone or be with his aunt's family. Dot as a third option sounded like a pretty decent alternative.

"My Dad's making me go."

"I imagine."

"Ought to be a big thing."

"Most folks are going I think."

"Maybe I'll see you there."

"Sure."

They walked on.

"I gotta run in here. See ya tomorrow."

She stood on the sidewalk, near to him, reaching for the handle of the hardware store door and Logan felt her slipping away. She had left him no option. Cut him off, more or less waved him away. "See ya."

He turned away so as not to have to watch her disappear into the darkness of the store. Logan tried to find another focus to drive away his anger. He saw the courthouse. It took up one narrow city block, and the lawn that set the building back from the street was the closest thing they had to a town square, though parked cars angled in from the street hid the grass from view. It was a symbol for—and an example of—all that was wrong with this middle-of–nowhere town. It could use another good fire.

And then there was that house. That fake house. You're not fooling me with this old-new shit. The plastic siding gives you away. So, whenever we get the balls to actually build something new around here it's either slap together bullshit like they're building down 74 or they have to make it look like it's been here a hundred years. Why not just make the roof sag, put some water in the cellar and three layers of wallpaper on the walls?

As vulgar as Logan thought the blue house was, with its wrap-around porch like it had welcomed visitors there for decades, the sight of it upset him for the same reason as it did his father.

She never really made an attempt to hide it.

"Mom?" Coming home from school one day, he'd seen her dark blue Camry parked on the gravel drive and he was surprised to see that she might be home. He made a quick pass through the house's main floor. Front room, kitchen, living room. No evidence that she was there.

Maybe she had gone off with friends. Maybe her car was broken down. He didn't know and didn't suppose he should know. His parents never kept him informed. If she wasn't home then this time became his again and he trotted up the stairs, humming, already anticipating the CD he was going to crank up. He twisted at the newel post on his way to his room but slowed at the wide-open door to his parent's room.

It stood open like an invitation, revealing a room awash in afternoon light. The usually forbidden room teased him with its expanse of clean, open carpet before the enormous bed. The bedspread, a blinding red, draped off the foot of the bed, and white sheets were a tangle of fabric and pillows like the cotton tops of clouds.

He stepped tentatively in, tip-toeing on the carpet, admiring the tall mirror atop the dresser offering a double of this sanctuary belonging to his parents. At the bed, he put two fingers to the sheets, his tanned, dirty boy's fingers against the pristine, and then he saw something. For a moment, his mind saw them as baby mice, the pink toes, attached to the pale underside of a foot.

"Mom?"

The tangle of sheets stirred. Slowly at first, then with quickness. She sat up and pulled sheets around in a blur and a flash of hair and what he believed were bare breasts. What he did notice was her glance to the bed beside her. A look at first of concern, followed by relief.

"You sick?"

"Oh, yes, honey." She reached out a hand for him but withdrew it when he came closer. "You know, I've been working so much."

It was true. She'd started in real estate as nothing more than a hobby. Her friend Holly worked at one of the two agencies in Sheridan and got her into it for the companionship. She sold one twenty-thousand-dollar home that netted her one grand, but recently things had picked up. While she'd not made another sale, she'd been out at showings in all times of the day. Disappearing into the setting sun after receiving a phone call.

"Can I make you some soup?"

"Oh, no. I'll be fine. I just needed some rest. But Logan…," she lowered her voice to a whisper, pulling him closer still, "let's not tell your father. I wouldn't want him to worry."

Logan stood back up straight. "Oh, of course not."

"Great."

"All right then." And he extricated himself from the room and the house as quickly as he could.

Thinking about that afternoon now as he stared hatefully at the blue house, he recognized the fact that, though he didn't really know then what was going on, something told him things were amiss. He knew from the way he had wanted to vomit as he wandered the pasture, the single tract, long since sold, that stretched out behind their home. The feeling was similar to the feeling after the shattering of the glass window. Guilt and a sickening anticipation of the inevitable.

Still in the street, there he fell then into imagining walking into the store behind him, purchasing some kerosene to torch the house. Maybe he could use the full Coleman can as a bomb. He imagined ripping off a strip of his t-shirt and lighting it as a wick that would slowly burn until it entered the can and the whole thing would explode in a rolling ball of smoke and flame that would eventually bring down the house.

Logan was imagining what he might say to old man Freid when questioned about the purpose of the purchase and staring stupidly at the door of the hardware store when it swung open. He hoped that it was Dot, then he didn't. Instead, it was a handsome man with what Logan imagined as a perfectly built male frame, the kind seen on television in some sort of shirtless repose that made him subconsciously question his sexual preference. The man barreled quickly toward Logan and as the boy leaped to the right to get out of the way, the man with his bundle of purchases moved in the same direction. They did this dodging dance one more time the other way before the man pushed through Logan and disappeared quickly around the corner.

Logan followed, scanning the sidewalk's edges for loose rocks that could be useful and when he turned the corner he saw the man climb into the cab of a pick-up with a logo on the door. Lucky Construction. It was the well-built home-wrecking home builder. A man named Lucky.

13

Bill ran the strip of black electrical tape across his badge. The roll of tape had sat there most of the day, in front of him on the desk. Each time he flicked ashes in the tray or snuffed out a cigarette, it was there. Under the glare of the fluorescents in his tiny office, Bill had sat over his paperwork. He spent much of the morning waving off well-wishers at his door and reading reports. Traffic-stops, domestic disturbances, and shot-dog calls. He had let his mind fall into the abstract, distant, objective, formalized voice of the report, before writing his own.

It went well, his mind remembered quite a bit of detail, until the first shots rang out. He had still been stepping up behind Terry, eyeing the corners of the house when the sharp sounds made him stumble backward, pulling the weapon from his holster. Then somewhere in this action, Terry went down, and he got off a series of shots before he was hit. He couldn't describe it with any clarity. He didn't want to write anything with certainty that might be proved wrong later. This whole thing could go to trial and what kind of idiot would the elected sheriff look like if he couldn't get the facts straight?

"Deputy Stegman was shot. I returned fire and was also shot." These facts could not be disproved, and the order of statements did not necessarily reflect the order of events.

It was quiet in the sheriff's office. Over the hum of the baseboard heater, Bill could hear some mumblings down the hall, the occasional bang and slam from the jail cells. There was no laughter. Along about lunch, the silence bothered him and he stepped from his office.

Deputy Parker was leaning with one arm on the wall, hanging into the dispatch area. The dispatcher today was Darla Lambert, a healthy young girl who wanted to be an EMT. Working for the sheriff's office required less training. Parker was making her laugh.

"How's that new baby, Parker?"

Startled, the young man stood straight. "Oh, great. Ain't sleeping for shit, but he's a tough little bastard."

"Where's everyone?"

"Schaffer took Elmer Conley up to see the judge. Holtzman's probably asleep under a tree." Parker turned to Darla with a wink.

"Summers?"

"Dunno. He walked outta here with fat ol' notebook 'bout ten."

Bill looked back down the empty corridor. When he looked back to Parker, the kid was giving him a look, like he was noticing something was wrong with him.

"Did you get the prisoners' lunch, yet," Bill asked.

"Naw."

"Get me a cheeseburger."

"Sure."

"No, wait…." Bill thought for a moment that it might be good to get out of the office, which sometimes seemed very much like the basement it was. To show his face in the diner would mean confronting a whole bunch of folks he didn't feel like talking to or making nice with. "Never mind. Go ahead."

He turned back to his office. "Don't get anything for ol' Elmer. Judge is gonna let him go."

Back in his office of wood-paneled walls, awards, a map, and pictures hanging. In one he stood in the back row of sheriffs from across the state. Another caught him in a moment of glee after winning that first election so many years ago. Elaine was pictured at his side. Above a high file cabinet laden with notebooks and loose papers, the flash of a camera illuminated Bill and Terry, shovels in their hands, standing proud and giddy in front of an open truck bed filled with a mound of bloodied armadillo carcasses. The sweat on their faces revealed hard work, while the cracks around their mouths showed their pleasure.

The armadillos were bad that year. They came north in droves. Conditions must have been just right for their propagation. Either that or the conditions were poor to the south, driving them northward. The sight of an occasional grey hump along the roadside or lumbering across the double yellow was not exactly uncommon, but when a man can't go a quarter-mile without that thud from the underside of a vehicle, despite swerving at every occasion that didn't risk collision with oncoming traffic or objects along the road, folks were bound to complain. Cars had to be pulled out of ditches, apart from trees or required alignment. And there weren't enough coyotes or loose dogs in the county to consume the animals on the road before the bright sun and humidity baked them into a putrid casserole. The Department of Conservation didn't give a shit, so folks called on Bill to do something about it.

Bill and Terry loaded themselves into his truck with a feeling of frustration. This didn't quite fit the job description, but they set out anyway, headed south, armed with shovels and squirrel rifles. They drove, pulling the truck to the side to scoop carcasses from the highway.

When they encountered the first live one, sunning itself on the opposite shoulder, Bill stopped there, flashers warning their presence on the strip of blacktop. Terry swung her door open and slid out her rifle from where it lay on the floorboards. "I got this one."

The sheriff watched closely as she took a few short steps to the front of the car, lifted the rifle and fired. In a quick flash of blood around the eye, the armadillo rolled onto its back.

Bill took a shovel from the bed and crossed the road. "Damn." The bullet from the small-caliber rifle had nearly pulled the tiny little head clear off.

"Shit." Terry smiled. "That's a lot more satisfying than shooting at beer cans."

As the afternoon progressed their spirits lightened as they scraped up piles of gray and red. Sometimes they wouldn't even bother stepping out of the car before firing on the beasts with the rifles as well as their pistols. The ones that might be found in the middle of the road either in a highway siesta or a struggle to get from one side to another would find themselves rolling along the pickup's underside. A thumping on the mud plate under the engine, the driveshaft, and likely dead by the rear differential and spare.

They laughed outright as Bill would swerve to catch them just right, smiling as the dozing ones never saw it coming.

The two of them were still at it after dusk, Bill reloading his rifle and Terry heaving another dead animal on the pile that had risen from the truck's ribbed bed, when a cruiser approached with lights flashing.

"I got a call of some folks shooting up the highway down here." Sam Summers approached, hitching up his belt.

"You got us, officer." Bill laughed heartily.

"We was just gonna fry 'em up, or just cook 'em in a stew." Terry smiled wide at Bill.

"Eww." Sam reacted.

Bill spent the afternoon cleaning his gun, unconsciously grimacing from the pain. He took his time with it, running the whisk down the narrow barrel again and again, with a pleasurable sound. The pistol sat on the desk when he got around to marking his badge for Terry's loss. He was running his old thumb over the black stripe slowly, again and again, pushing the tape into every crevice of the design, when a presence at his door caught his attention.

Sam stood there, his hands in the pockets of his trousers. "How's it going?"

Bill noticed the attempted relaxed tone. He looked across the desk, the gun, the striped badge, and saw how it might look. He pushed his government surplus chair away from the old tank desk and lighted a smoke. "It goes, Sam. It goes."

"Yeah." Sam looked down as he pulled a chair up to the desk. "Bill?"

Sam was judging him, he knew. Pausing in what he was about to say to see how it might be accepted. Bill forced a relaxed tone, "Yup?"

"You know those drugs at the Kelly place came from Harlan Lustig, not Jimmy Jiles."

"More than likely."

"We need to find out where he's cooking."

"Why don't we just wait till he calls up again with some fool thing and use it to snoop around?"

"I don't think he's gonna be calling us much anymore. Besides, he ain't making that much in that trailer."

"Maybe it weren't his 'tall. Could be he ripped off Jiles. It'd explain why he was so pissed off."

"Could be, but that'd mean he knew where Jiles was cooking."

"What do you think we should do?"

"I think we ought to watch him tonight."

"We?"

"You know I'd have asked her, but…."

"Yeah." Bill sucked on his cigarette, drawing it hard and holding it in until he felt his head go a little light. Sam leaned eagerly forward at him. He was always looking to get things done, as if he was cleaning trash out of a field and at some point, it'd all be picked up and the job would be done. It wasn't like that in Barnes County. Sometimes you just have to handle things as they come your way. "Suppose you're right."

"Great." He stood, pushing his chair back.

"The sooner we pick him up, the better."

"You wanna come by around suppertime? Natalie'll make us some stew for the road."

"Sure."

"All right." Sam disappeared down the hall.

Sam was a good cop, sure, but that didn't make him the best deputy. He came in to fill some hours and help get some things done. It couldn't be left to Bill and Terry to get it all done. They were all glad to have him. He had city experience and a professional attitude which was sorely lacking in these parts. And then what? And then it becomes Sam and Terry, with Bill back at the office doing the paperwork. Sam and Terry out on surveillance, making the big bust. Bill doing the politicking.

Bill caught himself thinking these things and chuckled to himself. Pain must be worse than he thought. He sat at his desk and dialed his sister, Francine.

"Can you have Angie run some dinner over to Logan tonight?"

"What's wrong, Bill?"

"Nothing. Bad guys to catch, you know?"

"Sure." She paused, but Bill noticed she hadn't yet agreed. He knew she paused because she had something more to say. "Why don't you have your wife do it?"

"Do what?"

"Take your son—her son—some dinner."

"I don't talk to her. I don't know where she is. You know that."

"He's in the goddamn yellow pages, Billy?"

"Who?"

"Lucky. Her boyfriend. Pay attention."

"Sure."

"Let her run off with the damn handyman." Was she shaking her head on the other end of the line? "Damnit, Bill, call her and tell her to quit her whorin' and come home and take care of her child."

"Francie!"

"She's your wife. Still your wife. She swore to God and everybody that she wouldn't take off with a man ten years younger and leave her hardworking man to take care of her only child. Swear to God I see that woman on the street and I'll slap her into next week."

"Don't you do such a thing."

"You don't call her and tell her to come home, I will."

"You'll send Angie over?"

"She ain't gonna be happy about it, bein' Friday night, but she'll go."

"Appreciate it."

"Swear to God, Bill."

"Gotcha."

"Okay."

"Okay." He hung up the phone.

His hands were tied, weren't they? He'd done the irrational, wronged husband thing already. And she ain't back. He'd cursed her in public, threatened him with violence and all it did was make sure that she never came around anymore.

The first report that Annette gave him at the diner set him on edge. It's easy to make a cop suspicious. The facts he began to assemble pointed in one direction. He stewed on this information for a few days, studying her face for something that might reveal her betrayal. He saw nothing that might show any bit of guilt. No new crease around her eyes that said she was getting some on the side.

The Monday following the report, he was back at work and Elaine was out of his watch. She had a freedom of movement that was dangerous. He held out until nearly ten o'clock before he hurried to his cruiser and headed out in search of her. No cars at the house, but at the second stop, the realty office of her friend, Holly, Elaine's car was in the lot of the little strip mall. He passed slowly by, looking through the windows into the tan light of the office. He did not see her within. On his second pass, Holly stepped out the door.

He slowed the car to a stop and the window rolled slowly down. "Howdy." Bill leaned his elbow out the window.

"Hi there, Sheriff Bill." She leaned to him with what might be seen as flirtation. Might be unless the history between them was known. Holly was a tall and lanky woman and had been such since she and Bill were in grade school together. Class photographs always had them pictured together in the back. At some point when the hormones kicked in, they became adversarial, primarily because they were attracted to one another. Nothing ever came of it, not even later in high school when she consoled him after her own best friend had dumped him after only a week.

Holly reminded him of these things, his own awkwardness. And she seemed to be everywhere. And in the years since she'd been his wife's good friend, he'd done his best to steer clear of her.

"My wife around?"

"She went over to the diner for some coffee a little while back."

"Thanks. I'll look for her there."

"She'll probably be here soon."

He nodded and the car rolled away from Holly.

As a policeman, Bill never wanted to be far from his car. He really wasn't up to running a block to his car should he get a call that required his immediate attention. So, when he didn't see a parking place in front of the diner, he circled the block to have another look. As he did, a large white pickup passed him in the opposite direction. Bill only glanced at it at the last moment and then he saw her. At least for that one quick moment, a woman that looked like his wife was sitting shotgun in the truck of some man. He was suspicious, he knew, but with reason.

He punched the accelerator and the 'police interceptor' model responded. He rolled through two stop signs and was back on the main street. On the corner in front of the diner, waiting for a car to pass before crossing the street, stood his wife. He pulled up quickly and cut her off as she walked. He nodded at her to get in. She did.

"Hey, baby. What're you doing?"

14

The Verdant River, as it flowed in its meandering line from the north county line to the south, cut its way through the limestone, the hills, ridges, and hollows formed over the centuries, and in the south where the land turned mysterious, where communities hid in gaps in the land, where each ridgeline looked like the last but upon looking back the last was no longer recognizable, the water, now wide and swift was detoured by a high solid ridge of rock and made a quick turn to the west. Here, where the water stalled in its change of direction opposite a cliff green with vegetation and a stripe of white rock, was a muddy strip of shore spotted with trees gone skeleton-like in the winter cold that served as a hangout for juveniles looking for a spot without supervision to throw themselves from a rope into the river, for teenagers seeking backseat privacy and quenching of incomprehensible thirsts, for adults seeking a private rendezvous point for felonious activities, illicit purchases they'd rather keep secret from the town and county as a whole, an area known in this generation and many preceding as The Bend.

The route to The Bend was not without effort. It required a drive down a thin dusty road that fell down into a narrow valley that twisted and turned and disoriented, keeping any attempt to understand one's whereabouts to a near impossibility, then the road climbed a ridge before sliding down a narrow descent carved into the side of the ridge, falling then into the river basin. Even once there, the road ran through trees and was set far enough back from the green, moving, sleeping snake of a river that one might never know that this was an area of such private actions save the various tracks that ran off the side of the gravel road and off into the trees. Between any trees set wide enough apart for a car to fit through, twin muddy tracks served as proof that many had come here to this spot or the next set of tracks to hide their activity from the general public.

On a Friday night, The Bend was likely to be an active spot and before settling himself for a night of clandestine activity, the manufacture of methamphetamine, Harlan Lustig headed there to make some spot sales and search for more of those buyers like the late Dale Kelly who made his work simpler and more profitable.

The air down there was always pleasant to him, thick with moisture and the excitement that came from doing something you shouldn't but you desperately want to do. It put everybody into a state and made them a little susceptible to pressure. Just as teenage virgins were more likely to let their panties slip below their knees at The Bend, a little experimentation with illegal drugs was not off the table. Besides, Harley just might get a chance to see some young girl squeezed into the backseat with her ankles up around her head.

Harley had, of course, learned about The Bend from Jimmy Jiles. Being alone with Jimmy in his abused little Hyundai always made Harley a little nervous. By this point, he'd come to realize that the man could not be trusted. He'd been smacked upside the head, been yelled at, had that little girl's gun waggled in his face so many times that he knew anything was possible with this man. In each instance, Harley made himself so unassuming and non-threatening that any violence against him would hardly be worth the effort. Besides, he knew that surviving as this lunatic's sidekick was likely to give him a reputation as one not to be messed with.

They had stood on the soft green and brown of the soft riverside when Jimmy threw the rope swing out over the river in the coming evening's dusk. It whipped and cracked over the river while spider bugs skittered across the water's surface.

"This here rope," Jimmy spoke as if he was finishing a lengthy statement.

"Yeah?"

"Left him swinging out over the water."

Again, the man made him nervous. "What?"

"And it wasn't like the nigger was after some white woman."

The words raised his hackles. In St. Louis, he'd heard the word uttered from many dark lips, but knew that from any others those lips were likely to encounter a fist or two, or worse.

"Just cus he was a nigger."

"What?"

"The Klan."

"Here?"

"Right here. They used to meet here in their sheets and cross burning right next to the river.

Harley had a vision of the burning cross's reflection on the water lighting up the night. "When?"

"Dunno. Fifties or sixties. They say that ol' nigger's still around here peeking in at kids making it in cars, giving the boys a squeeze when they swing out into the water."

The two of them had wandered around the area, making sales, talking and drinking with groups sitting on the hoods of cars under the trees. After some time and some success, they were headed back to Jimmy's car with heads blurry and thick with drink, when they came across a car in the dark, rocking on squeaky springs. Jimmy smacked Harley's arm to make sure he'd seen.

Jimmy crouched down and stalked to the car on exaggerated tip-toes. In the filtered moonlight, Harley saw an expression of shock and then an arm waving him closer. Together they looked through the glass at a young girl, a teenager, straddling a boy in the backseat, giving him everything she had, one hand bracing herself against the roof, young proud breasts swinging painfully, pale in the dim light.

They were spectators there for some time until Jimmy brought his burning cigarette to his lips for a long draw. As he pulled air through the tobacco, the tip glowed a bright red, enough to catch the eye of the show's starlet who reeled back in a scream at the sight of these two gaunt drug dealers leaned into the window.

In a moment of screams damnd laughter, a shirtless kid built like a football player, big through the arms and shoulders but soft in the middle, withdrew from the car, all finger-points and shouts. As the kid approached, his postponed ejaculation apparently turning him violent, Jimmy ceased his laughter and stood as upright and rigid as a brick wall. And the kid struck him as such.

The sportsman ran into the dope head, intending to run through him but instead found himself on his back on the soft earth, having been pushed backward over Jimmy's foot twisted around his ankle. Jimmy then descended on him with a knee to the sternum that expelled the air from his lungs in a pained huff. As the kid struggled for breath and the girl started up her screaming again, Jimmy pulled the shiny little gun from his pocket, holding it above the boy's face for him to see before pressing it into the kid's eye.

Harlan found himself looking around as he heard voices from all around, approaching. Looking to the girl, he was in time to glimpse the breasts again, so magical, as she dressed beside the car. Jimmy was whispering something into the kid's ear, looking as he did like an aggressive lover intending to excite his partner with breathy words or a tongue in the ear.

When Jimmy stood, the tough scampered back to the car which started with a flurry of exhaust and light. Folks jumped out of the way as the car, with the boy and his lover inside, dodged trees on its way to the road. The onlookers retreated into the dark as the dust and night settled back down on the scene.

"What was you doin? Just standing there?"

"Looking and learning."

"Ha. That's right. Looking and learning."

On this night, the trees, usually full with leaves, stood bare at intervals like frightening tombstones in the darkness, illuminated by headlights. Harlan switched off his beat-up car and headed off on foot towards the smell of marijuana.

He made his rounds, pushing his drugs, looking for faces so strung out that a large purchase was the only way to get them through the next week or that night. He made some money but no stronger contacts. He was feeling disappointed at this and the fact that he hadn't had the chance to observe any paramours behind steamed windows, but he did come across a couple sitting on the hood of an old Pontiac.

He used the usual approach, simply asking if they were looking for anything, but he didn't bother hearing the answer because his mind was too occupied analyzing the pair. The girl had hair so red that it seemed to emanate light in the shadowy night. She sat leaned back on locked arms, her puffy winter coat falling backward, emphasizing large round breasts pressed upwards under a sweatshirt. The boy she was with was not much more than just a boy. Years younger than his companion, the kid, hair all in his face like he was too cool to be in the world with everyone else, sat with legs folded, slumping forward.

"I'm sorry, honey, what's that?" Harley sat down on the hood next to her.

This made her draw up defensively. "We're cool."

"Oh, yes." He made the review of her form obvious, glancing at the boy to dare him to make a move to defend her. "You got anything to smoke?"

"Reds," she offered.

"Like anything stronger?"

"No, man."

Though he sensed her trepidation, her voice was so soft it made him think of clouds. He wanted to keep her talking. "I got some crank that'll rock your socks."

"No, thanks."

"How 'bout a little bump? A little something for a Friday night?"

"We're cool."

"I'll tell you what. Whenever you're ready, you come see me." He leaned closer, though the boy stared at him. "I'm out in a trailer on 419. Near the washout. Door's always open for you."

"Sure."

Feeling dismissed, he stood, then felt a little angry about it. "What the hell you doing out here, then? I know you ain't climbing in the back seat with the pansy." He waved a hand at the boy.

"We're waiting on someone."

"It ain't me?"

"Him." She motioned behind him and Harley turned to see a pair of headlights bouncing slowly over the rough ground.

When the car came close dand the ignition cut off, leaving a stirring silence and headlights burning, Harley approached the figure getting out of the car. It was an old car sales technique, separating the couple, making a pitch to the man that appealed to his independence from the woman. The guy was more genial to Harlan than his girl, but he was sent away without a sale none the less.

Now, if the boy wasn't there, he'd head back to them in about fifteen minutes to catch them as they got hot and bothered, but if anything was going on that involved that sulking boy, Harlan didn't want to see. It was time, instead, to pack it in and get to work.

15

The two men were silent as the narrow road they drove turned to a shadowed strip of gray in the settling dark. Sam didn't want to turn on the lights until he had to. He wasn't interested in alerting the Lustig guy to their presence unless necessary. The sound of the gravel pinging the underside of the truck ceased momentarily as the road dipped and passed over the concrete washout. It still amused Sam that the county was so cheap that they would rather have folks trapped by overflowing water than to build even the smallest bridge. When they rose on the small incline, the truck slowed and both men turned to their right. The thickness of bare trees opened. A small plot of land revealed a darkened trailer and no car in front.

Sam felt himself grown heavy in his seat. Bad enough that he might have missed Lustig for the evening, but he had pressed Bill into coming. Bill was tired and had been through more in this week than a man should reasonably be forced to experience. There was a chance that this would be good for him. Get him back up on the horse. A man can be made to feel pretty impotent by failure. Or the perception of failure. And with any luck tonight they could have reasonable cause, some hint of evidence that would allow them to arrest Lustig.

That was really what Sam was hoping for. Bill in his state might be more interested in making an arrest or even pushing for a warrant. If only they had looked in that clearing to see Lustig pulling glass jugs from his trunk. Maybe there was something else.

During his questioning after the killings, Lustig gave up nothing. He was just visiting. He knew nothing about any drugs. And, yeah, he used to know Jiles, but the man was dangerous. Without anything against him, Sam was not going to get anything incriminating out of him.

Sam turned the truck around at a gate and drove back to the Lustig place, stopping in front. He rolled his window down and sniffed the air a couple of times like a drag on a cigarette, drawing the air into his lungs. Nothing. No chemical scent that might clue them into some sort of illegal activity.

Bill radioed for anyone to let him know if they spotted Lustig's car.

"Damnit, Bill, I'm sorry."

"Well, he's somewhere."

"Yeah, but where?"

"I don't know. But it might be the place we're looking for."

The excitement of surveillance can be a good time. Fun, in fact, but disappointment kept them silent as they cruised the county, stopping at structures they knew to be vacant. This wasn't what Sam had hoped for. They were shit out of luck, he felt.

Sam and Terry had been on surveillance the previous summer and it had been fruitful. To Sam, it was always "surveillance," not a "stakeout." He wasn't willing to give in to the trivializing of his profession that pop-culture pushed. They'd had a guy dead to rights. Everyone knew he was cooking, knew where it was done. They probably had enough to get a search warrant for the property, but the real goal was to catch him in the act. Some of these guys make a party out of cooking, so not only could they catch him, they'd be likely to get his band of associates.

The two deputies sat across the road, backs against a log while Terry used night-vision glasses to call out license plate numbers of the cars in front of the house while Sam wrote them down. A dusk-to-dawn light hung from a pole in front of the shop where the lab was located. It was a sort of garage or large utility shed. Light could be seen coming out from under the door.

Sam chuckled to himself.

"What's yer problem?" Terry whispered to him.

"This is going to be easy."

"You bet."

"These guys don't have much upstairs, do they?"

"No, shit. Probably couldn't put one full brain together between 'em."

Listening closely through the chorus of crickets and night birds, a thin strand of guitar rock could be heard. It was a warm, damp night with only a sliver of silver moon just now rising in its arc through the stars. Sam felt his body, his legs, his arms, warm and soft like he'd just come out of the bath, while his heart kept a hard and steady beat in his chest.

"D'you ever wonder how folks end up like this?"

Terry sighed and leaned back some. "You think they had any choice about it?"

"Coulda gone to junior college, got a job at the Forest Service, something."

"Like they're folks ever told 'em that."

"Probably true."

"I knew his parents. Buncha drunks in Max Hollow. He spent his time drinking and smacking her around. She spent hers fucking around."

"You don't think he could have made things any better for himself?"

"I'm saying he didn't know there was anything better."

Sam had a hard time with Terry's point of view. "And you feel sorry for him?"

"Fuck no. He's a low-life. He's a fuck-up and dragging the rest of us down for it. A man can't learn to follow the law needs to pay for it."

"I'm with you there."

"Ain't like we got these laws for no reason. Cause he's a dipshit don't give him a free pass."

"Damn right." Sam was happy to settle in this agreement. He wasn't one to believe in destiny or fate. Folks make themselves who they are. This guy they were after tonight, Harney, had made his own dumb choices that led them to this night. It wasn't like he had to do it. And now he was going to pay for it. And that pleased Sam.

Just then the door squealed open and the two of them raised binoculars to watch the figure that emerged. At first the light directly above shielded the face from view, but as the figure moved on, it became obvious that it was a female of about nine or ten. A girl. Tangled hair past her shoulders, a tank top, pajama bottoms. No shoes.

She carried a cracked glass jug and dragged a bag of trash.

At the open dumpster that sat near the road, she swung the trash bag in her left hand and flung it up above her head and in. With the jug, she used two hands but the jug clanged against the lip of the dumpster and fell and shattered in the gravel at her bare feet. She squealed and leaped back. The girl seemed to contemplate the hunks of glass there, then turned and went back inside with a slam of the door.

Sam and Terry looked at each other. This changed things. While they could bring another charge against Harney, they couldn't just bust in there with guns blazing. Sam thought they were defeated.

Terry rose then and Sam believed she was ready to pack it in, but she pulled the radio from her pocket and called dispatch.

"Get Parker and a couple others. And wake up Bill," she commanded. "And call Child Services. They got a girl in there. We're going in."

Sam's heart rate which had been slowing jumped up and he, too, rose to his feet. As he did, Terry was starting through the trees towards the road.

"Where you going?"

"I don't know that we want to wait."

Walking gently on the gravel, Sam saw the girl's bare shoulders in the dim antiseptic light of the dusk-to-dawn. His ears heard again that phrase "Child Services." He was not unfamiliar with this term, and it still raised his hackles.

Back in Pennsylvania, in that little house pressed into the hillside that ran down to the Ohio River, Sam's wife made them a supplemental income from watching his brother's kids.

Things were tough on everyone and somehow the two families struck an agreement that seemed fair and equitable to all. The fact was that his brother's children, a boy and a girl, were in need of other parental figures and Sam and Emily thought they'd step in and lend a hand. Sam and Emily's own family was on hold. It was as if they were waiting for the right amount of money to have children, when things would be more secure for them. Then when the kids, Cory and Allison, became near full-time figures in their house any inclination Sam had towards children evaporated.

They weren't the best kids. Just eleven, Cory, and nine, Allison, they were used to being ignored. It wasn't like his brother John and his wife, Tammy, were relaxed parents; they were ignorant parents. The kids dug their hands into everything, jumped off the arms of the couch and into the chair, hit each other with closed fists, and stole food from the cupboards. This isn't to say they weren't friendly kids. Cory was happy and eager, even thankful, to have his cuts and scrapes tended to. Allison liked to be held, her hair pet.

This responsibility exhausted Natalie, leaving her drained when sometime around six or seven PM, often with the smell of a quick round or two at the bar on his breath, John would pick up the children. Sam's hours as a policeman were not consistent for any more than a week or two at a time, so he wasn't much help to his wife.

Through this, they survived as a couple and even as a pair of couples. At least for a few years. In these years Sam witnessed changes in the kids that unsettled him. A stash of magazines, the pages a blur of tan and pink, was found by Natalie under some shrubs behind the pump house after one afternoon of wondering where on earth the kid could have been for hours on end. Sam had trouble seeing him after this as anything other than a little pervert who couldn't keep his hands off himself. This also concerned him because hormones were also having a developmental effect on Allison. And, though she seemed unaware, her tanned legs were long and gathered the attention of male drivers as they passed on the busy riverside road in front of the house. And the spaghetti-strapped tank tops she wore made evident a future that made both Sam and Natalie concerned.

These physical changes seemed only symbols of the further changes to come, a period of darkness that continued to eat at Sam whenever he saw a young girl who was on the cusp of an adult form of beauty, whose innocence blinded her to the threat that beauty posed to her innocence. Like one who, at two in the morning, walked innocently into a room of men on high on drugs unaware of the risk posed. Of course, this assumed that any innocence was left.

Nothing tore Sam up as much as the sight of his wife crying. He'd made it home to that small house in Ambridge in the late afternoon after a shift that began at five in the morning and he entered the house hoping to find a sanctuary away from grimy streets, patrols that took him down narrow sloped alleyways where drunks slept, where drugs and sex and other things were bought and sold. Home was like a hushed and shadowy cathedral while the tourists bustled in the heat outside.

Natalie stood in the arch between the kitchen and the living room, her hand to her mouth as if she could physically keep herself from crying. A rock formed in Sam's gut. His mind raced through a million horrible possibilities. Most involving death. "What is it?"

Water came from her eyes like water flowing over the rim of two twin sinks. Her hair, worn long then, came from her head at angles as if she'd done her best to pull it all out of her scalp. Sam grew angry as he looked at her because the more she looked at him with those eyes, the more she looked wronged.

"John called." Natalie's voice came as if through rain. "Ally…."

"She okay?"

"She said you touched her."

"I what?"

"Molested…." She couldn't hold any of it and she broke down in sobs, coming to him them, burying her head in his chest, in the side without a badge.

He held her to him with one arm and pulled her along as he went to the phone that hung on the wall in the kitchen. Calling his brother brought little other information outside an expletive, a damnation, and the supposed fact that that the police were on the way to his house.

Whenever things went poorly in their little house, and they did every so often in those days when two hot-heads looked after two troubled children, the house felt too close to the road. Like the hillside was pushing the house forward into the road and into the lane of a speeding semi.

Sam remained in his uniform, expecting the Ambridge police department to show up at his door. As he waited, Emily was able to calm herself enough to explain the accusation.

Allison had been overhead at school talking explicitly about sex acts. The teacher called the house, John and Tammy confronted their daughter who then sought to push blame elsewhere and onto her uncle.

While no charges were ever brought and Sam's innocence at least partially upheld, his brother never seemed to get over the possibility of something having happened. The whole scene tainted their life in Pennsylvania, made everything ugly and unbearable. Getting out was the only option for Sam and Natalie.

Seeing the young girl going back into the building, back among men that were breaking the law and likely drunk or actually on drugs, pained his heart. For innocence lost. For false accusations.

In the moonlight and the gray half-light of the dusk-to-dawn, they dashed across the road and put their backs against the boards on either side of the door. The risk of it all was first on Sam's mind. These sorts of characters tend to get a little paranoid and there's a good chance that he and probably someone else in that shop had a gun. There was back-up on the way and they could wait. Maybe through closer surveillance, they could get a little more evidence that might give them probable cause. Terry, on the other side of the door, looked equally anxious. Maybe a little excited. Maybe a little nervous.

He wondered if she was acting a little rash, if something about this life, about being a cop out here, in this community, made her extra-confident, taking chances that didn't need taking. Sure, they knew the judge and he wasn't likely to throw anything out if they didn't have a warrant or enough probable cause. It was a scary world, though. Here or in Pittsburgh.

The gray light shone down on her face, lengthening her nose, making dark shadows of her cheeks. She looked nearly matronly, not like a foul-mouthed county cop with one hand on her pistol grip, ready for action.

The door squealed open then, making Sam jump as he pulled his pistol from his holster. The girl had barely emerged into the night when Terry pulled her by the arm, the child emitting a scared squeal, and turned her away from the door. As she had done this, Terry had also managed to nod at Sam and kick the door open with her foot, allowing Sam to enter the building with his gun drawn, shouting to see everyone's hands.

He'd gone in knowing it was what was to be done and the fear disappeared. His thoughts went underground and his eyes scanned the room for threats, for hidden hands, while noticing something sharp smelling cooking on a butane cook stove. Only when they all lay on the concrete floor, three guns having been removed, did Sam realize the danger he'd faced and overcome.

"Two-seventeen to two-ten." The radio in the cupholder between Sam and Bill crackled.

"Two-ten."

"You looking for a light-blue Buick? Eighties model?"

"Affirmative," Bill spoke, looking at Sam while he drove.

"I passed it sitting in the ditch along forty-one. When I turned around and went back, it was gone."

"When?"

"Half-an-hour, twenty minutes ago."

"Christ." Sam banged lightly on the steering wheel of his truck.

"Thought I'd catch up with him, but I didn't."

"What's yer twenty?"

"Forty-one, north of the Headrick place."

Bill nodded to Sam. "Ten-four. Let me know you see 'em."

"Ten-four."

They had missed him. He was lost in the stiff wind of a cold front pushing along the Ozarks. Sam felt pretty bad about it. He dragged Bill out into the night when he should have been convalescing, recovering from wounds. It was going to be a hard day tomorrow and here they were, wandering the countryside looking for a piece of shit Buick on the off chance that they might catch Harlan Lustig engaged in illegal activity.

At a little after midnight, Bill said, "That's it."

"Okay." Sam had wanted to call off the search earlier, but if Bill was willing to go on then he certainly was.

"Governor's coming tomorrow. We're having breakfast together."

"Geez, Bill, I'm sorry."

"S'alright. I'd rather be out here than with him."

"That means there'll be reporters here."

"They been calling all week."

"What'd you give 'em."

"Very little."

"There gonna be talking to everyone."

"Suppose."

"We probably don't want anyone else from the office talking to them."

"Probably right."

Sam looked to Bill, who was staring out the side window at snow beginning to fall. "I'll make sure no one says anything."

"Thanks."

16

The snow fell soft and steady over Barnes County in the early morning hours of the day of the funeral of Deputy Terry Stegman. By the time people woke, the roads were stripes of white, the color of the fields dampened, the skeleton trees candy-coated. It fell on everyone, everywhere. It fell on plains, on forests, hollows, and it fell on the Verdant river, each flake becoming part of the moving mass, the cold slithering waterway that passed silently through the county, off to become rolling and wide elsewhere. For a time, the river was the only thing that moved. For a time.

Annette set off to town early, worried about road conditions between her house and Sheridan. The Sheridan Cemetery. A series of hills on county road F were notoriously bad, prone to icing over, sometimes prohibiting uphill travel, sending downhill vehicles into a rapid slide. Annette had once wet herself some after her Oldsmobile slid quickly and sideways down a hill. It wasn't an experience she'd like to repeat.

She'd had breakfast at home, knowing the atmosphere at the diner would be somber. It was going to be a hard day as it was and she wasn't likely to find much enjoyment in commiseration. Things would be happening there without her, but she could not worry about that. It wasn't likely to be anything of interest anyway. Nothing worth repeating. It might give her friend Alice a chance to find something worth sharing. It was usually, nearly always, the other way around. Alice was hungry for information, licking lips for tidbits of salaciousness. Annette usually had something worth telling her, something about townsfolk or the old farm families they'd grown up with. There wasn't as much information these days. Not enough of those old characters. As friends passed, went to homes, and got just plain old, they became less interesting. Sometimes their kids stayed and their lives made for good stories, but a lot of them found their way out. It wasn't nearly as interesting telling stories about folks that moved on to Springfield or Little Rock or Memphis. And sure, other people in the area were up to activities that could fill the afternoon stories, but no-one knew them. And what did it matter if some woman from a trailer was cheating with a man from another trailer? That kind did that all the time. Maybe that was why Annette and Alice spent more time talking about the men and women from their shows than they did about real people.

The gold interior of her Oldsmobile was close with the canned warmth from its heater where it sat parked on a narrow, sloped curve, near where two black men were erecting a canopy. Annette watched them in their progress, between the intermittent swipes of the wiper blades, working in the gentle snowfall, pausing occasionally to wipe the snow from their faces or to knock ashes from the cigarettes that dangled wetly from their lips. After struggling with the canopy and finally figuring how to operate its crank, and getting the legs firmly planted in the soft earth, they began lining up chairs. One man, large and more rotund than the other, paused and sat at the end of one finished row. When the other, arms heavy with more chairs, turned and saw the first, Annette saw him stop short, dropping two chairs into the snow as he gestured.

Just then she felt a vehicle pass on her left and she watched as a news van pulled one tire up the curb and onto the grass as it tried to park. The van, belonging to Springfield station KPGE, finally rested its tires on the wet blacktop and a man stepped down and out of the driver's seat. Annette turned off the wipers.

She must have dozed. The sheet of glass in front of her was solid white as if it had been painted over with her inside. She held a hand to her chest, hearing car doors and hushed voices outside, and quickly she pushed on the column that began the struggling twin arcs of the wiper blades. Seeing that other people had arrived, she patted her soft cheeks, tied a plastic cover over her hair to protect it from the elements, and went out into the cold.

Annette was in a daze, as if still asleep she had simply walked from one dream into the next. Others, like her, had skipped the memorial service and had come directly to the burial and they all seemed to be wandering around, a little lost. Annette remembered how she had her eye on a chair under the canopy, somewhere in the back, not too obvious, with a view of most everyone. This allowed her to focus and she stepped from the blacktop and into the snow towards her destination. She was forced to pass a group of soldiers in dress uniforms. She stumbled as she looked at them instead of the placement of her feet. They were looking solemnly past her.

Turning back to town, looking down the long slope of gravestones, she saw the procession snaking slowly through town. Lights, blue and red, flashed, headlights blared into the gray day, as the cars drove so slowly past people lining every sidewalk, all sorts of people out in the snow to watch Terry pass. Men with hats in their hands. People holding up signs, tributes. Everyone was out to see Terry pass.

Annette groped at her purse for a tissue. Her tears blurred the day even further. As she wiped her cheeks, her nose, she moved ahead to find her seat, feeling conspicuous standing out in the open, in the middle of everything.

Annette stood then in the shelter and shadow of the canopy, out of the way. And watched as the majestic procession climbed the snow-covered road to the gravesite, the lights of police cars, cars from every jurisdiction within probably a hundred miles, the only color in the day. People came from every direction, from the long line of cars when the procession stopped. The few rows of folding chairs where she prepared to sit would be lucky to hold a quarter of the people that were gathering around a six-foot-deep hole in the ground. So many sad faces, so many she'd never seen before. A solemn, mourning hoard.

The pallbearers carried the dark wooden coffin, faces grimacing with their burden, through a line of saluting, uniformed police officers in every color of uniform. Bagpipes played. She saw the grandson of Clem Summers who had come back, one of the few to ever return, look almost pleading to his wife in the crowd before his faced steeled before the rest. Billy Wallis, bandaged neck, poor man, lifted it like it was the hardest thing he'd ever done. Surely it must have weighed a ton, to him. The sheriff nodded to someone behind her and Annette turned to see his son, the boy with the unfortunate haircut. The boy, though, didn't look back at his father; instead, he held his face tightly pinched, his eyes fiery, burning rays at someone. Annette leaned her head back and forth trying to look through the black and grey coats, but all she could see of interest was a girl with short hair and her arm around a bulky boy, her head tilted up towards his, appearing to be locked in a kiss of the sort seen on late-night cable. Inappropriate.

While the minister from Varie Baptist Church droned, his voice full of rhetoric and prayer, an attempt to explain that what appears unjust is just, that what is sorrowful and difficult should give us hope, a man was pushing his way backward out of the crowd from his position up front. Franklin Redbird, one of the hard-working and perpetually poverty-stricken clan descended from Cherokees who had pushed through the area so long ago, made his way to the back and she saw him take a quick drink from a bottle in his coat. It should certainly warm him up some, but it wouldn't do much for those red eyes.

From under a tree further up the hill, a bugler began to play taps. The somber song sounded more mournful than ever.

There was silence then. Snowflakes fell large and thick like ash upon the heads bowed in prayer and sadness.

From out of the snow clouds and low sky a helicopter suddenly came into view, its whirring blades nearly mute. It hovered over the assembled crowd. And after a respectful moment, it tilted its nose in a nod or salute, and then rose slowly up and away as if it had come to pick up the poor deputy's spirit to ferry her off to heaven. The cold shook Annette's bones.

"Two-twenty-one." A loudspeaker from one of the cars blared out into the dampness. "Barnes County two-twenty-one... Barnes County two-twenty-one...," the dispatcher repeated. "Barnes County two-twenty-one, end of watch...."

17

Summer hit Barnes County hard, making the air thick, making one gasp for air and want for shade. The fields and trees once brown and dead were lighted up green, populated with long, lashing grasses and fat leaves hanging like tongues. Among the living flora, the large forested areas of the county were populated by all sorts of fauna that moved about comfortably in the damp underbrush beneath the canopy of leaves. Sparrows, bob-whites, and grackles, black squirrels with tufted ears, even lynx with lopped off tails were alive and moving about in the forest, their noises filling up a sleepy morning.

Logan could hear all these creatures as he sat on the forest's edge, hearing the nonsensical warbling and repetitive songs of the birds, the chirping squirrels leaping from limb to limb, he could even hear the grass growing, the leaves taunting him, and hearing all of these things only made him want for all the living things to perish. Some sort of atomic fire that would reduce all around him to ash would be greatly satisfying. And though it was the coming of summer that had been responsible for the return or rebirth of all of this around him that expired, carbon dioxide or oxygen, he was indeed grateful for summer's arrival. The second week of June not only brought the first days of ninety-plus temperatures, but it also brought release from the asylum of high school.

It never felt more like a prison or other formal, penitentiary institution, as in those last few weeks before the end of the school year. He could see the end of his sentence, red X's on a calendar marking the final days of his internment and if only he could make it through each last one without trouble, without incidents of violence, and before the ever-restless inmates rioted, he just might survive to see himself free on the outside.

It had been nearly unbearable. Each day filled Logan with so much rage and dissent that he could barely contain it. He felt like he would burst. He fell into reveries during classes, fantasies of confrontations of so much violence, a release of his anger that drew much blood and gore. On the last page of his notebook, he created a list that grew to nearly thirty names by the last day of school, a list of those around him who deserved some sort of violent retribution. Not last on that list: Dot Baxter.

He was angry, certainly, to see her wrapped around that big Brutus at such a sacred ceremony. He had wanted it to be him, Logan, attracting these lust-filled kisses that even the air of mourning could not hold back. Logan had even dared to ask, placed his heart upon a shelf, and she rejected it, only to turn around and go inside the hardware store where the oversized son of the owner and object of her affection was shelving cans of Coleman fuel and proceeded to ask him to accompany her to the event. Logan certainly held some resentment and anger over the whole scenario and the thought of it made him cut moon-shaped arcs into the palms of his hand from the clenching of fists. It was a betrayal, he felt, not just of him, though he thought there must have been some malice directed at him in the scene, but it was also a betrayal of Dot's character. She was better than that. She was different. She was set apart from all the brutes, the simple-minded ruling class. Dot had let her morals slide, put aside her high character, and allowed herself to be swayed by what they thought. It was a suicide of sorts, a giving up on life apart, a giving in to the standards of the surrounding community.

It made him sad and angry. Dot was on the list because she did not deserve her life any longer. Her violent death would save her from this life. But the first name on the list belonged to her beau, Doug.

Doug's name would have made the list even if it hadn't been him with his tongue wrapped around Dot's at the funeral. There was a one-sided animosity that went back for many years. He'd been one of those kids who had always made Logan feel inferior. He was better in every way. His hair always held the popular style naturally, he was athletically built. His jeans always fit so well as to make apparent the ideal form of his bulge, and his behind on the reverse. He was the object of the desire of many of the girls. An ideal up to which no others could live.

In seventh grade, Logan was still buying into the styles and standards pushed on him and there was little else he wanted other than to look like Doug. Logan only looked like a discount store knock off. He was thin and his hair fell flat. His pants were always a little too short. Gym was generally likely to be torturous. His inadequacies were apparent in every way. A soccer game gave him the opportunity, he thought, on a level field to challenge the likes of Doug on a sport where they didn't have an inherent and well-developed advantage over him.

He'd been in back as a defender and when the ball came his way he managed to make his presence known. He stripped the ball away from the opponent and was looking for someone to whom he could pass the ball. In his panicked hesitation, he was swarmed. His team shouted at him to pass, the opponents taunted him. Doug pushed himself into the scrum, but Logan was still managing to keep control of the ball. Until Doug kicked him in the shin. No accident, the kick resulted in a six-inch scrape up Logan's thinly haired leg that immediately drew blood and sent him whimpering to the ground amid some laughter and shouts at the scored goal.

The strip of pale skin on Logan's shin still meant that Doug would have made the list, even if he had not been responsible for the fall of Dot Baxter. And despite the existence of the list and the bounty of rage, Logan had no course of action. It was the absence of true things to do, real actionable items that sent him out into the summer day to find the edge of this forest on the south side of town. He sat in the shade of an oak a hundred or so feet back from the dirt road, watching a pair of horses, one a dirty white and the other a glistening red, as they leisurely lunched on the long grasses.

There were things he could do, he knew. He contemplated these things daily. A gun safe in his father's closet sat unlocked, ammunition stacked on top. He was not unskilled with a gun and he could easily dispatch each member of the list without wasting a single slug. But he didn't want to go out Columbine fashion. Those wannabe Goths made the thing all about them. They were the stars of the show. They wanted to be big shots. And then, what? They put the barrel under their chins and ended it. Cowards.

There was no moral in that event. No lesson learned. Christ, it only emboldened the pricks, gave them one more taunt. More than once someone had called him Klebold. No. He wanted it to be about them, about what comes to people like that. Let them learn that fucking with kids because they're small or quiet might get them a bullet in the brain, a horrible explosion that showered the innocent in the blood and bits of the guilty.

Summer, maybe, had saved him from what he might have done, but he felt like a man who had carried a large burden a long way and was grateful to set it down. And still, his muscles ached from the weight. He was free of seeing these people day after day, away from girls like Dot, but what was he to do now?

He stood, still feeling the cracks in the bark of the old oak against which he'd leaned like creases in his back, and began high-stepping through the pasture to the road. He had headed out of town, heading south, as soon as his father left that morning. Logan knew that his father would be after him to get a job. He had always been put to work every summer as long as he could remember. But now that no-one in his family had a working farm any longer, gone were the days of grooming horses and cleaning stalls, helping repair fences, clear brush, paint barns. He would be expected now to get a real job, one that required punching a clock, answering to a boss, doing what he was told and in return getting a piddly paycheck. Labor he understood when it benefited someone, family, directly, but selling himself to someone who only sought profit sounded like a bad deal. It was a turn onto a long dead-end path that led only to a lifetime of being owned by someone else.

And where was he to work? At the hardware store with Doug? That would be his luck.

Logan shuffled his shoes down the dirt road, trying to find a tack that kept him on the dusty, khaki-colored dirt and out of the difficult sliding gravel. The sun scalded his scalp and he had not gone very far before he lifted his head, looking for shade. What he did see was a car parked in a field, the grasses grown up around it so that all he could see was the hump of roof, a metal turtle warming in the sun.

He looked down the length of road in front of him which disappeared over an incline. No cloud of dust indicated a car. Behind him, the road curved off gently a half-mile back and the length of it was vacant, save the flattened snake he'd kicked around sometime earlier.

A gold Ford Taurus ten or more years old, the car had been forgotten about. For Sale was written in white shoe polish across the windshield like the qualifying numbers on a drag car. Logan circled the car once and could not stop himself from trying the driver's door. It opened with a blast of hot air. He felt then that instinct of fear, that chill and unsettled stomach that accompanies doing something "wrong," something that would get him in trouble. The sensation antagonized him. He slid into the car.

Feeling his face going damp with sweat, he began to look for excuses that could be used should someone show up suddenly. He was looking for a place to get out of the heat, but, as his eyebrows caught sweat rolling down his forehead, that didn't make much sense. He leaned over to open the passenger door, hoping for a cross breeze. As he leaned, he found the key to the ignition under the floor mat.

Logan did not have his license yet and his Dad was doing little to help him learn how to drive. It wasn't as though he didn't know how to drive. Especially a big automatic like this one. He'd seen it done. He'd spent limited time behind the wheel. And it seemed pretty obvious.

He could slip the key into the ignition, drop the car into gear and be out of there in a flash. He saw for a moment the power of mobility. He had thought that morning of going to The Bend and, in some way, that's where he'd been heading at his slow pace. With a car, though, he could be there in a hurry. He could be anywhere.

It wasn't actually a possibility, though, was it? The son of the sheriff couldn't drive around the county in a stolen car. He would surely be caught. His fingerprints were already all over the car. His hand shook some as he reached to put the key back where he'd found it, but the shudder caught his eye, make him realize the extent of his fear.

It was this fear that held him tight, that squeezed his chest daily, that stopped him from doing anything. It was this fear that kept him in his room, kept him from speaking in class, kept him from fighting back. Would it be the end of the world if his Dad caught him? Hardly. Would it make life more miserable, sure, but in the meantime, he would have lived some.

The car struggled to start, the starter grinding dryly under the sun. When it caught, Logan stomped on the gas and the car rocked and twisted. The grasses bent down in front of the car as he tapped the pedal, motioning the car slowly to the road. He was careful, steady, cautious as he straightened the car out and looked at the stretch of gravel through the windshield. He felt the edge of panic, a fear that could send him running from the car, leaving it idling. "Fuck you." He stomped again on the pedal and the car spurted gravel and slid over the road until Logan sorted out the right pressure on the gas, the right grip on the wheel.

The way his gut sank against the speed, the way the gravel rumbled the car, the lingering rise and fall of the road's texture, took him back to being a passenger in the empty shell, the long bench seat, of his father's police car. He wasn't normally allowed. He was more often the single passenger in his mother's car, but she'd been so busy, not around.

Logan had sat obediently quiet, his elbow on the door's armrest, his hand gripping the handle. His father's habitual grimace always seemed more severe when he wore his uniform. Logan supposed he must have seen him smile once, though he couldn't remember it, couldn't think of the occasion that would give him enough joy or pleasure to show it. He rarely ever spoke to his son and he hadn't told him where they were going. As usual, Logan kept his mouth shut and went along.

The car hummed pleasantly over the highway, air blasting from the black dashboard too coolly. "Was that Mom?"

Logan slid forward in the seat as far as the seatbelt would allow when the brakes quickly slowed the car. "Where?" His father shouted.

The question had jumped too quickly from Logan's lips. If he'd have bothered to think about it, he wouldn't have bothered. He was surprised, though, to see his mother's blue car this far from town, turning down a small county road. "Back there."

His father pulled the car onto the right shoulder before turning the car around without slowing. The movement was hard on Logan's head.

"Where? Where!"

"Here. Here." Logan pointed at the dirt road that started past three trailer homes on a small lot, various items and implements spread in the thick grass around them as if for a yard sale. He felt his eyes watering.

The car slipped and slid over the gravel and up the road. Logan could see a cloud of dust, like a brown fire burning and remaining just out of reach as they chased it. She must have seen the lights on top of the car approaching and ditched herself down this road on the chance that it might be her husband or anybody that might recognize her. Logan knew that they were pursuing her and that she was fleeing. He didn't then understand exactly why. She'd been funny, ever since he'd found her that spring lying in bed in the middle of the afternoon. She was always distracted and made-up, smelling like she and Dad were headed out on a date to somewhere nice when they weren't.

Logan had seen her once when he was on his way to a friend's house—not a friend, really, a study partner. She was standing with a man, in front of a truck, the house behind them nothing more than a frame. She scratched the back of her calf with the top of her other foot. Logan, in his usual gait, grew closer to them slowly and he studied her to be sure that he was correct. She put her hand on the man's thick forearm. When she looked in his direction and his beliefs were confirmed, she then turned quickly away, her back to him. The man then looked at him, said something to her. She turned back to him and the man walked away and joined the others constructing the house.

It had been odd and Logan had thought he'd seen in her face the same thing he knew in his own when he was on the verge of getting in trouble. This chase, he guessed, had something to do with that.

Logan was scared or at least thought he should be. They were going so fast, closing in on the dust cloud, but his father's hands were tight on the wheel, his eyes locked forward. He didn't look afraid. Even as they passed through a group of homes pressed close to the road, dogs barking on the ditch's edge.

Soon, he thought he saw brake lights, dots of red through the brown. Trees near the road had grown tall, throwing the whole of the road in shadow. Then the brake lights disappeared and the smoke before them dissipated, clearing just enough to see a line of trees directly in front of them, a black arrow in a floating yellow box.

They turned in a violent motion that threw rocks and dust all around them, ending with a dropping stop as they found themselves leaned into the ditch. By the time all of the dust around them settled, they could see no dust cloud down the road that now headed south towards town.

In the gold Taurus, Logan eased off the gas, letting the car settle into a calmer pace.

After some struggle, he found The Bend and parked the car in roughly the same spot where Angie had taken him the night before the funeral. It had been like a glimpse of another world. Of how others live. He'd seen for an evening how life could have been. But he didn't experience it. He was only an observer. He was still himself in that other world.

That was really the thing. He could never stop being who he was. Even sitting on the hood of Angie's car he'd remained that sullen, quiet kid, afraid to make his presence known in the world. He could have been, for that night, a twenty-year-old drinking Southern Comfort and hanging around, instead, he'd had only one sip and spent the rest of the night paranoid that his father might sneak into his room to smell his breath as he slept.

He had been thrown, that night, by Angie's presence. She had a larger-than-life presence that made him want for more out of life but intimidated him, making him afraid to look at her, as if she were the sun. She had a fluidity as if her joints were well-greased. A maturity. Logan felt the sexuality about her, like an odor, her body more mature than those that usually distracted him at school.

Sitting under the bare-armed trees, he could have pretended that they were together. That they would soon find their way to her back seat. That she was his cousin didn't matter to his imagination. Sure, it was not permitted, and maybe a little gross considering they had the same grandfather, but it had the same likelihood of happening as the moon falling from the dark canvas of sky to land on them and press them into the earth.

He had sat there on the hood in the silence and the chill, next to her, thinking that this was what life could be like, that life held this potential, and someday he might actually live a moment like this and be part of it. It was painful but pleasant.

Then that drug dealer showed up to insult him and bring back the real world. Skinny long-haired prick. But what was he to do? Like it would have been worthwhile to have his teeth smashed in just to stand up for himself. Being called names by some low-life wasn't going to change, wasn't likely to change Angie's opinion of him. She didn't think much of him, to begin with.

He came back this morning in an attempt to bring back something of that night, to step out of the world. Though he had already accomplished that by taking the car.

After parking, he walked away from it, leaving the key in the ignition. Maybe someone else would take it and he wouldn't be responsible any longer.

18

Evening was coming on quick, a heavy sheet pulled over the landscape, devouring his features, and leaving nothing but black. If only it would take him as well. Swallow him up, instead of leaving him to fumble along in the dark. At the same time, Frank wanted to flee, to run away from it, to get to someplace where the sun still shines brightly, where trees and fences and buildings were drawn with sharp, distracting vibrancy. Someplace where he could be drawn into the physical world around him, and not in the dark where there would be little else besides his mind wandering through memories, pushing and pulling at him, not letting him escape his misery.

Frank also thought he might be better off being somewhere other than where he found himself, among trees and rocks and scrub.

He had been at a bar. A dismal place at the end of an aging strip of stores. It was falsely sterile, as if someone had poured antiseptic over its surfaces, the grime still resting and festering in the crevices. The bartender, the bar's owner, was so earnest and eager that Frank could see he was destined for failure. As the man in his t-shirt leaned back against the bar to watch the television, swinging his dirty towel around his hand one way and then the other, Frank wanted to grab him around his thick throat and tell him of the misery that awaits him. Even when you're on top of the world and all seems perfect, magical and bathed in light, it is false. It is magical because it is not the natural state of the world. Even if you begin to think that this high place is where you exist now, it only serves as a greater punishment when it is all ripped away from you. Give up on all these hopes and dreams now, my friend.

Instead, Frank left money on the bar and left the man to his empty bar with its television displaying cars racing around and around, not often enough crashing in a terrific split of metal and smoke.

In his truck he'd been restless, wanting somewhere to go, but he didn't know where. The long shadows were making him sleepy. An idea in the back of his mind was pushing him, subconsciously directing him until he realized where he had driven himself. He was in an area of rocky terrain, of ridges and valleys, near the river, where roads were as wide as cow paths, where society gave up the county back to the earth. He pulled his truck off onto the rocks. On the other side of the ridge was where he'd grown up, where, conceivably, his family still lived.

Out of the truck, he slung his empty fifth over the bed of the truck and into the dry creek. It shattered flatly.

His past seemed so far from him, like a movie he'd seen, on the couch with Terry, when it was late and he was tired and he had not been able to pay attention. He had a family, like anyone else. A mother who had given birth to him, once held him in her arms, pressing his black hair against his head, whispering words of love. Any displays of love were no more trouble than this. She was not loving. She was caring, she ensured that Frank and his brothers were fed, coddled when they were injured or sick, but even the youngest born was not shown any more love than was necessary.

Over the ridge, he climbed was a settlement established when the Cherokees were pushed through the area. The story that passed among the children, cousins of cousins, was that the Redbirds fell behind, lost their way. Others claimed that they had hidden themselves in the narrow valley in order to not be pushed west into land dry and uninhabitable. Either way, it was in the small sliver of land where they settled and stayed. Here where they grew an over-large extended family.

When Frank got to the top of the ridge, curiosity pushing him on, his legs were sore and he was beginning to feel sorry he'd done it. The exercise sobered him some. There in shadows and the darkening evening was the old, literal homestead. A single farmhouse sat over Jay Creek, its boards replaced again and again after floods that rose up in this valley. Rooms had been tacked on, using scrap lumber. Several small outbuildings dotted the fenced pasture where goats ate the grass short. Chicken coops, tool sheds, grain bins, all of which served as bedrooms for Frank's generation.

It was ugly. Just ugly. Junk sat in piles. Animals had trod the land bare in spots. The meager crops looked weathered and ill. How could anyone live here, he wondered. Yet, this had been his home. And he had not thought much of it, either way. The children there had only gone to school occasionally, when it was easier for them to be away rather than running between the feet of the men and women working. And when there was work for them, school was forgotten.

Most of the men, Frank's father among uncles, grandfathers, older cousins, made their living as handymen or day laborers. They would often roll out early in the morning before light made its way down in their valley, the lot of them loaded into a pickup truck, arms and other limbs hanging out of the bed as it bounced up the road, away. Frank remembered watching them, and he wondered if he felt jealous of them. He should have.

By the time Frank was of an age when his youthful energy could be put to use, the Redbird men had earned a reputation as a hardworking clan. There was much pressure on him. If ever he dared to stare off into a blue sky for a moment, he was likely to receive a soft blow, a board to the back of his head. It was work and work was good. He came home tired and hungry. He ate and he went to bed.

Surely, he had missed things living in this shithole, things other kids experienced. Some of the same rituals happened here. One day it had been his turn to drive the truckload of men to their jobs, and they all laughed in their caps and black hair, as he struggled with the clutch and tried his best not to cry in front of them. His schooling, though, had been haphazard. He was confused by many things. He could not distinguish among the stories heard as to which were true, which were fables, and which were myths. He confused reports of buildings that reached up to the clouds in faraway cities, with fantasies of Johnny Appleseed or Paul Bunyan. The myths of his own heritage, of thunderstorms as gods, of the existence of bugs and pests borne out of sins, from an old lady who lived in a shoe, or a boy that climbed up a beanstalk to the home of a giant.

The buildings below him, the cow chewing hay with boredom, the two boys coming back from the river, shirtless and chasing one another, were disappearing into the dusk when Frank wondered if it was odd that he was disconnected from his past. He had willfully severed himself from this life, from these people living in this hovel with their poverty and their head lice, but what had happened in the past before them? He knew nothing. Sometimes the men would talk, lawn chairs and stumps around a fire, cans of beer crackling in their hands and, as a boy, Frank would listen. Sometimes falling asleep to their voices under the stars.

Had they ever talked about death? Did they ever say what happened to someone after they died? What would happen to Terry?

Burial was just a ritual, Frank knew. A ridiculous and pointless ritual. And no one had asked his input, asked what he thought would be best. They had let themselves into her house, the sheriff and another deputy, to find clothes for the funeral. They buried her in the dress that she wore to Bob's funeral. Were they trying to be funny?

Not all who died moved on, that much Frank knew. Sometimes they hung around. Down there in the dark was a dead tree, a barkless mangled tree that looked to have been struck by lightning, was inhabited by Frank's great-grandmother. He remembered her as a bitter old woman who smoked and barely spoke. So large and big-breasted that she hardly ever moved from a chair that sat just in front of the old house. Until she died she was always there, cigarette in her mouth, shucking corn, splitting beans, occasionally brushing ashes from the slow slope of her bosom. Frank remembered the twisted tree mumbling to him in that same small voice, her old wrinkled face suddenly appearing in the knots and grain of the lifeless trunk.

He had heard, too, the story of the nigger hanged at The Bend. That was how it had been described to him by his brothers who had taken him to that place one summer night. They told him of the white-cloaked men, black eyes cut out of their peaked hoods like ghosts themselves, as if they had been there, too. They had led him, the black man, by a rope, chanting and shouting. A strange sacrifice, they tied him up to the tree, the rope around his neck, and let him swing out over the water as he died. Frank's brothers told him, and he had been foolish enough to believe, that he still haunted The Bend and that any boys who came there had to, at least once, swing out and let themselves fell into the water. Or else, the hanged man would haunt him, white eyes would appear out of nowhere, everywhere. Frank was crying as he did it himself, feeling a little like he was dying as the rope slipped from his hand and he fell through the dark and into the cold water.

Frank hoped no such fate had trapped Terry. She was good, she had a good life, she deserved better. But it had come too early for Frank. Too early.

Dark had come. A small light came from a window in the house. An oil lamp. They had no electricity. He was disgusted with, glad he was cut off from, this life, these people. And he was not happy about where his thoughts were leading, so he turned to go.

Under the trees, under the deep black sky. Frank was blind. The ground below him tilted, but he could not distinguish up from down. His leg tentatively stretched out, toes reaching for earth. His hands were held up defensively. He felt like an idiot. As if he knew what was coming.

He had made his way with some success before a rock underfoot gave way. He tumbled in the dark, bounding and twisting, colliding with trees and rocks and the hard ground. He closed his eyes and held his breath. He was being beaten, kicked, tortured, and it felt deserved. Something about it felt right. He wondered if he might die.

He would float upward into the blackness and the burdens that he felt, the tightness around his chest, the pain in his head and his heart would dissipate outward. And he would be free.

He would never again know anything like Terry. Like the way she stirred him. Like the way her eyes reached and shook something in his core.

"How could you not know when your birthday is?"

They were in the shop, hitching up the scoop to the front of the tractor when she asked him this. They were preparing to do some work on one of the cow ponds, and Frank had admitted to Terry that he was always fond of fall because that was when he was born. In that season. But when she asked him when his birthday was, he had to admit that he didn't know.

"It's not something that was important."

"Not important?"

"It's not like they're a bunch of calendars down in that holler."

She looked at him, to see if he was getting upset. "I guess not, but then you're left without any day to celebrate." Again, Terry looked up from her spot between the yellow scoop and the blue tractor where she was connecting the hydraulics. "You never celebrated your birthday, did you?"

"No." Frank was standing there, with nothing in his hands, nothing to do at this moment.

"Then I tell you what." She stood upright, wiped her hands on her jeans. "We'll make today your birthday, and we will celebrate it."

"No." He looked out of the dark shade of the shop out into the bright day outside.

"But don't you think I'm about to sing you Happy Birthday or anything. You get that out of your goddamn head right now."

It wasn't what was in his head, but the thought of it made him smile. He directed the smile at Terry.

"Come on. Let's get washed up, go out, find something special to do."

"What about the pond?"

"It'll wait."

"I was wanting to get it done today." His protest was earnest.

Terry looked at him, eyes into his, studying him. She glanced at the shop's open door then came to him and kissed him.

Her kisses were otherworldly, supernatural, signifying a power, an existence that went beyond the physical. As Frank's tumble down the ridge near the hollow where he was raised was halted by a tree, a rough-barked one with short broken branches, these kisses were proof to Frank that death couldn't take Terry.

She existed elsewhere. She was part of the stars in the coal-black night. She filled up the black expanse. She was part of everything, yet she wasn't here. She wasn't here to kiss, to touch, to be kind, to curse, to be all the things that she was. She was gone from him, yet there wasn't a thing that didn't make Frank think of Terry.

He was on his feet again and making his way to his truck when he realized he was crying. He found it distinctly unpleasant. An insult after everything.

Frank backed the truck accidentally into the creek bed and rocks spit out, banging against the trees and the fender as he stomped on the gas to get away.

19

Days off from work were nearly frustrating for Sam. At least they had become that way. There always seemed so much to do. Indeed, he was often called on, during these days at home, to go assist in serving a warrant, to help in the arrest of a figure who had been on his watch list. And while it seemed disruptive and Natalie would shake her head at him as he talked on the phone, nodding his acquiescence, he was often thankful for his return to duty. In this way, things around their farm had become somewhat neglected. The dark grasses of their yard had grown long and soft after the wet spring. A slow leak had developed in one of their large watering troughs that were going to be necessary for the survival of the heifers and the new calves in his fields.

These things pestered him as he lay in bed, next to his sleeping wife. It was his day off and though he had much to do, he should be sleeping in. He was tired, had been itching for an extra hour's rest for weeks now, but the sun had risen and the day was calling him. It angered him. He'd been a little angry lately. An extra buzz radiated through him, made his temperature rise quickly, the tone of his voice tighten. Rest was supposed to cure it, help calm him down, relax the tightening in his jaw. Yet there he was awake, watching the increasing glow of the bedroom's yellow curtains, listening to the clicking of his dog's claws on the linoleum downstairs.

He had his excuse to get up and that was the problem. He felt he needed one. He had barely stirred because it could wake Natalie and she would scold him for waking, for not getting the necessary rest. He didn't need her scorn.

She slept beautifully. Eyes closed gently, peacefully, lips pursed just slightly as if on the verge of a smile, hair brown with hints of red radiating as it lay across the white pillow. She curled herself towards him, a leg stretched in his direction, the bed covers spreading gently from the high point of her hip. He could touch her now, just to appreciate her form, that sloping thigh, but it would be interpreted sexually. Indeed, the sensation would quickly turn sexual for him as well.

Natalie stirred a bit as he watched her, pulling the pillow to her, pressing herself further into the bed. Then her eyes fluttered open, brown with just enough green to appear occasionally otherworldly. At the sight of him they exhibited, in the many lines that surrounded them and the heavy lids, a bit of disgust, then closed.

"Ugh. You were so mean to me. In my dream."

Of course, he thought.

Turning and stretching, she said, "I was trying to move the couch and you wouldn't help."

"Maybe I didn't want it moved."

"You told me to do it myself. Bill was coming over. Maybe to stay with us. And you yelled at me about it. Like I was cheating on you."

Were you? he thought. "Why was he going to stay here?"

"Don't know. He didn't have anywhere to go, I guess. You didn't care."

How was he supposed to react to being told he was an asshole--in her dream?

"You didn't really like him anymore."

"Silly."

"You were a jerk."

"Thanks."

"I'm still mad at you."

Sam rolled onto his back. "You remember when the Governor was here for Terry's funeral?" It was as good a time as any to tell her.

"Of course."

"I talked to one of his guys afterward."

"Yeah."

"He told me I should run for sheriff."

"Against Bill? You wouldn't."

"He said the Governor wanted me to. They want to show they're trying to make a difference down here. By bringing in someone with experience in a city."

"He's been here for over twenty years. He knows what he's doing."

"That's what I told them."

"And?"

"They said the whole thing didn't make them look good. They should have been more careful."

"No one would have done it any different."

"They said I would have handled it different, coming from Pittsburgh.

"You told them you'd have done the same thing."

"I didn't get a chance."

"You told them you wouldn't run against Bill. He's your friend."

"Sure. They told me to think about it. They said I'd do a better job, understanding the problem better. New blood would be better."

"He grew up here. His family's from here. He knows everyone."

"I know."

The dog let out a muted bark from below.

"I'd better let him out."

Natalie rolled away from him, settling herself in again. "You were such a jerk."

"Great."

Outside, with the old dog, the dog which had spent his days stressfully tethered to a dog run, his chain connected to a high wire that scratched and scraped with his pacing, behind the tiny Ambridge house, Sam was still thinking of the offer from the Governor's office. Of course, it wouldn't be the Governor himself with his hardened hair and cheeks reddened by weather or excessive drinking, but his men, political strategists, those looking out for the Governor politically, as well as the future of the party, who would talk to him, taking him aside while others walked past the snow-covered graves, back to their lives and putting death behind him. Sam's mourning quickly passed in the face of pressure. It was so efficient and direct, how he imagined things in Washington were handled. Men that he didn't know and had no real interest him in him had nearly pushed Sam into running against his friend.

He had declined, there on the spot. They, of course, would not accept his refusal, demanding that he think it over, it would be for the best. And he did think it over, falling for the flattery, the assurance that he was the better candidate and would be the better man for the job. They had promised support, extra hands, money. Sam had walked away from them, imagining himself shaking hands, asking for votes, campaign signs with his name, speeches, a victory party at the diner. And there was all he would change at the department. He saw shiny new desks, well-lighted offices, deputies fit and eager for work, a county eventually clear of criminals. He could be the best thing to ever happen to Barnes County.

But there was Bill. He was a good sheriff, a good man, who cared for the people he was elected to protect. He deserved the job. It was true that his laid-back ways couldn't handle the post-millennium, the post-9/11 world. He was a sheriff of the old west, not the type of sheriff who knew what to do about an area being overrun by drug addicts and drug dealers. Was it really right that he continued in that post?

Spring had brought heavy rains, and now the summer was coming on strong, and Sam had not called the number provided him, had practically put the whole idea behind him. Yet, somehow there remained the notion that he was destined for greater things. In some ways, he didn't much care about the condition of his black cows that grazed in the morning haze. He only cared about the length of the lawn for what someone might think about it, what assumptions might be made about the character of a man whose front yard was becoming the home to ground-nesting birds.

The old dog raised a couple of quail from the grass near the roadside and Sam thought about this debate going on in his head and wondered at the vanity of it. He had never seen himself like this, but here he was, desiring the admiration, the votes of others. He was a sucker for appeals to his character.

He did not see himself as a vain man. He was a simple man who wanted simple things, thus the old dog who would continue to run about for only a few minutes more then tire and return to heel at his master's side, this majestic farm, a wife of so many years. Does a vain man dream of these things? Where is adulation in this? Where are the people to encourage him, the bootlickers and hangers-on that the vain need around them? Christ, if he even wanted any sense of that he would have at least had children; what choice do they have but to love you?

Sam walked around the far side of his shop. It was the only place around that he could not see from his window that didn't disappear into trees or over a ridge. It was a neglected space and so Sam felt the need to check on it every once in a while. Though he didn't really know what he might find out of the ordinary there. The shop itself, a metal building delivered on a truck and assembled by a team of men in only three days, was built on the site of the old barn whose wood roof had sunk and finally collapsed before they bought the property. The building was incongruous with the age of the house, the natural setting. It gleamed in the sun.

If it wasn't vanity then what brought him back to Missouri? Was he not here to prove that he could succeed where his father had failed? He had refused to consider taking a job at the steel mill in Pennsylvania out of some sort of pride as well. His brother could follow their father into failure, but Sam would not. He was better than those grimy men. That was what he believed. Even if by better he meant something as simple as a landowning Missouri farmer. He could have pride in that.

And where does law enforcement fit in this? If he was discovering on this morning walk, this small bit of leisure on his day off, that the life he had built for himself was based on some sort of pride, a self-righteousness that elevated him beyond others, then his career for the last thirty years surely had the same origins.

The job in Pittsburgh had come out of his function in the Army. It was what he knew and a bit of experience in law enforcement, even if it was against one's own, gave him a leg up on the others in the academy. Being in the military police had been no real treat. He had chosen it then to keep himself off the battle lines in Vietnam but found himself instead on some other battle line that pit him against others who wore the same uniform. Pulling drugs off men, chasing down soldiers who had gone AWOL or who had gone drunk to the wrong whorehouse, men guilty of fragging, of purposefully injuring themselves, men charged with crimes against people who were supposed to be innocent but to the war-weary soldier, whose name had been pulled out of a hat and was ripped out of his hometown, thrown into a uniform, shouted at and abused and thrown into the jungle with a machine gun, all looked the same, was not the easy safe job that Sam had been hoping for. In many ways, he didn't feel much better than these men. He was only one stupid mistake away from being one of them.

As a police officer in Pittsburgh, he couldn't help but think that he was better than most folks he came into contact with, but it left him with the general feeling that there really weren't too many good people in the world. The thing was that he knew right from wrong and it was his job to prevent wrongdoing and find those that did wrong. Maybe one could find vanity there. Maybe one could find vanity in the pride with which he did his job, the pleasure that came with doing well. And if others should hear of his success it should only help them to become better officers.

Would he have done anything differently? Could Terry's death have been prevented? He didn't want to fault anyone, but the answer was yes. When someone makes a mistake, it is natural to look for things that could have prevented it. And maybe, from his experience in the city, he would have been warier. Things in Barnes County, though, aren't done that way.

On one of those days so hot that your scalp feels like it's sprung a leak, Sam and Terry responded to a domestic disturbance call. They tell you that these are the most dangerous calls and it's true because love makes you do crazy things. These sorts of calls were pretty common in Barnes County and for the most part, they were relatively tame. A man had knocked his wife around with the house showing evidence, broken furniture, kids cowering in bedrooms and the wife won't press charges. Or a wife that came at her husband with a knife, leaving him bleeding with several shallow cuts on his forearm, but because they couldn't pin down who started it, the best they could do was separate them for the night and pray they didn't get another call.

This call came in the middle of the afternoon when everyone should normally be hunkered down in the shade and air-conditioning, while Sam had been cruising a c-store that he suspected of being a front for selling drugs. He sat parked in his car near the road, running the plates of the cars in the lot through the system. He heard Terry respond first; she was about five minutes away. Sam called in quickly; his ETA would be about eight minutes.

No officer should respond to a domestic violence call alone, but he couldn't tell her to wait for him. She was his superior and she would do what she wanted either way. Indeed, when Sam pulled into a group of trailers on a dead-end road that hid on a blind curve south of town, Terry was out of her car talking to an overweight couple who were leaned against the trunk of a car and pointing to a trailer that sat up a slope from the dusty dirt road. He parked his car on the grass next to the road and Terry came over to him.

"Now, why they didn't bother saying they heard shots when they called, I don't know."

"Shots."

"Sure, heard a couple shots before they decided to call it in. But did they bother telling us that? Shit no." Terry tapped the butt of her handgun and nodded in the direction of the trailer. As they began up the sun-soaked expanse of a southern-facing slope, the couple behind them disappeared back into their own home, either for the shelter of cool air and shade or for their own safety.

Terry led the way, pausing just before going up the steps to listen for activity. Movement inside shook the trailer. Sam felt the shifting as his hand pressed against the hot aluminum siding.

"Woolsey," Terry shouted. "Mike. Come on out. Need to talk."

Of course, Sam thought, she probably knows him.

"I don't wanna have to tell your momma that you gave me a hard time."

There was a rush of movement inside and the door whipped open revealing a harried woman with sunken eyes and a fat lip. "You tell her her bastard son got no right and I'd just as soon kill his ass, he come near me again."

"Ma'am. He in there?"

"In the bedroom. Won't come out."

"He's got a gun?"

"Son of a bitch shot two holes in the ceiling. Here." She pointed. "Sunlight coming through. That'll be great when it rains." The woman raised the volume of the last phrase to be sure it was heard throughout the home.

Sam stepped up to the screen door. "Why don't you come on out and let me get me some information from you." He took her out into the yard where the sun was brightest and the heat most intense.

"Michael. You come on out now. I need to have a word with you."

Sam pulled a small spiral notebook and pen from his breast pocket to begin to take notes as the woman told her story. Looking up, his eyes dropped to the slack breasts under the woman's white t-shirt. They swung like small sacks of grain and made him think of his wife's body, involuntarily comparing Natalie's tight and frail form with the softer, younger body before him. The thoughts, the sizing up of a stranger disturbed him and he looked away. To Terry, in her uniform, hand poised on the butt of her piece.

Terry was sturdy, built like a woman who knew hard work and wouldn't shy from it. She wore her hair short, not unlike how a man might. Curls and tangles that likely became unmanageable at any length. Skin tan and creased. A face as tough as she was, yet somehow captivating. Somehow the face lingered with him, her visage better known to him than his own.

There was then a crash of glass and a man with a freshly shaved head, making Sam think momentarily of a cantaloupe, with his head out a window, began shouting the sort of nonsense a man shouts when a woman has ruined his world, somehow driving him to the point of madness. He swung a gun around wildly, sometimes using it to flagellate his forehead, other times pressing it against his temple with a squint of his eyes.

When the man finally held the gun out the window pointing it vaguely in the direction of Sam and the woman standing out in the yard, Sam moved to wrap himself around the woman and shelter her while pulling out his gun. After this quick, involuntary action, Sam turned around to see that Terry had already diffused the situation by twisting the gun from his hand and holding him by the wrist, pulling him forward out the window. Sam went to her side and together they yanked the man from the window, dropping him on the dirt. Sam then stepped over him and cuffed his wrists behind his back and looked up at Terry. Together they smiled.

Then the woman came running over, screaming, and began to kick the man on the ground, until Terry finally, after a moment, pulled her away.

It was how things were done. Maybe in an anonymous city, where the background, the family, and their history are not known, a cop might be more cautious. Sam, on his own, probably would have done things differently. In this situation, and probably others. And maybe that would be the better way.

20

Harley sat slumped low in the driver's seat, smoking and watching the trucks pull in the truck stop off I-44. He listened to the tobacco burning as he sucked air through the filter, a crackle not unlike the sound of wheels over the small gravel on the side of the road, both sounds occasionally punctuated by the blast of air brakes. Morning wasn't his favorite part of the day. He preferred a slow start, squinting, crusted eyes watching the smoke fill the air. But he was on a mission this morning and headed out early in order to get to this truck stop.

His time spent behind the County Mart had led to a discovery. Well, at least an idea. Most of the brightly colored goods that lined the shelves of the store, offering consumers a variety of choices and the false notion of freedom, arrived in drab boxes wrapped tightly in shrink wrap upon pallets. This would have to include the coveted main ingredient of methamphetamine, ephedrine, or pseudoephedrine. All of these cold medicines that were so damned expensive and purposefully hard to obtain would have to come in one of those muted boxes. The trucks, Harley knew, came roaring down 19 from I-44 and it wouldn't be surprising to catch that tractor-trailer bound for the Sheridan County Mart stopping here to refuel or rest.

It was a long shot and he sort of knew that, but the logic to him felt solid. He hadn't thought about the details. He would sort out what to do whenever he saw that Country Mart logo painted on the side of one of these trailers.

He was excited and proud of himself for producing such a plan. He would brag about it to whoever would listen afterward. It was a complete pain in the ass to get Sudafed. Sometimes he would pay people or trade for a discount. And sometimes it took a tankful of gas, driving around to every drug store, convenience store or supermarket within fifty miles to get enough of the stuff to make a decent amount of meth. Now he was going to the source. Who else had thought of that? Not Jimmy Jiles. No, most of the time he had known Jimmy, Harley had been the gopher, fetching tablets from all over the area. Someone somewhere would be proud of him for this.

Harley chuckled then at the thought of calling up his father to explain to him how he'd found a way to bypass the usual method of obtaining the fundamental ingredient used in the manufacture of an illegal drug. Sure, it would take a crime to do it. But it was one in many.

His father couldn't care. No matter how ingenious. Jesus, even if it had been something legitimate, his father wouldn't look on it too highly. There was too much ground to make up. Too many burned bridges to repair. Keith Lustig was a straight-laced man, boring to the extreme. Risk taking to him meant wearing a Hawaiian shirt on a Saturday. Maybe that's what happens when a man who studied to be an economist becomes a CPA. Risk-taking meant the potential for loss and any loss was intolerable.

Not that any of this made him a bad man. Maybe that would have been inspiring. Maybe if he had ventured to raise a hand against his son things would have turned out differently. But Keith and his ever-devoted wife, Nancy, were dull. The evenings of Harlan's youth were spent with his mother, hair always in some ridiculous perm, knitting some scarf or afghan that would wind up lying across the back of a couch or chair, across the foot of a bed, while his father sat in his lazy boy with some thick book on accounting rules or economic theory in his lap, his glasses sliding down his nose. All the while Matlock or Murder She Wrote played on the TV and young Harlan went steadily out of his mind.

Keith and Nancy spent most of their time ignoring his existence, ensuring that he never disrupted the calm, dead air of the living room, but they had plans, assumptions for him. It took him until he was sixteen and not living up to expectations for Harley to understand that his father expected him to succeed where he had failed. Harlan was to be what Keith could not. He expected Harlan to do exceedingly well in school, go to a good college, for which they had of course been saving since his conception, and become an economist, teaching in a prestigious school until finding a position in an economic think-tank or the Federal Reserve. Somewhere there was surely a fully mapped-out plan, full of details and options for minor contingencies.

What Keith couldn't foresee was that the son would abhor mathematics. Maybe it had been the flashcards that appeared at the dinner table from the time he was two years old. What was likely more disappointing for the walking dead who were his parents was his lack of drive. On all things, Harlan couldn't care less. Sure, homework may be due, but it didn't matter much to the boy if he got it in, even if it meant some minor form of public ridicule. His teachers would make some feeble attempt to shame him in front of his peers ("Harlan? Do you not have your homework?"), and his response ("Maybe tomorrow.") would leave them steaming. And Keith and Nancy had no effective method of enforcement. They didn't show emotion as it was; he had no shame or anger to fear.

The psychotherapist he saw at thirteen told his parents that he was acting out to get attention. Horseshit. If anything, he had fallen into the muted complacency his parents lived by. He couldn't see why anyone would get worked up over something as arbitrary as a grade. It was all pretty subjective. He understood that his father had certain aims which the man did his best to explain with a great amount of logic and Harlan, the boy, would nod his head in agreement and consent. He could see the point, but it didn't have to work the way it was suggested.

A tall man in sweaters and a soft beard, the psychotherapist, had talked about feelings and tried to draw from the young teenager his opinion and sentiment about things trivial and mundane and even things fundamental as if Harlan had any options, any control over these things. And though the bearded man had not succeeded in finding some maliciousness in his ambivalence, he had succeeded in establishing in Harlan the notion of questioning what seemed apparent and unmovable. Things which he had believed were as solid as the concrete of the city's sidewalks might not be as formidable and set as he had thought. And this included the previously inherent authority of Keith and Nancy.

His newfound ability to question and even dismiss led to the shunting of Keith's ambitions for his son and the premature expulsion, as mutual as it might have felt, of the boy to the streets of St. Louis.

When a boy of seventeen, who had previously believed his fate to be necessarily sealed and his will completely sublimated to a parent, finds himself free in the world it is liable to lead him to a life of recklessness.

Sitting there in his car, Harley pitched the still burning stub of his cigarette out the open window. He was strongly confident in his inability to change the past, but he knew the future was in his hands, that every action was a willful action. He could prove who he was with what he did, and that was his intention this morning.

With a great creaking and groaning, a crushing of gravel and dispersion of the thick air, the larger-than-life Country Mart truck came to rest among the many long trailers in the lot. When the driver emerged, Harley thought he looked awfully small to be operating such a large thing. It gave him confidence to know that he wasn't one of these old toughs, hardened and violent from time spent alone on the road.

Over-the-road truckers were likely to keep the trailers locked, but these guys who had to hit ten different stops in a day and still make it home for dinner were less likely to bother slipping a padlock through the two holes of the latch. And should this assumption prove false, Harley had bolt cutters in his trunk. It was amazing how often those came in handy. Today, though, they were unnecessary.

Quietly and calmly he lifted the latch and turned the handle, raising the gate just enough to roll himself inside, and then he pushed the rolling door closed. He waited for his eyes to adjust to the dark, but after many seconds he realized that was not going to be able to see his way around without raising the gate some and allowing the light to penetrate the length of the trailer enough for him to be able to read the cartons within. He was frustrated by his lack of foresight. If he'd have been a smarter person he would have brought a flashlight.

He went back and opened the gate just enough to make the metal of the front wall of the trailer glow some, then he began his search. Harley was amazed at the variety of items that were held behind shrink wrap on each of the pallets. Everything from toothpaste to windshield washer fluid, from glucosamine to cap guns. He'd gone past two pallets, looking only at the cases that faced out, not yet bothering to tear down the stacks to get at what might be hiding in the interior boxes. He had only a limited amount of time, as long as it might take the skinny driver to finish a plate of biscuits and gravy or eggs and hash browns.

The third pallet provided a bounty and his grin could not have been any wider as he leaned so far over to read each package's contents that he nearly read upside down. A white box, with red letters declaring Pseudoephedrine Hydrochloride. He tore at the shrink wrap and he had the distinct image, as he used both hands to tear apart the layers upon layers of plastic, of what it might be like to rip into a man's belly with both hands. He went about his task frantically.

In the gap that the box made, like a brick pulled from a wall, he saw behind it another box, some other variation that would prove just as useful for his purposes.

Now a reasonable man might have turned away at this point. Seen that enough was enough for today, accept the small but significant victory and move on. And Harley was aware of this, somewhere, in a place deep inside, buried under the idea of a major victory, of succeeding against expectations, of being set at a task and opportunity and not letting it slip by, no matter the risk. Buried equally deep was also the understanding that things were unlikely to go his way, that no matter his success his luck would soon turn against him, and so he was not surprised to hear the rumbling start of the truck's engine followed by the jerk of the whole large vehicle being set into motion.

Harlan scrambled over boxes, trying to get to the door, a box under each arm. His feet slipped and stuck and he fell, rolling over the corner points of many boxes until he heard of the whir of blacktop beneath eighteen wheels and the continuing ascent of gears. He had missed his opportunity for a relatively simple escape. It would likely grow more complicated from here. Harlan stacked his boxes neatly by the door and went back for more.

The truck had gone about twenty miles down the highway only turning once with enough force to topple him over, making him knock his head on the outside wall and he'd come up with a total of five small cases. Though he could continue his hunt, he'd grown bored of it and knew he'd better find a way out of his predicament as soon as he could. Peeking through the gap to ensure that no vehicles would be close enough to see him, he then lifted the gate and threw the boxes in quick succession far from the truck and off into the soft grasses of the ditch. They would likely suffer no damage but Harley couldn't throw himself that easily and guarantee his safety. Though he contemplated how he might tuck his head and roll, the risk exceeded some threshold and he was simply going to have to wait until the truck slowed to make his escape.

He closed the gate and sat down against the side, pulling a small folded paper from the pocket of his jeans. He was exhilarated and hardly needed it, but the drug had become like a comfort, a reward. It was something pleasant after a hard day and something that might lift his spirits. It was a minor reward, like dessert. A treat that he felt he deserved. He didn't understand the danger of it, though it reminded him of the way he used to feel about a stiff drink. A beer was something one consumed in the normal course, but a stiff drink instantly made one feel better and, in the beginning at least, it sustained. It grew, though. He deserved it and soon enough he needed it. It was one at the end of a long day and then if one was good, two was better, then the morning was as difficult as the day and another drink would help. And it had gotten to the point that he wouldn't leave his apartment without a bottle in his pocket, the tight, caramel taste of bourbon in his mouth.

He had had no trouble in leaving school behind. His parents had given up on him and he gave up on fulfilling even the most minor of ambitions held for him. He sought out and obtained the cheapest apartment he could find without concern for the neighborhood, the neighbors. He took a job at White Castle and began a new life without much worry or excitement.

Only after a couple of weeks of noticing the stares at his walking down the street and into the apartment building did he realize the warning that the landlord had given him. He had stood with the man, oval-shaped in a hooded sweatsuit. "You're not exactly like everyone else here, you know." Harley had thought the man was referring to his age. He knew he was likely younger than the others. "S'alright."

The man pushed the lease to him and Harlan had held up the form on the freshly painted wall and signed. The landlord was white, with a broad, pocked nose, glasses with thick black frames. He had some food in the corner of his mouth. He had parked his pickup in the alley.

The stares Harley saw daily came from blazing eyes in dark faces. He was the only white person he ever saw from the moment he got off the bus until he saw himself in the mirror in the tiny studio apartment. He felt small and young, stupid and naïve when he finally had this realization. It didn't come out of any hatred, but maybe a little fear. Though it was the late eighties and people of Harlan's age were in the full trance of urban culture, he had been raised in Webster Groves, an upper-middle-class neighborhood of St. Louis. His interactions with anyone of another race had been, he only realized now, entirely limited.

What he really felt wasn't so much fear as shame. Shame that he had been so stupid not to realize that he was in a black neighborhood and the landlord's attempt to clue him into that fact had sailed over his head, but also shame that he should feel any different about his situation simply because of the skin color of his neighbors. Shame that some sort of racism existed within him. He didn't believe that one could grow up without hearing jokes and prejudice. And somehow it had instilled in him something he thought immoral. To counter this he took a freshly acquired pack of cigarettes and went out that night to sit on the stoop.

His new smoking habit was something he'd picked up in the few weeks he'd worked at White Castle flipping burgers and taking smoke breaks with coworkers. Harlan had felt an incredible amount of freedom at being able to establish his own identity. These people did not know him, he had established no patterns of being the one who said very little and staying out of the way. He had the opportunity now to be loud and even a little bit wild and no one would know he hadn't always been like this. So, when offered a cigarette, he accepted. He also accepted when offered a swig of a whiskey bottle.

In a very short period, Harley went through so much change that he hardly felt like the same person anymore. He'd begun smoking, drinking, and other than his manager at work everyone he hung around with was African-American. Looking back at it from this point, here in a semi-trailer, he hardly felt like he had ever been this person either. It was that person who he had come down to Barnes County to escape.

With a down-shifting that jarred him, Harley knew that his opportunity was coming. The truck slowed and slowed, and he lifted the gate, again slowly to ensure that no farmer would see him or run him over when he chose to leap to the ground. The coast was clear and all he could see was the bare highway behind the truck. They were coming to town and he would have to go now or risk being seen by many and being caught.

He hung with one hand on the handle, his heels on the crossbar below the truck's bed, and swung as the truck began to make a left turn. Harley flung himself from the trailer in a very ungraceful move. He'd had the intention or hope that he might be able to stay on his feet, but he'd misjudged the truck's speed and fell to the hot blacktop in a motion that tore open his jeans at the knee and scraped the flesh from his palms. He quickly rolled himself into the ditch.

21

The bacon popped and sizzled in the pan as Annette pulled the biscuits from the oven.

She ought to be down any minute.

With a spatula, she stirred the viscous eggs, bright yellows and hazy whites like cataracts, in their pan. The table was set. Grapefruit juice in small glasses painted with wildflowers. She'd even made coffee. Just in case.

Of course, she'll have to wake up sometime soon.

She was hardly a child, Annette knew, but still, her granddaughter had sat in the passenger seat sulking as she drove her down from St. Louis, looking out the window as if she had scolded the sixteen-year-old girl.

"Pretty country ain't it, dear?"

"I guess."

"You know our family's been here since before this was a country?"

"Figures."

"Sweetie?"

"Nothing."

Talkative, ain't she? This was bound to be a fun summer, Annette thought. She'd driven all the way to St. Louis and back a day ago and she really hadn't paid her any mind. Annette had been worried from the drive and quite tired from the concentration it required. It had rained on the way back, so it was slow going. And it was always difficult seeing her daughter.

Lily had had a hard time growing up and things had not gone well since she'd gone out on her own. She was living in a rented basement in a run-down area of the city bordering an industrial area of warehouses and chain-link fences, large tanks and tubes, some bellowing steam, others fire. Lily had been happy with Annette's idea to take Rachel for the summer. It was the best thing all round. Lily had called Annette sometime in the spring, just before the shootings and she had gone on and on about how she couldn't control the girl, was worried about her, didn't know what could be done. A pause at the end of her delivery offered Annette the opportunity to step in with an offer that would please everyone. Well, maybe not the girl.

Rachel was said to be hanging around a new crowd, kids that scared Lily for the music they listened to and the clothes they wore. Annette understood how this could be, many things in the world proved frightening. Lily said she had no reason to believe her daughter was doing drugs but it was probably only a matter of time. Some of her new friends smoked cigarettes.

Annette was happy to help out when Lily was having trouble. As the mother of her own inconsolable and uncontrollable daughter, she would have been grateful for someone to step in and lend a hand. But no, it wasn't the same. Lily had been a grown woman when Annette thought she needed help. Lily and a friend had taken an apartment in town and she was working a county over, in Austin, at a company that assembled lamp parts from China. For Annette, it was just a matter of time before she found a reliable man to marry. It was not a short amount of time and the man she found was far from suitable. And grown women don't always want their mothers' meddling.

She had a whole summer to help set the girl on the right course, but judging from the look of her, it was not likely to be an easy task. She would have to find a way to tell her that streaks of pink in her dark hair were not exactly flattering. People would stare. Maybe she could take her to the salon for a coloring and a perm. And those pants, two or three sizes too big, black, with pockets. Those were the same ones she'd worn the day before. And then a big t-shirt. One could nearly mistake her for a boy. Annette supposed she should be grateful for the pink in her hair as some sign of femininity.

"They say… you see that ridge, there, on the other side of the water?… well there was some folks, Headricks among them, who'd come to find a place to settle and they camped here at this bend in the river, where the land levels out…there's even a beach through them trees…. Well, as soon as they'd set up camp and lit a fire, Indians appeared on that ridge and killed them all with arrows… never even had to cross the river to scalp them."

"Geez."

"It's the truth. It's what they say. Probably would have happened again in the Civil War. A group of men from the county (not sure that anyone on the Headrick side was there or not) … they set up on that hill hoping to catch a unit from the north camped out on that same shore. They didn't come. They were supposed to be coming down the river, but I don't know how they ever believed that. Why it's probably quicker on foot, the way this river wanders around."

"We getting out?"

Annette had pulled the car to the side of the road as she told a couple of the many stories she had about The Bend.

"We could."

Rachel opened her door and crossed the small road and was making her way through the trees and toward the river while Annette was still struggling with her seat belt.

Annette walked slowly under the trees, trying to not let her small foot slip in holes hidden in the shade. She really wasn't much for long walks anymore. And she certainly wouldn't have volunteered to walk around down here. It was morning and probably safe. Relatively. It was one thing to drive the small road; it was something else to stroll around like one actually belonged here.

As she came closer to the water she saw what must have been the reason for Rachel's haste. She was talking with a boy, dressed similarly to Rachel, who was awkwardly leaning on a rope swing. The boy had a disheveled appearance much like Rachel and she must have been so desperate to be around someone of her own kind that she might have jumped out of the car even if it hadn't been stopped.

She came closer to them and caught their attention.

"Well, hello. Logan?"

"Mrs. Headrick?"

"What're you doing down here?" Annette saw that he looked a little sick, his face a little tight. He must have been nervous talking to Rachel.

"Just hanging out."

Annette looked up the length of rope to where it hung from the tree. "Good. You should enjoy your summer."

Rachel then gave her a look, the meaning of which she was unsure though the sentiment was apparent.

"Well, I'll just be over here."

Eggs in a bowl, biscuits on a plate, bacon on another, tub of margarine next to the salt and pepper before her, Annette sipped her juice. Listening for movement upstairs.

22

The Dairy King was situated on 34, at the south end of Sheridan and, during the summer months, it became a popular place. In addition to ice cream (they'd lost the franchise some years ago) they sold the closest thing to fast food that Sheridan had to offer. It had a clientele similar to the diner, except a couple of generations younger. Bill made an effort to check in every once in a while.

He always appreciated his greetings at the Dairy King. At the diner, he was treated with deference; here was treated with respect. Nods, "How ya doin', Sheriff?"

"Good, Tom. How's it going?" Tom was the business owner. Along with coaching girls' T-Ball, he had a boy in Iraq and a daughter who was a senior and a star on the volleyball team and working at the counter as well. She gave Bill a smile that made him feel guilty.

"Busy, busy." He hooked his thumbs in his belt and nodded to the seating area.

Looking around, Bill saw many familiar faces and a couple of strangers who caught his attention for a moment before he turned back to Tom. "Looks good."

"What can I do for you?"

"Nothing. I was just wondering if you were hiring?"

"You looking for a little walking around money, Bill?

"No, no. Logan. Hoping to keep him busy this summer."

"I'm staffed." Tim looked around at his teenage crew. "I'm sure I'll lose one sooner or later. I'll give you a call if something opens up."

"Appreciate it." Bill turned back to the room.

"Sure I can't get you anything?"

Two males, early twenties, hair to their shoulders. Pale. "Well…

how 'bout a soft-serve cone?"

"You got it. Chocolate or vanilla?"

"Just vanilla."

Bill took his cone, a napkin wrapped around it to keep the melting ice cream off his fingers, and walked outside. He took slow, leisurely steps on the narrow sidewalk and the strip of shade next to the building. He was looking at license plates until he finally found the one he was looking for. Colorado. A brown cargo van. Tires nearly bald. He tried to look through the windshield but the sun's glare didn't allow him much.

Next door to the Dairy King was what used to be an old Sinclair station. The pumps were long gone but the two bays were still used for auto repair. The lot was lined with cars for sale, orange numbers beneath layers of dust. He started judging the cars while enjoying the cones.

Trust wasn't something to be cherished to Bill. It had served him wrong before. Distrust served more purpose for him. Two guys like that come through this town, they're up to no good. Could certainly be drugs. More than likely. But a van like that? Could have a girl tied up and gagged in there. Could be looking for a girl to take.

He thought then again of Tom's daughter, the athletic Laurie and the smile she'd given him. He couldn't help thinking about going to the 3A volleyball championship game and seeing her in the tight shorts all the players wore. The bare arms.

Elaine had been gone for nearly a year. And it caused his mind to wander sometimes. It wasn't like they'd had a private life that would have been worth telling anyone about, but she got things done for him. Things that weren't being done for him now. Things she was doing for that damn contractor.

When a man is convinced but has no proof he feels like a bigger fool than he might had it happened right in front of him. The truth was that he'd doubted his belief the whole time. All the evidence pointed to her stepping out, but until he came home to find her gone he didn't know. Logan was spending the night at Bill's sister's after painting their barn all day and Bill came home to an empty house. No note; just her things gone. He was amazed by how few things she had.

Elaine had her clothes and makeup, things that occupied their bedroom and bathroom, closets and drawers. Nothing else in the house she took. No pictures. No furniture. Not the china her mother had given them as a wedding present. Not the wedding album that sat on a shelf in their living room. Not even her magazines that arrived in the last few weeks and remained unread.

When he went to bed that night he wasn't angry. Maybe a little, because a night with Logan out of the house was a rarity and he would have pushed her a little harder that night. Instead, he heated up some soup out of a can and took the weekly paper up to bed. He turned out the light when he couldn't hold his head up anymore.

The next day and the day after, he wasn't mad. It hadn't been easy lying to Logan that his mother had gone on a trip to St. Louis with Holly, but he felt he could breathe easier now that she was gone. He had no need to worry. All the things that had made him wound up and sick to his stomach were no longer a problem. And he was alright until the night he saw her car outside Marelli's.

Marelli's was Sheridan's Italian restaurant, run by actual ethnic Italians from St. Louis. After retiring from a career at McDonnell Douglas, Alonzo Marelli and his wife retired to one of the large houses across from City Park and, finding the town sorely lacking in any sort of "ethnic" food, they opened a restaurant on the corner of Main and Highway J. It held only ten tables, but by virtue of its location, where everyone who came into town saw through its café curtains the white tablecloths and wine glasses, it was filled every Friday and Saturday night.

The flash of red and blue from the top of Bill's cruiser on this particular night where he stopped in the street to read the license plate of Elaine's blue Camry probably caught the attention of all the restaurant's guests, but only Elaine stood from her seat, managing to catch Bill's eye. He was out of the car before he really knew what he was doing. It was the first time he'd even laid eyes on his wife since she left without warning, without a word of explanation. It wasn't only this that spurred him on. If he'd have seen her car in the parking lot of the Country Mart he might not have felt compelled to storm in there after her, but to be at Marelli's on a Friday night was likely to mean that she was in the middle of some romantic evening.

When Bill pulled open the door, every eye in the restaurant was upon him. They were all probably expecting some such scene, having observed the married woman at the table with the younger man, the small candle burning between them. The teenage hostess moved toward him to offer assistance, but something about the look of his face, the swiftness of his movements made her back away. The well-built contractor, sandy-haired and young, had a hold of Elaine's wrist as if he'd just pulled her back down to her seat. The intimacy and presumption of the gesture enraged Bill even further.

"So, this is him?" Bill tried to restrain the words. Of course, he knew it was him. His existence, his name, his appearance had been shared with him from a multitude of sources. Well-meaning, they were, looking out for him, but each mention of his wife stung. The mention of her new man cut him deep.

"Bill." Elaine looked past Bill to the staring eyes around them.

"Whore."

"Now, Bill." Lucky pushed his chair back.

"A little late to try and protect her integrity there, buddy. I ought to…."

"Stop it." Elaine reached for him.

"You, too. You both deserve to have the shit beat out of you." He was practicing restraint, the anger, the stabbing nature of it overwhelming him, but the thought of a physical outlet, bold acts of violence, made the anger spill over. He began to shake. He picked up the edge of the table and slammed it back down.

The lovers moved to right glasses and keep plates out of their laps. And then there was a gentle touch on the scalding skin of Bill's bare elbow.

Terry appeared next to him, nodding with a look that said everything. It said she knew how he felt and that he had every right to feel it, but here was not the place and he'd really be better off containing himself right now.

He had felt his eyes grow wet and walked out of Marelli's without another word.

Bill, standing still among the dusty used cars, kept one eye on the door of the Dairy King, the other on the van.

"You looking for a new car there, Sheriff?" Dennis Shultz, in greasy jeans, a mesh cap, a t-shirt a size too small and a couple of years too old, came his way. Shultz really was an unfavorable type, not the kind he'd want to buy a car from, but he'd proved to be a decent informant on more than one occasion.

"How you doin', Dennis?" The men shook hands. "I'm gonna have to get a car for Logan sooner or later. Turns sixteen this fall."

"Well, he's gotta have a car the girls'll like. Something sporty."

The two young men came out then and climbed into the van. Bill excused himself from Shultz and tossed the remaining ice cream cone in his mouth. He felt the cold shock an old crown in the back of his mouth.

They set off south, out of town and Bill hung back, knowing just the distance that would make him appear like nothing more than an average car in the rearview mirrors, the lights on the roof imperceptible at that distance. No one kept to the speed limits and it didn't much matter. This limit, though, did serve as a justification for stopping anyone.

It wasn't easy being a suspicious man. Not only did it make him doubt everyone he met, it made him doubt himself. These kids, though, were an easy mark. Everything about them said that they weren't from anywhere around here. They weren't your rural meth freaks or head-bangers, instead, they were lefty liberals. Hippies. Despicable.

He'd had encounters with their kind, those that protested against a war while he was over there with wet socks in his boots, a t-shirt in his helmet to keep it from irritating the scar it was creating, those that were said to spit on returning soldiers. He'd worked too hard for that treatment. If they wanted peace so damn much they could start with a little respect for fellow citizens, those Americans who'd, without option, risked their lives for them. In most ways, he hadn't really been bothered by their kind after his return, mostly because he brought his own troubles back with him.

War had offered him a perspective that he would never have known without the inundation of those images for years on end. Bad things happen. That was maybe the primary lesson learned. Bad things brought on by the proximity of angry, tired men for extended periods, by drugs and nightmares. Bad things brought on by an enemy with no mercy, with no sense of the standards of war, who'd just as soon hide in a house full of women and children or put a gun into the hand of one of those women or children to do the killing for them.

Bill had, of course, seen men killed. His men, as he ascended rank. Boys still in their teens who'd disappeared after the whistling approach of an incoming shell, lost parts after snagging a tripwire, bled out waiting for help while bullets sailed over a paling body. That was one of the moments he still recalled. It had surfaced from his memory and shown itself to him on many occasions in the last few months.

An angry kid from upstate New York who blamed his parents for not helping him get a deferment, a Democratic father insisting they needed soldiers for Johnson's war. Wilson deserved better and he told everyone so, getting into a fight one night with a farmer's son from Kansas after telling the larger boy that he deserved to be here, deserved to be part of war's fodder because he was poor, while Wilson shouldn't be here at all. Wilson got beat bad, but it took none of the fire out of him.

Their patrol that day had taken them to a clearing no wider than a city street, but they needed to cross it. The options were weighed and two by two they started across, eyes scanning the opposite shore of that gulf for any activity. There were two quick shots, the sound of a bullet sinking into a tree and everyone dropped to the ground. They scrambled on their knees for the shelter of the trees, only then turning to spray the opposite tree line with bullets. Bill realized that one of them still lay in the low grass. He didn't hesitate long to rush out there, planning to put his hands in Wilson's armpits and yank the boy out of there. Staying low while bullets popped repeatedly.

"Let's go. Let's go," Bill said when he reached the boy. The slits of Wilson's eyes showed only whites. His dark green uniform had a spot that looked like raspberry jelly. Bill could not mess around long. He ripped the buttons off Wilson's shirt, pulling it open, and snapped the chain of the boy's dog tags. He pressed one into the dying body's slack mouth and the other into his own chest pocket. And he left him there.

He'd seen this moment again many times in the months after Terry's death, the dead body, his charge, the raspberry stain. It wasn't a lifeless face that stuck with him, not the person Wilson had been. It was the nearly weightless metal of the dog tag, the glinting metal, the pressed letters of identification. A name, social security number, blood type, and religion. Even following a quarter-mile behind the two long-hairs in the van, he could feel the light metal between his fingers.

They were going just less than ten miles over the speed limit and this didn't seem enough reason to stop them. Speeding was one thing, but reckless driving was another. And he was hoping, or more or less convinced, that he could get them on something else, drugs or worse. Judge Bryson would likely think he'd been harassing the kids if the reason for the stop had been something as simple as a minor speeding ticket.

The judge had enough respect for Bill, but their sense of justice differed some. Bryson appeared more concerned with personal relationships, his social standing, than making sure people get what they deserved. Just before Elaine left, they'd been invited to a party at Judge Bryson's house on the other side of Sheridan Cemetery. The house was a large Georgian thing, columns and an extensive second-floor balcony that, from the house's hillside perch, overlooked the many treed ridges to the south. The place had belonged to Sheridan, the town's founder himself and built, it was said, with such a view so that he could, from his death-bed, see his old Louisiana.

The house had a mystique because it sat there, behind its big white fences, allowing everyone to spread rumors. Rumors of all sorts. It was the only house in the county with full-time help, a wisp of a woman now in her forties who had served as a nanny to the Bryson children, a cook, a maid and more. Rumor said that she didn't live in the house's traditional maid's quarters because they'd been turned into Mrs. Bryson's workout room, complete with mirrored walls, exercise equipment, yoga mats, and a TV that hung from the wall, and the woman had been moved to a windowless room in the cellar. It was also suggested that the woman, whose hair was as long and straight as she was, served in other capacities in the house, in the bedroom, and when she could be seen sulking around the County Mart, it was easy to believe. It was said she served both the master and the missus in this capacity.

Bryson had been born with some privilege in another county and had married the last descendant of Sheridan. This was held against him by most until they needed favors. The party was populated with these sorts of people milling about on the front lawn, past the pig spinning on a roaster, manned by the owner of a place called the Roadhouse, a place just outside town limits and the jurisdiction of Sheridan's police and liquor laws. Bill's officers were often called there on Friday and Saturday nights. Also, as entertainment, Bryson had a drummer-less band playing traditional country-western.

The people that wandered around with drinks in their hands or sat on concrete benches balancing paper plates on their knees while stuffing pulled pork sandwiches into their mouths, included all of the town's prominent, those who occupied the town's largest houses, along with many of the county's prominent who occupied the largest farms, though Bryson was thought of less favorably outside the town's environs. Among this elite were others with less stellar reputations, like the owner of the Roadhouse who was said to sell cocaine. Included was a former pastor who'd been forced to give up his post after being arrested on suspicions of child molestation. No charges were ever brought and the accusing parents left the community. Another party-goer was a woman who, along with her new husband, was said to have fed her last husband to his own hogs. Another was a private gun dealer who was supposed to be the man to see if someone wanted a handgun without a waiting period, an untraceable weapon, or a weapon with more firepower than was needed for hunting or normal household protection.

These associates said more to Bill about Bryson's character than did his track record on the bench. Bryson wasn't reluctant to sign a search warrant though he didn't always follow through when the case came before him. The company Bryson kept explained everything to Bill and despite the nudges and nods to Elaine, she didn't much seem to care. She must have had other things on her mind that night. He walked around as if alone in a bright setting sun making long shadows out of this menagerie of characters.

In the long arrow of road in front of him, the brown van made a quick turn onto a side road. Bill sped up.

23

When the sun finally stretched to Frank's closed eyes where he lay long across the bench seat of his truck, he awoke. It wasn't so much awakening as it was a simple shift in slippery consciousness. It felt at that moment hardly different from the dreaming he'd been doing, the stiff-drunken dreaming that replays moments and actions without end. Though he'd left the unnamed bar when it closed, in his sleep Frank had still been there, trying to get another drink, trying to stay out of a conflict that had arisen around the dartboard, trying to strike up a conversation with a woman with long black hair and a tight-fitting shirt. He covered his eyes against the sun, his lips and tongue gone dry and fat.

When conscious enough, he sat up against sluggish muscles and retrieved a small bottle from his glove box. Opening his mouth to receive the liquid he hoped might provide some stasis, keep him away from the painful, powerful decline he was experiencing, the pain in his jaw revealed that he had not been able to avoid the dart throwers' argument. Maybe the two men had been friends and that had given them license to call each other names, to dispute the outcome of their contests. Frank had sat at the end of the bar, where he was least likely to be pulled into a conversation, where he could sit and let each new drink wash over him like a warm breeze, like a world rushing by while he sat blissfully with closed eyes.

Maybe the first time the guy spoke to him, he hadn't really heard, maybe it came from so far away, from so far outside his lumbering thoughts that the request could not have been registered, understood. The bigger one was pushing him for an objective opinion, and Frank didn't give a shit. Somehow, he'd given this impression, or maybe he'd said as much because he received a shove that knocked him loose from his stool. Face to face with this man, older, shorter and thicker than Frank, he could have gotten riled up for a fight that he would likely have won. Brothers teach a boy fight. His adolescent survival had depended on the success of thrown punches. But he was too far gone to bother getting agitated. He'd earlier felt the sharp sting of failure. But standing mute before the pair was obviously the wrong response because before he'd had a moment to raise fists to his chest in defense he received a punch to his jaw that sent him back against the bar, where he fell to the sticky floor between the stools.

He struggled to right himself, hitting his head on a stool on his way to his feet. He hadn't thought yet what to do, except to save himself from the indignity of lying on a barroom floor, but before he could do anything the friend seized his shoulders to hold him back. It struck Frank then as odd. It felt almost like a hug, like someone telling him to buck up. Maybe the friend really sought to protect him, Frank, by standing between him and his attacker. While standing in this embrace, Frank still drew two open-handed smacks to the head, ruffling his hair and drawing the bartender out from his foxhole behind the bar.

By all means, Frank should have been thrown out on his ass, but the bartender was wise enough to determine the conflict's aggressor and who was likely to sit peacefully, elbows on the bar, and continue ordering drinks. And this is exactly what Frank did, occasionally forgetting the pain in his jaw but never quite letting go of the evening's earlier indignity.

He'd been seated earlier in his crouched position on his stool, a roadhouse gargoyle, and couldn't keep his eyes from focusing on a pair of women sitting in a booth. One's back was to him and he never had a notion about her, but the other, hair long and black, nose and jaw straight and thin, glowed in his mind like an apparition. She was a beauty and, at first, nothing more, but each time he turned away from her his mind went to another subject, another beauty, unlikely and tragic. He thought of Terry. He thought of the way her beauty had snuck up on him. It had been this realization of her beauty that allowed him to see his attraction to her.

He'd never met a woman so earnest and kind. Terry took no bullshit and yet she seemed to care about him. In her he found something that he felt had been missing his whole life, a limb restored when he'd lived his life without it. It changed, though, when he realized that she was much more to him than just a good person.

Bob Stegman had taken off early that morning with a trailer of calves to an auction, leaving Frank to handle the day's chores. In the afternoon, Frank had gone out to assess the remaining herd. By horse, he went out through two closed gates and one open to where the black animals grazed as casually as any other day. To Frank, it had felt different. Knowing that Bob was going to be gone from the ranch meant a sort of liberty he rarely felt. It resulted in a good feeling, a raising up of the heart somewhat, but he noticed then that he was hurrying about his task.

He had to count them, locate them all, and check on the conditions of ones that had some sort of ailment, real or suspected. And he was to repeat the findings to Terry. One cow might have had some sort of eye infection. Maybe she had scraped it on brush or a branch or maybe it was some sort of affliction that was going to require medicine or even a visit from the large animal doc. Frank bounded down from the horse when he saw her, the eye soft and wet like a cracked egg in a dish, and she struggled to get away from him as he put his hands on her head, pulling the eye open to look for discoloring, a discharge. It was gross and wet, a tear trail all the way to her mouth, but nothing to be concerned about.

Another one had shown what might be a limp last time they brought them all up for some fattening sweet grain. He found her a little way from the others up in the trees. He didn't like seeing that and ducked beneath low branches to get to her. Frank pulled a thin broken branch from a tree and smacked the deep black hindquarters of the cow. She leaped, ran ten or so paces in front of him and stopped to pull again at the soft grasses in the trees' shade. She exhibited no limp.

Frank pushed the horse to get back to the house, jumping off and back on at every gate as if he'd just had an extra cup of coffee. He had not, though, recognized his own eagerness.

He found Terry on the cool screened porch in the house's northeast corner. She sat on a dusty couch, leaned forwards towards papers spread out on a low table. She was punching numbers into a calculator when he came to the screen door.

"Afternoon," Frank said, pulling the screen door open, waiting to be acknowledged before entering.

She took a moment, finished her calculation, and muttered to herself, "Shit." Then she raised her head to him and, with a nod, "Everything's more expensive than you think it's going to be."

"Is it?" He asked, entering.

"It is." She wrote the figure down. "How are the ladies?"

"Good, good." He stood to the side of her papers, conscious of the light.

"Sit," she commanded, shifting papers until she located a small black binder. "What's the word on fifty-two's eye?"

Frank sat slowly in the large chair in the corner, the one occupied by Bob on late summer evenings, sweating bottle of beer in one hand and a smoldering cigar in his mouth. "Still wet, but nothing funny. I'm sure she'll get over it soon."

"Great." She made a notation then looked up at the horizon. The sun was getting low in the west, the fence posts casting long shadows. She might have been watching the far tree line for turkeys. "Oh," she turned to look at him, "what about that limp on thirty-four?"

"Sure. She looks good. Wasn't favoring it at all." He felt a slight chill as she looked to him for the answer. Maybe she didn't look at him directly, look into his eyes as he answered, or maybe he'd simply taken to noticing each action she took with some sort of clarity.

"Great." Again, she noted something in the binder, her pencil moving swiftly and purposefully. "Great. Not a thing to worry about."

"'Cept the price Bob got for those calves today."

At first, she looked at him like she didn't know what he was talking about, but then she smiled. "There's always that."

Frank nearly shook his head for the attempt at a joke, and for even mentioning Bob's name. He was aware that he didn't want the thought of Bob in her mind at all. Why should he not want her to think of Bob? What was so special about this moment? Why did it feel private? Special?

He looked then at Terry, his eyes passing slowly and carefully over her high cheekbones, the sturdy nose, the lips held slightly open as she again looked in the distance. Frank wanted to touch her, to feel her face under his fingers. He dared even to think then about what it might be like to press his own lips to hers. He reddened and turned to look across the near pasture. He knew then that what he felt for her, what he'd obviously been feeling for her, was more than one might feel for a person who was merely nice to him.

Frank was only twenty-five when he came to this realization and this feeling was entirely new to him. It wasn't like he'd seen love. His father was barely visible, always working, and his mother was around, involved in some sort of labor, often with an unrecognizable child in her arms. His brothers had demonstrated lust and wanting, but no one mentioned "love." Women, even the girls he'd known for the few years he'd shown up in public school, were seen as little more than pack mules, good for a handful of purposes and nothing else. His understanding of his own existence was not much different. He knew displeasure, sure, but real pleasure was only imaginary. Or, on occasion, fleeting.

His brother, Washington, had been frequenting the house of a high-school girl, an overabundant girl with parents who spent each evening out at a bar. She was only sixteen, Frank's age, while his brother was two years older, and she saw him as exotic and was willing to do anything he wanted. So Washington had been happy to tell him when he stooped through the low door of the grain shed they shared as a bedroom. Washington told him of things so carnal and physical that Franklin could scarcely believe them to be true. Bodies could not contort in such ways; no person would willingly have such a thing done to her. He was assured that none of it was fabricated, that she was as eager as he described.

One night after being ripped from pleasant dreams of walking under trees on a fall day, leaves falling around him like snowflakes of red and gold, Franklin called his brother's bluff. "Prove it."

"I'll do you one better." Washington's breath smelled of alcohol. "You can do it to her."

"No way." He didn't believe it and wasn't really sure he wanted to.

"Shit, yeah. Tomorrow night we'll go over, and I'll get her to let you stick it in her. If she don't, I'll suck it for you."

"Fuck off."

Such favors were not required. After waiting in the car for what must have been an hour or more. Franklin was waved into the single-story house to find a girl, her pants unzipped below a large soft belly, lips raw and red. She'd been leaned back on the couch until she saw him, sat up, took a drink of something pink from a bottle and held out her hands to him.

Giving himself over to the manipulations of an easy teenager had been one thing, and even the feeling that lingered through his body the next day was not at all similar to the sensation he felt in his body, in his heart, at even the thought of Terry. And maybe his attraction to the black-haired woman at the bar was a way to displace these feelings with something simpler, something physical instead of emotional. Or maybe it simply was physical, simple desire taking over his actions, making him mistakenly rise from his barstool and sit in the booth across from the beautiful stranger.

Her friend had disappeared to the ladies' room and the woman had looked around the bar, her eyes meeting Frank's. Her eyes did not ask for a response, they did not call him over, but they were a cue none the less and Frank spun on the stool and planted his feet on the floor. He leaned forward and put the closed fist of his free hand, the other being occupied with ice melting into his whiskey, on her table and sputtered, "How's it going?"

He'd not intended to sit down, understanding that doing so without being invited was simply rude, but his legs were weak with what was being asked of them. The nerves and liquor forced him to drop to the vinyl.

"Do you mind," she asked.

Frank wasn't sure what she meant. Had she asked him a favor? Did she need something from him? He looked around as if someone else might have the answer for him. "No," he responded.

She looked at him then, dark eyes looking at him, to him. They were not observing, they were engaging him, colorless eyes, the skin around them also dark and lined. He could not, though, discern their message.

Finally, they opened up from their narrow focus into an expression that Frank read as exasperation. "My friend will be back in a second."

"Oh, sure." He pushed himself to his feet, her bottle of beer rocking on the table. Looking back at her, still struck by her beauty, he wanted some sort of farewell, a sign-off, a parting shot that might somehow correct the impression he had given her. He felt only his mouth hanging open and he spun to return to his stool.

Still sitting in his truck, his drink having put the necessary gloss to his eyes, the calmer sheen to the day, a mellowing of the squeezing of his head, Frank rolled down his driver's side window with laborious cranking. The sun had turned the cab suffocatingly hot. The remembrance of the previous day having returned to his consciousness with larger, more disturbing and fundamental ideas and failures behind them, Frank needed to get moving, to find new ways to push these things far, far away. He needed to do something other than return home to a lonely and neglected farm.

24

The dark grasses in front of the Stegman farm were long, with tufts of seed waving from longer blades. The lawn had not been mown once this season and the sight of it bothered Sam in ways he knew better than to explore. He knew that it attracted the attention of others, whispers hissed around the diner about the apparent neglect. Some suspected that Frank had been kicked out after Terry's death and that her family had left the property to go to ruin. And who knew what happened to the cows or the horses?

Sam knew that the horses had been gone for a long time, soon after Bob's death, when Terry and Frank came to the same realization as many other ranchers, that an ATV was much more logical transportation around the pastures, requiring less maintenance and care. Sam also knew from Terry's probate lawyer, who also served occasionally as public defender, that everything Terry had was tied up and wouldn't be changing hands anytime soon. And if everything could be released and the appropriate taxes paid there was still a dispute over the will.

After Bob's death, Terry had made some changes to her will. The property was to go to her family, to whom it had once belonged. All else, any livestock, personal property, along with all money and investments would go to Frank. The trouble was that both, Terry's family and Frank, wanted it the other way around. Frank wanted the land, wanted to be the first in his family to own property other than the communally-held hollow where he'd been raised. Terry's mother wasn't interested in land so far from their other holdings, and she had every reason to believe that Terry's finances and investments were worth much more, the money left over from an insurance policy and other dealings would likely mean more as a penciled figure in her mother's green paper ledger.

Sam imagined that Frank was surely in quite a state over everything, the loss of Terry, conceivably his only real associate, along with his future being held in limbo.

Pulling up to the farm, Sam didn't see Frank's truck in front of the small old house, but he turned in anyway. He drove between the houses, past the equipment in their shadowy stalls, and parked near the back of the barn, in front of the gate to a small holding pen, a corral of white steel pipes and a maze of gates and chutes which Sam had used as a model during the creation of his own ranch. About thirty cows were grazing just beyond a second gate and they crept closer when he stepped out of his truck. They studied him as he lowered the pick-up's back gate, pulled a fifty-pound bag of sweet grain to the edge and swung it up on his shoulder.

Sam's round face reddened as he lugged the bag to the gate, veins bulging at his temples, a pain in his lower back as if he could feel the compression of his spine. He let himself through the gate and threw the bag down next to a trough, long and low, that sat in the center of the holding pen. Some of the older cows began their low, guttural call as he cut the bag open and hefted it up again to pour the pellets along the length of the trough. Maybe they were talking to him, a "thank you" or maybe just "come on, hurry up." Or maybe they were calling to other cows somewhere out of sight.

After opening the far gate, letting in the slow, heavy herd, he backed himself up to the gate, leaned against it and put his fingers in the pockets of his jeans in an attempt at leisure. Maybe he should go get his trailer and haul them all back to his own ranch so they can get the care they need. It would take all day and be damn near impossible without some help, the kind of help Frank was always good for. The heifers (there were no calves here) orbited the crowd at the trough, occasionally trying to nose their way in, only to be chased away.

Despite court orders, Frank had sold off twenty head, nearly half the herd and Sam appreciated the single action, defying authority to ensure the safety of the farm. It was the only admirable action he'd seen out of Frank since March. Phone calls had gone unanswered, leaving Sam to seek help from other lent farmhands, notably less hard-working. The property had obviously been neglected and there were the stories he'd heard around.

He'd been seen pissing against Sheridan Cemetery's rock wall and stumbling back to his truck to drive away. Supposedly he'd been making the rounds of the bars or any place with a neon sign in the south of the county. The rougher parts.

One such place sat in an alcove around a blind curve on the main north-south highway. Sam had been there many times to block traffic while troopers scraped car parts, glass, and fluids from the road, or on other occasions to check on reports of gunfire in the parking area or to extricate an unruly or simply passed out patron.

The bar resided in an old house in which the owners still lived upstairs and was backed up against a limestone cliff and every bit of the narrow strip between roadway and hillside was scraped clear of vegetation and covered with white rock to accommodate a Saturday night of pickups, Dodge Dusters, and second or third-hand Hyundais.

Stacey Earl was a meth dealer and general bad man. Maybe having a girl's name and a first name as a last name had turned him from an object of ridicule to an outlaw, rejecting morality. He was known to operate out of this bar in the open, visible to all. Sam's fellow deputies were executing a warrant on Earl's house on a Saturday night and Sam sat undercover in the back seat of Natalie's car, with an eye on Earl's car. He was to alert Bill if Earl, for some reason, left the bar and might surprise them as they ransacked his house, ripping apart the cushions of his couch to look for stashes of money, drugs or guns. And then if they found what they were looking for in the house, they were to come to the bar to pick up Earl.

Seated in the backseat, his radio at a whisper in his lap, Sam monitored the action on the radio. He was a bit sorry to not be a part of what he considered to be the excitement, but he wasn't about to trust this responsibility to any lesser deputy. Many were known for dozing in the middle of the day, in the middle of their shift, and would likely be drooling on themselves in the darkened car at nearly midnight. He watched there as people walked slowly to their cars then sped off without a glance either way down the road. During the height of the action, calls of "we got it" over the radio, a couple were having at each other in the backseat of the neighboring car. Sam struggled not to picture the horrible pair these two had made outside of the car now unclothed and raw behind the glass.

"Two-two-nine?"

"Two-two-nine," Sam answered into the radio in a whisper.

"Two-twenty-one. I'm in route to your twenty."

"Ten-four."

Sam hitched his holster to the belt in his jeans and slid out the back door of the car, on the opposite side of the car that was rocking in small quick fits. Standing, he pulled his long flannel shirt over the gun and badge on his belt then walked to Earl's car, a battered old Suburban with flaking paint and rust holes, and let the air out of the front driver's side tire. It might not stop him if he wanted to run, but it sure would slow him down.

A county cruiser sped into the lot and slid to a stop just in front of the narrow front steps, wrought iron handrails the same as they had been when the building actually served as a home, before the small road became a highway and someone decided to put linoleum in the living room, bring in booths, chairs and tables and a barely operational jukebox and turn it into a bar.

The place was much more brightly lit than a room of its dimensions should have been. Each cigarette smoldering in aged lips, each uncollected empty bottle and glass, each bleary eye was lighted like a window display. Sam stood at the door next to Terry, eyes scanning for a man with a look of an abandoned mangy dog.

Earl was sitting at a short bar of five stools conversing with a homely blond with a pair of missing teeth on the right side of her smile and deep cleavage that would, none the less, draw eyes. The bartender's wide-eyed recognition of the threat of a uniformed officer forced an involuntary move towards whatever she likely kept just behind the foul water of the bar sink. Her shift and change of expression made Earl swivel on his stool, bringing his brown beer bottle in his hand along for the ride.

Sam saw the man's focus shift to the door behind them, escape being his primary instinct. A quick look of the room revealed no other means of escape. "Whoa! Whoa!" Earl said loudly enough to ensure that any guests that may still have been distracted by their conversations or general intoxication turned in their direction. As an

Allman Brothers track played into the hollow silence of the room, Sam knew this wasn't going to be simple.

"Stacey Earl?" Terry's voice commanded the question like a formal declaration.

"Yeah, so?"

Terry stepped confidently and swiftly forward, but her movement drew a quick reaction from the crowded room. People stood and moved toward her and Earl. Not quite a direct threat, but Sam put a hand on his gun.

The plan had been for him to stand by the door to make Earl less inclined to dash for the exit, but now Sam came forward to be a somewhat taller presence next to Terry.

She took a hold of Earl's wrist and pulled the bottle from his grip and only then when she had control of her suspect did she turn to the room. "Stay back now."

There were murmurs then, people talking to each other, quietly voiced protests. The general objection to his removal apparently emboldened Earl and he whipped his wrist away from Terry. The crowd yelped in approval and Sam leaped in to help Terry wrestle Earl's arms behind his back. They slid around the sticky linoleum Other hands became involved, pulling at the man's shoulders and arm, the officers' forearms, in an attempt to free him.

"Get back," Sam shouted and, though his words were without a doubt loud and forceful, he knew they also displayed an emotion that he wasn't interested in sharing in this situation.

And though hands pulled away, curses and obscenities filled the room. Sam knew that he had somehow upped the ante. His command had been perceived as a challenge.

Terry had Earl cuffed and he struggled less. Sam reached in with his left hand grabbing the man's upper arm and they began to pull him backward out of the room. For this second, Sam felt a patter of victory in his chest but this sensation was quickly followed by a shifting at his waist, a tug at his belt that meant that someone was grabbing at his gun.

Sam had been well-trained in defensive moves and acted with instinct, a closed fist swung down and back to dislodge someone's grip by striking the wrist, but even as he did this the fear that leaped in him pained his chest as if he'd been struck. And though it wasn't advisable, he unholstered his weapon and raised it for all the room to see. "Who else here wants to go to jail?"

A beer bottle unseen by Sam sailed by him, striking the sticky bottles of booze behind the bar. Chairs and tables turned over and fell somewhere behind the men closest. Sam pulled at Earl, wanting to extricate him and Terry and himself before things escalated further, and Earl fell off his feet, nearly pulling Terry's smaller body to the floor. Someone grabbed at her then in an attempt to drive her to the ground but she struck back with an elbow, making contact with a man likely too young even to be in an establishment like this.

Sam couldn't read fear in her, but as she stood she also grabbed Earl under the arm and her other hand pulled her radio from her belt. "Two-twenty-one to dispatch. Ten-sixteen." Officer in trouble.

They moved backward the ten or twelve feet to the door but they were met with trouble every step of the way. From whichever way Sam wasn't looking he was struck with some sort of blow, a fist swung from a distance, a kick off-balance, a beer bottle or two. And the closer to the door they got, the more Earl's protest grew frantic, panicked, his fate becoming apparent.

A pair of men blocked the door, one with a stomach that showed round and pale beneath his t-shirt, the other tall with shoulders of a man that once played sports but grew slack over the years. Sam gestured with the dull black metal of his gun for them to move. It took a second time, slowed this time with the hollow of the gun's barrel hovering at a spot just above the level of their heads, before they moved.

Outside they were met with assistance, other officers who quickly hogtied the still-struggling Stacey Earl and tossed him dismissively in the back of a cruiser. Sam and Terry took the chance then to lean on one of the cars and catch their breath. They looked at each other with wide-open eyes, acknowledging the danger they had just been in, the fear they had felt, and saying nothing. Several of the bar's patrons watched them from the narrow concrete front porch.

And now Frank had been spending time in places like that. Sam feared what could happen to him, or who he might become. He knew that some sort of intervention was going to be necessary, though he could not see it, could not see himself throwing an arm around the stinking shoulders of a hungover Frank and finding the right words to explain to him that simply because the life of someone he cared for had been stolen too soon it did not mean that he should throw his own away. Sam could empathize. He wasn't a quitter, wasn't likely to throw things away. At least not consciously.

25

There was a magic in the air, a palpable scent, something kinetic, a sensation of the world's swirling molecules that Logan felt as he drove in his stolen car. It was possibility, opportunity. It was a kindred spirit, a female counterpart. Someone who had sensed his difference, knew that his outlook differed from all those blind and deadened by a society that taught them every day how to think and behave. Television shows that kill an independent spirit by fostering a false version of freedom based on American enterprise and an abundance of consumer choice. She was also someone who sought to make her stamp on the world a visual one, a declaration like a middle finger raised to the world, the wardrobe of resistance. She found him as one can see, can find a fellow revolutionary, and offered him compassion, companionship. A cell phone number that provided direct access with the absence of intermediaries. She offered possibility, opportunity.

It was a victory for Logan, an affirmation that his intentions bore fruit. Each day as he dressed he acknowledged that he would likely fare ridicule but his clothes and his hair were intended to separate himself, not only to tell the rest of the world to go take a flying fuck but so that someone like him would see him for who he was. Someone who might appreciate his difference. He had held unarticulated fantasies of someone, a Dot Baxter maybe, who would appreciate him for his differences and come out of her own shell, shed herself of the costume of commerce and join him in rebellion.

He would never have had the courage to imagine a girl, one like Rachel with sunken eyes and features only an artist could create, would seek him out, find him there at The Bend as he sought solitude and refuge from the world. She came to him boldly and casually as if it all had been arranged previously. And it made perfect sense that she came from the outside. She might as well have come from another plane of existence, one where she saw his value. Their contact had been brief, but electric, and she left him with seven digits to memorize, numbers that he dialed the next day, his fear overpowered by compulsion as if she were drawing him forward.

And that was what she was doing to him now as he drove to her. It was a feeling like a tether around his squishy insides, each pull squeezing and drawing him forward.

As Logan had wandered around The Bend that morning, he had come to the conclusion that he would return the car to where he had found it. The exhilaration was exhausting. He had succeeded in his rebellious act. He had defied the grip of guilt his father had around his throat, but there was no need to keep it going. No need, at least, until Rachel showed up. The Headrick place was far from town. If was going to see her again, and he needed to, he was going to have to drive out there.

He had stashed the car close to town, where a narrow drive led through trees to a hollow where a trailer had burned to the ground some months earlier. He could not take the chance of returning it to the high grass from where he had taken it. And he needed it to be closer at hand. Any fear that he might be discovered, that his father might read his face for the thrill and guilt and know, dissolved in the excitement of things to come.

"I'll tell her I'm going for a walk." Rachel was also involved in deception, also pushing aside real-world complications.

Logan parked the car between the pale green siding of the house and a row of decorative bushes grown large and long-armed with decades of neglect. Rachel had said the house was abandoned by her grandmother and they would have a place to be, away from the heat and the day and the world.

He pulled back the metal screen door gently but still, it sounded of metal on metal, a tangible timbre that made him shudder. He twisted the front door handle with delicacy, felt the tongue of the latch free itself from the frame, but it took an extra, forceful push to free the door from the seal, the sound of rubber lips smacking. A suffocating smell of heat and must and mold, old perfume, grease, and rodent droppings choked him, his eyes beginning to water.

Shades were drawn in all the windows yet the bright day's light came lazily through, lighting the rooms the dusk of sunrise. The house may have been left vacant but it was left inhabited by furniture stationed in the positions that they had likely held for a century. The place had the look of a museum, a replicated room left to be overtaken by the dust and the mice.

A sound came to Logan from somewhere in the house, a hollow sound like wind, or a moan. It unsettled him and he felt the hairs rise on the back of his neck. Until the sound was choked off by chuckling.

"Get out here," Logan added a forced laugh at the end of the command.

Rachel appeared from through a door frame and Logan felt an easing in his chest. She was as she had been, magical and mysterious, beautiful. "Check this out." She turned and disappeared.

Logan followed her into a bedroom, a bed unmade and covered over with clothes thrown down in haste. "D'you do this?"

"This is how it was." She rifled through the work clothes and shirts, a man's clothes, pulling out a brown suit. "She must have gone through it all, looking for a suit to bury him in." She held it up to her chest as if she was going to try it on.

"Who?"

"My grandma." She looked up at him, read the confusion on his face. "My grandpa." Rachel held the suit up to Logan, pulling down the sleeves as if he had it on. "My mom said he killed himself." Rachel turned and tossed the suit to the bed. "She's full of shit most of the time."

"No way."

"Well, she said it was a hunting accident, but it's not too easy to accidentally shoot yourself in the head with a rifle."

"Suppose not."

"Come on." She pushed past him, her shoulder purposefully striking his shoulder, sending a rippling sensation through him. He followed her, watching the way her form moved, the sliding joints, beneath her baggy clothes, the gentle bounce. It was like she'd come directly from his imagination as if he'd built and ordered her online. He had a feeling like he wanted to devour her, to swallow her, to envelope her, to take possession of her, to make her his, part of him.

Was this what his father had once felt for his mother? It was hard for him to imagine. The thought involved his father feeling a strong emotion that wasn't anger. They had once been young lovers, giddy kids in love but he couldn't remember any display of as much. Still, he could see it. Or at least he could see how a man, such as his father, could be motivated by his mother. Certainly, she was still motivating men to irrational action.

Logan had often been repelled by his mother's sexual nature. Who else around here wore tight running pants? Form-fitting and revealing the curves and mounds, the textures of private areas. As a boy, he'd been close to these areas, these private parts on display and constantly in his line of sight. And when she began her escapades, parading around just out of sight with a man ten or more years younger, he knew it. He sensed it, he could smell it. He could see it in the way her hips moved, the fullness of her lips, the way she would touch herself. At dinner, or in the car, she would run a hand over her forearm as if she was caressing the gentlest sleeping animal. Logan found himself imagining what else she might touch similarly.

Was this her reason for leaving? Was it because she wanted sex? Was his father unwilling? Or was she just the type that would never be satisfied, that needed some reinforcement of self-esteem that would only be sated, temporarily, by the lust of a younger man? Or was she just a whore?

And somehow, she felt justified in this as if it was the most logical thing in the world to up and leave her family. How could she do anything else?

In the kitchen, the smell made it obvious that the rodents had control of the room. Rachel stood with a hold on the handle of the old humpy, refrigerator, "Dare me?"

"At your own risk."

He watched her face as an expression of disgust spread across, cheeks and lips pulling back, eyes narrowing to a squint, brow lowering. Logan felt like he was touching her face, his own eyes feeling the changing expression, the softness of her skin, the features, as if he controlled it, as if he were her creator. She threw the door closed and recoiled, drawing back until she pushed her body into his. "Blech."

"You knew the risk." Logan noticed how nicely she fit in the hollow of his shoulder before she pulled away. He was distracted from the beginning of imaginings that could be inappropriate, at least while standing, by something in the sink. Bottles of liquor, some standing, some lying like drunkards on the street, filled the old porcelain sink. He rifled through them, clinking against one another, looking at the crystallized remnants at the bottom of each, hoping.

"Whatcha got there?"

"Bottles. All empty." He put his disappointment into his words for her benefit. It would have loosened him up, made him daring, given him the courage to do what he'd wanted the moment she came to him seeking his attention at The Bend.

Logan's cousin, a tough farm kid with a buzz cut and his four-wheeler, had stolen a small bottle from its hiding place behind a coffee can of tools on the workbench in his father's shop. They'd ridden out together on the ATV, Logan doing his best to keep his thighs from gripping his cousin's behind, to a forty-acre parcel that sat low and surrounded on three sides by trees. The field had once been used for crops and under the grass, the land still rippled.

As they passed through the open gate, his cousin laid on the throttle, standing slightly and rode them quickly across the washboard. Logan did his best, squeezing the vehicle's body between his legs, but it shook and bounced him horribly. His brain, he knew, had rattled loose inside his skull.

When they crossed the field and his cousin slowed quickly before striking the fence, Logan dove from the ATV into the grass. Laughing at him, the cousin, withdrew the tiny bottle of liquor from his pocket. From the boy's thick hand, he poured some of the bottle into his upturned mouth. Logan, having raised himself to his feet finally, watched as the older boy shook his head vigorously, screwed the tiny lid on the half-empty bottle and threw it at him. Having not been given the opportunity to decline, refuse, or protest, Logan mimicked the move he'd witnessed.

It stung his throat and mouth like medicine, like someone poured foul and scalding water in his mouth. His nose burned and his eyes went glossy. He couldn't immediately understand why people would subject themselves to something so horrible, but it didn't take long before, following a short lesson, Logan was driving the four-wheeler at increasing speeds over the ribbed field. It was stupid and dangerous and something that in his right mind he never would have attempted, but the liquor had given him courage.

With a similar dispelling of his normal fears, he might be brave enough to make a move on Rachel, might be able to turn from his position at the sink, reach a hand to the small of her back, pull her forward to him and put a serious kiss on her. And if there was a lot of liquor who knows what else he might have the courage to do, what uncharted territory he would be willing to explore.

"Holy shit!"

Her shout startled him out of his inappropriate visions and he dropped the bottle he'd been holding and it crashed into the others in the sink.

In the cabinet above the refrigerator, behind a tub of Crisco, a tin of Folgers, Rachel had discovered a cache of liquor more than fifty years old. Not just whiskey, the liquor was of every sort that might fill a liquor cabinet, from vodka and gin to cognac and vermouth.

The fear sank in. He could see it coming. They would drink, sitting, lying lazily on the couch, the floor, a bed, and they would be close, enough for him to smell her, to see the small capillaries beneath her skin. They would touch. He would have to make a move to kiss her. And they would be entwined, engaged, undressed. And they would have sex.

In the expected delirium, they did.

26

Mornings came on funny when he wasn't high. The normal waking with the sun was unsettling to Harley. It gave him a taste of what it must be like to lead a real life. And he didn't like it. He'd woke on the couch when the morning sun pierced the gap in his eyelids. He'd completed a batch around midnight and hadn't felt like going through the labor of beginning again. And then, when he sat up alert on the couch, he realized he had no cigarettes. He rummaged through an ashtray and smoked the two good drags he could get out of one before deciding he was going to have to go out.

His hands on the wheel were shaky and despite the sweat starting to bead at his hairline, he held his arms close to his side in an attempt to stay warm. The morning sun had a way of lighting up the trees, the blacktop in a new way, a way he never saw in the bright hazy sun of midday or the lazy setting sun of the evenings. He felt as if he was in a foreign country. Whatever that must feel like.

As he drove, heading to town, amazed by the number of cars on the road in front of him, Harley thought about what it must be like to travel abroad. He realized the forests and roads of Europe were as alien to him as the surface of Mars. It could look just like this, the sun reflecting off damp leaves, roadside grasses looking like they'd be soft to the touch. What did he know besides this? Did California look like this? He didn't know and couldn't quite imagine. He'd never had the opportunity to travel beyond these two states on either side of the Mississippi, Missouri and Illinois. A vacation for Harley's father meant a week off to do work around the house. Travel was a waste of money.

He was going to town. There was a gas station on the west side of town, just past the roadhouse, but where two county roads crossed and a gaggle of homes and buildings crowded the intersections, Harley noticed what used to be a gas station. The pumps in front of the low cinder-block building had been removed, leaving two raised curbs on a small slab of concrete. A few cars were parked casually near the building, just beside what brought Harley to slow. A metal advertisement for cigarettes. The numbers for the price had been removed, but the sign looked deliberately placed to draw in people like him. Then, the sight of a lighted open sign.

He did find it odd that there was no sign above the door, no encouragement for patronage other than the swinging metal sign and a faded beer poster (a busty woman in a glinting silver swimming suit) in the window. It was how things were done around here. Accountants did people's taxes from basement offices. Veterinarians operated out of their barns. An auto repair place was identified by the name on the mailbox. Even bars didn't always bother with a sign over the door. These people didn't seem like they were running these businesses to make a living, certainly not a killing. They were just filling the time, filling a community need. In St. Louis, somebody who approached business so casually wouldn't find themselves doing it for very long.

Standing in the angled morning sun, Harley again noticed how his body dragged. He definitely had not slept enough, not last night, probably not for a week before. He was going to have to catch up at some point.

The store was musty and dirty. Whole lengths of shelves were bare, pegs held nothing. A cooler in the back had some beer, some soda, but no orange juice, which Harley thought for a minute he might want. Just the cigarettes, then. From a doorway in the back where the sound of a television moaned, a man emerged. A ball of a man on spindly legs, he held under his chin a bowl from which he shoveled cereal into his mouth as he walked. The band of his sweatpants was pulled up to the widest circumference and Harlan could notice beneath the burial mound of a belly, the man's parts swinging. The man's bald head reflected through thin hairs. His graying mustache had milk in it.

"Two packs of reds."

"Sure, sure." He scarfed down two more overloaded spoonfuls through his oversized lips before setting the bowl on the counter and retrieving the packs from the rack.

"That all you need?"

"Yep." Harley was rummaging through his pockets, trying to retrieve only dollar bills and he was struck by the sincerity of the man's tone.

"You sure look like you could something to get you up, get you going."

Harley only looked at him.

"I got just what you need. I'll even make you a deal, give you a little early morning, first-time-customer discount."

"What?"

"Jesus, forget it."

It wasn't until after he got in the car, lighted a cigarette, and pulled his car back on the roadway that he finally sorted out that the man was trying to sell him crank. Trying to sell him crank. The insult stung. It was like trying to offer the CEO of GM a leadership course. Who the fuck was this yahoo? Fat fuck. He thought for a minute that if he'd Jimmy's girly gun with him he just might go back and teach him a lesson. Let him know who was in charge around here now and if he thought he was going to deal around here he'd better at least choose his supplier wisely.

The cigarette was beginning, though, to take hold and calm him down. He began to think about why the man tried to push, to sell to him. Sure, he might look tired but that was a by-product of hard work, of labor taken seriously. He certainly didn't look like a user, did he? Sure, he'd been using some, just for fun, really, just to keep moving at three in the morning. He wasn't one of these guys with bad teeth, sores, and scraggly beards, whose eyes held a look of perpetual desperation. No. He wasn't one of these people and never would be.

Thinking about using made him think about using. It would really help this morning, would perk him up, get him going. He thought of the floating feeling, the stars in his eyes, the crawling scalp. He tapped his fingers on the steering wheel. He inhaled deeply the cigarette smoke. It was good, wasn't it? It was always a good time. Why shouldn't he enjoy himself? Life wasn't all about hard work, was it? And it helped him stay motivated, made him feel like jumping, like shooting baskets, like raising a barn, like driving ninety miles an hour, like a convulsing rock star on stage. A little would be good.

He was driving fast now, hurrying home, with the sun behind him. The traffic to town was in the opposite lane, bright sun in tired faces. Here they were, the proletariat, on their way to work, guzzling coffee in preparation for selling a day's labor, their physical activity traded for an arbitrary signifier, paper that represented something valuable, something representative that has actually become valuable in itself.

He'd done it too, sold himself for a paycheck, enough to buy ramen and beer. The old White Castle days. It was a life for a while, a simple life working all day. Working every hour allowed spending the rest of the time drinking until sleep overtook him. Sometimes he went out with co-workers and even the boss. The store's manager was a tall, skinny white guy who'd managed only a semester at Washington University before abandoning it for a career track in restaurant management. It didn't seem to require much more than the ability to tell people what to do, and even then, he wasn't too good at that. He wanted to be everyone's friend, to be just like everyone else, even though he was older and, unlike everyone other than Harley, he was white. But like Harley, he'd adopted the lingo, the slang, the way of speaking, even the common mannerisms and gestures.

Harley resented him. Maybe because he'd invaded his turf, the sole white guy who doesn't quite get it but is treated benevolently, more or less. Maybe it was because in his new adopted culture he was supposed to resent the white boss. Or maybe it was just because he was a lousy boss. After only a few months on the job, Harley found himself arguing with him about how things should be done. But he was willing to buy alcohol for the underage staff, so he was tolerable.

During one late-night close, Johnny, the name the grown man went by, had made a run to the liquor store, the duration of which Harley spent entangled in the walk-in cooler with a girl whose uniform pants fit her so tightly that Harley though he knew exactly what her ass would look like without clothes. What made the activity more exciting was that it was clandestine. Harley was busy courting a new girl, Brittany, a small girl whose curls stretched to her belt. She'd begun to show him the level of attention that led him to believe he was making progress. She was also closing on this evening and if she drank it might just speed the whole process along.

The quick petting session with the other girl was interrupted when

Johnny returned with wine coolers and rum. Harley was at the point that even the thought of alcohol excited him. The big bottle spurred him along and he rushed the others to finish their work so they could begin drinking. Johnny was not going to let them have even a sip before their work was done, though he sat behind the tiny office window counting the money from the registers, stacks of green bills across his desk while sipping liquor from a kids' cup.

Those who didn't have better things to do than hang out with the boss piled into Johnny's Lincoln, its soft-top torn to rags, and went for a drive. The car floated gently, adding to Harley's quickly drunken sensation, though Johnny seemed eager and proud to give it full gas and squeal the tires at each turn. They roamed through what Harley guessed must have been every part of the city, though from his position slumped low in the back seat he saw little more than the street lights and bridge trestles pass, while bottles clanked around his feet. He'd chosen his seat hoping to get Brittany to sit next to him, maybe leading to some shadowed fondling. Instead, he sat hip to hip with a guy with a pork allergy so eager to be part everything that he leaned forward the whole time. Brittany sat in the seat in front of him, out of sight.

They passed the bottle and a joint around until they began dropping people off. It was then just Johnny driving, Brittany in the front passenger seat, and Harley there in his corner in the back seat. He'd grown sullen and quiet in this state, the hopes for excitement leaving him disappointed. He was glad when they pulled up to his building, the Lincoln swinging wide into the alley. He was just shutting the heavy door when he heard Brittany speak up. Her voice, though, had mixed with the sound of the door closing and he was about to rip it open again when she stood from the other side. "Hang on."

She grabbed him by the hand and pulled him around the corner of the brick building out of sight of the Lincoln's front half, its sloped trunk still poking out into the sidewalk. "Sorry, we didn't get to hang out tonight."

"I was thinkin' we'd be macking in the backseat all night." His courtship method was really this simple and vulgar. Brittany, though, giggled at him, pressed the hand she still held against the outside of her thigh. "Not tonight, baby."

"'Ight then."

"'Ight." She fled from him then, turning and out of sight.

Harley retreated inside the building and up to his apartment.

Inside the small studio, his sullenness was gone and he didn't feel ready to sleep. He lighted a cigarette instead and wished for a place other than the bed to sit down.

He leaned against the wall, soft with layers of paint, and after half of the cigarette had been turned to ash, he noticed that he'd been hearing a low rumbling. He pressed his head to his window and tried to look down at the alley's floor. He had to open the window to see, but there it was, the Lincoln still parked there in the alleyway, its engine still running.

"What the fuck?" He didn't know what was going on, but he didn't like it. He felt something like pain. He was weak like he'd gone days without eating. "Hey," he shouted but no one anywhere stirred. Everyone knew better than to get involved with a man shouting at three in the morning. Something was going on that he wasn't going to think about but stirred him none the less. His fists clenched, he paced the room, until keeping the thought back was impossible. He raced down the stairs and outside into the dark.

"Hey," he shouted at the dark car, rocking slightly on soft springs. Mute to any other words, hands tied from any real option, but a word appeared to him then, a bull-horned announcement in his head. Rape. Rape. He's raping her. That white man is raping that black girl. He had to do something. "Hey."

The night was cold and dark and the amber streetlights did little to illuminate the street. The alleyway was cast in a dark shadow. And Harley shook. At the building's corner, frighteningly close to the Lincoln and near the spot where Brittany had held his hand, encouraged him with a press of his hand on her thigh, were some broken bricks fallen from the building itself. The sight of this decay and collapse more than anything called him into action. If it hadn't been for the sight of these physical remnants of what was once properly structured and built, he might have stood there above the glinting concrete sidewalk all night. Instead, he heaved one nearly complete brick into his hand, stepped back and threw it at the Lincoln's back window.

There was a satisfying concussion of sound as the brick bounced from the window, leaving it dented, pitted, shattered but intact.

The car shifted and bucked with interior movement, as Harley stared at it until the driver's door quickly creaked open, making contact with the alley's wall. A figure taller, larger than he remembered, emerged, shirt untucked. "What the fuck!" Johnny threw his arms out wide, stepping towards him.

Harlan backed into the street. "What're you doing in there?" He heard the shaking in his voice, heard it bouncing back from the walls of the cavern-like street.

"Fuckin' her."

"You're raping her!" His eyes were going wet and his voice rose high.

Jimmy laughed once with a loud expulsion of air. "Oh, no. She wants it, man. She be needin' it." And as if the thought of it overrode all else, he returned to the car.

Harley could hardly believe it. Johnny was going to return to it with him standing here helpless on the street. To his relief, the brake lights lit up and the car started and backed into the street, sending Harlan scampering back to the sidewalk. With a squeal of tires, the Lincoln sped down the street and he bent, scooped another deteriorated brick and chucked it down the street, striking nothing.

He returned to work the next day not knowing what to expect and not knowing else to do. He had known something had turned for him but he couldn't name it, couldn't see how it manifested in his actions. He felt weak, yet hardened at the same time. He was, he thought, prepared for anything.

The sight, then, of Johnny walking in the restaurant door with Brittany at his side seemed just about right, while also making him a bit sick to his stomach. He stood in front of the grill, flipping burgers that had turned from frosty red to a withered and moist gray and Brittany sought him out there. She came and stood next to him. Too close. Too close for whatever sickness she had. He did not turn to look at her. He could turn to her, hold her, let her release her suffering into him. But she hadn't suffered, had she?

She came closer still, her soft hip pressed against his.

"Did you come in with him?"

"I guess."

"Did you fuck him?"

"Harlan."

He looked at her then, a look that burned with disgust, that saw every flaw, the malformed head, the slight curve of her nose, the dark skin of her chin that looked nearly gray, green.

"Yes."

He looked around the kitchen, the stainless-steel tables, the fryers, the laminated posters on the walls giving instructions, excuses. Harlan wanted to strike out, to exhibit some extreme act of violence, something physical that would release the tension in his muscles and demonstrate to all what he felt. Something that would display the finality of the feelings. All that he could come up with was to toss the long spatula skittering across the grill, over the grease-laden burgers and then walk, past Brittany, past his coworkers, past Johnny bent over a register, past customers, and out the door and into the afternoon.

It wouldn't be the last time he walked out on a job, the last time things welled up in him to such an extent that some final, definitive act was necessary. And maybe he felt bad about this trait for a while, maybe at one point he thought he might want to calm down enough to handle a job, to be one of these people headed to work. But as he looked at them, tired and squinting, he couldn't even feel bad for them. They'd fallen into that false American dream, believing that hard work was going to lead them to something. Suckers.

Instead, Harley was headed home to cut crank into two thin rails and ride that train off into the day. While these people were off working, taking orders from bosses, grimacing with pain in the backs, wrists, feet, he would be high. He stepped on the gas to get home in a hurry. Something was calling him.

27

"Did you really put them both in the same cell? They're in their gettin' their story straight right now."

"Oh. Good point."

Bill looked at this deputy. Idiot. He was surrounded by this sort. He was irritated because Parker was spoiling his mood. After bringing in the two long-hairs from the van, Bill had gone to his office to get his own story straight, to write up the report and the charges. He wanted to make sure this part was in order before he really laid into them. There would have to be more charges than just marijuana possession and public indecency.

They'd pulled off the highway to take a leak and when Bill came along one of them was still shooting a stream into the ditch. And in the ashtray, through the open window, he saw the remnants of a marijuana cigarette. It didn't take any more than a little poking around then to find the baggie among some trash on the floor. Not enough for intent, he knew by looking, but enough to take them in, charge them, seize the van and see what else he could get on them. New charges are good.

"Put the driver in the interrogation room and then give Howie a call and see where he is with the van. When he tows it in I want you to give it a good going over. See what else you can find."

Parker left without a word, apparently knowing he'd screwed up. Bill had been giving direction for so long that it came as second nature, almost. He could give an order and chastise in the same breath. He didn't seem to have trouble making others listen to him. When he was younger he had thought it was his height, and maybe it had been. He had also taken to telling things as they were, no need to pussyfoot. It was the way his father had been with him, and the way he was with his son. It didn't look like Logan was going to end up the same way.

Telling it like it is often led to the kid crying. At least when he was younger. And now that he was a teenager, Logan had turned it all against him. Bill was sure that he'd started dressing like a goddamn zombie because he thought it would piss him off. Bill wasn't going to give him that satisfaction. If you want to go through your life looking like a freak, that's something you'll have to live with. Kid was probably lucky he was the sheriff's son or else he'd end up with a black eye nearly every day of the week. At least he wasn't getting into trouble. It looked like they were going to take him on at the diner and a job might just straighten him out some, keep him busy.

Elaine had always been pretty good with him. In the summers, she had kept him occupied with chores or made him come home for lunch. But this summer was a little different. Who knew what the kid had been up to this week? No one had said anything yet. That was good.

It was different without Elaine. For many reasons. He could do his dishes. His uniforms went to the cleaners anyway. And Logan had to clean up his own messes around the house. There was hardly reason to go to bed at night, though, except exhaustion. Logan probably suffered more. He wasn't going to say it, though.

The problem for Bill was that he was a man whose wife had walked out on him. That's what burned him. That he had somehow failed and she up and left without so much as a thought as to what it looked like, what folks would say. He felt like a bull who walked around with his head low because he no longer had anything swinging between his back legs. And everyone knew, everyone he looked at looked back at a man whose wife'd taken to fucking somebody else.

He had an election coming in the fall and how would everyone feel about him now? He had a role in this community that she had undermined. Lucky anyone listened to him at all anymore. He had to hope that folks would vote for a man whose wife had left him, whose son went around looking like a misfit. A man who let his best deputy get shot in the head. Right in front of him. Isn't that what they'd say? That he was somehow negligent. That they hadn't done the right thing, hadn't been safe and that was the fault of a sheriff whose life had suddenly turned up empty.

Would they be wrong? Was it not his fault? That was thought in his head. It was his fault. He could have done something to stop it. He could have been first to the door. He could have made sure they had sufficient backup. He could have viewed the scene with more suspicion. They didn't think he was there. Was that his fault? It was. Simply because he could have done a million different things to prevent things from turning out the way they did.

Upon swinging open the interrogation room door the van's driver, looking a little sick, jumped. His eyes darted as if looking for an escape.

"So, tell me again what you're doing down here."

The kid moped through his excuses, trying to talk plainly and straightforward, but his voice jumped with fear. His friend's father lived down outside West Plains. They were going to spend the summer working his ranch and fishing.

"And where you come from?" Bill was doing the tough cop routine. He usually started as the earnest, interested questioner, and he knew it was hard to go backward from this point. If he was going to figure out what these kids were up to being nice wasn't going to get him there.

"We drove from Boulder. Colorado."

"And you were going to ranch and fish?"

"Yes."

"You in college there?"

"Yep." The kid tossed his head, flicking the unwashed hair out of his face, and folded hairy arms across his thin chest.

"Those your drugs?"

"I told you I didn't even know it was there."

"You think that matters to me, kid?" Bill leaned forward.

"Probably not."

"That's right. Your vehicle, your drugs." He pretended to jot something illegible on the statement form in front of him. "What else we gonna find in that van?"

"Huh?"

"We gonna find a wad of cash or did ya already make the deal? We're gonna rip it apart, you know?"

"There's nothing there, man."

"You think I believe that? You think I believe your story?"

The kid shook his head.

"So, don't bullshit me, kid."

He shrugged his shoulders.

Bill set his pencil down, slid the papers away some, and leaned back in his chair. "Look at it from my point of view for a minute. I'm gonna believe two guys looking like you two come here from that college in Boulder to work on a farm? It ain't true. So, either you're down here to make a deal on some meth or something worse. Maybe my deputy's gonna find some hair or some blood in the back. Maybe you two just got done raping some little girl and dumping her body somewhere in the Mark Twain National Forest."

Bill stared at him there until he turned away. "So, if that ain't what happened, how 'bout you start telling me the truth."

"I told you the truth." The boy was whining, nearly pleading.

"Fine." Bill held up his hands, feigning surrender. "You're used to writing papers in that college, right? Maybe it'd be easier for you to write it down. Here." He slid the blank form across the table. "You write me a little story and tell me the truth. Take your time, now. It's gonna take us a while to pull that van apart, find what you got hidden in there." He stood, folded up the file and leaned down to set the pencil carefully on the table. "Careful with that. Break that tip, it might take us a while to find a sharpener."

Bill shut the latch firmly to make sure the kid heard it, to make sure that metal on metal sound, the scrape and ring sank in, that it found a place deep inside where fear would grow like cancer. He liked his job. Maybe it didn't make him the nicest guy. Maybe it made it so that he didn't trust anyone. Everyone had secrets. The question was just how to get to the secrets about something illegal. He probably should have been on the lookout for other secrets too.

The passenger was sitting on the edge of the mattress. Bill had taken his time with the door, giving this one time enough to think of his response, his stance. The kid only sat there, his hands hanging off his knees, hair hanging around his face.

Bill sat in a similar position, with the creaking of his belt, pistol, handcuffs, mace, ammunition, hands gripping his knees with a sigh. "Welp…"

The kid only raised his head slightly.

"Your friend's in there now writing up his whole statement. Said he had a lot to get down." Bill turned to look at the young man, his slumped shoulders, long enough to be sure the prisoner knew he was looking. "Gonna explain all about what you did to that girl."

He sprang up, mouth open.

"Oh yeah," casual as could be, "said it was so awful the only way he could tell me was by writing it down."

"No, no. Wait." He waved his hands.

"What?" Bill leaned back, but it wasn't comfortable, didn't portray the right attitude. "You wanna hang it all on him?"

"You got the wrong guys. There's no girl. We're just going to my dad's place."

"That's your story?"

"Yeah, yeah."

That stupid, soft-faced Parker kid. "Well, you better give me your story. 'Fore I start to think your friend's is the truth."

The kid sat.

"Start with buying the drugs."

"What?"

Bill chuckled some to himself. Folks sure could squirm when they thought they were in deep shit. "Tell me."

"I dunno. It must have been a couple a weeks ago."

"You don't know? You buy so much dope you can't remember from one day to the next?"

"Bobby said he got it from some guy down on the mall. Some dropout."

"What mall?"

"Back in Boulder?"

Bill jumped up, scaring the kid backward on the thin mattress. "Don't give me that shit. Tell me the truth."

"I didn't even know it was there."

"The truth!"

"I was going to see my dad. I wouldn't want anything like that in the car."

Bill envisioned grabbing the kid by the shoulders, the bone and skin fitting nicely in his palms, and shoving him against the wall, shaking the truth loose from him. There had to be more. The first story is never the whole truth. Even if that's the story they stick to. Even if it's someone picked up on possession, or his son.

It had been one of those trying days when his demands had been split between the administrative, the political, and true law enforcement when he pulled into the gravel drive to see the shattered front window. The fury appeared out of nowhere making his forehead and scalp sweat, the blood in his veins pound. There was only one party responsible for this: Logan.

He slammed the car door closed and hollered the kid's name. Logan had been growing hostile, a sullen look on his face worn out of anger at his father. He'd done it on purpose, that was a given. And he was going to make sure the boy admitted it.

Playing catch. That was the line the kid had given him, after finally coming whimpering out from behind the barn. His face all wet and ready to accept a punch, it seemed. Playing catch. It was insulting. Did Logan really think his old man was that stupid? "I'm no idiot, boy." Playing catch with a plate glass window. He'd done it and now he was lying about it, with that sad-sack look on his face. Bill wanted to make a point, to let him know that he'd committed a grave error. Throwing him through what remained of the window might make him understand. And in these thoughts of how to make Logan understand, the boy sobbed, "I'm sorry." And before he thought, Bill had reached forward and shoved Logan to the ground. "Bullshit."

28

Once in a while, Sam was struck by a memory of his early childhood in Barnes County. They weren't really memories, though. They were impressions. Certainly, he had seen much of the area before they had run from there. And on occasion, a corner, a certain overhang of trees, a long low barn, a narrow driveway rising away from the road at an angle, would take him back. Back to riding as a passenger, mute in fear of his father, to these many odd locations to purchase tractor parts, to sell off used equipment, or to sit around in lawn chairs while his dad drank beer from the can.

On this afternoon, with the sun slung low and flashing from behind trees, Sam was driving along a dirt road, flanked on one side by precariously tall pine trees held back behind a tightly strung fence, adorned every twenty yards with a sign of the US Forest Service. It was this sight that took him back, made him recall the sensation of that bold and mysterious badge declaring that this was government property. What did the government need with this land? What were they doing behind that fence, buried deep in that pine forest? As a child, he had imagined cement buildings that held laboratories where they conducted experiments on animals or people. Or maybe it was here that they were building the next generation of atomic bomb. Or maybe it was here that they worked in collusion with the communists to keep us all held tight in fear.

Thinking now, that old fear having appeared in his heart again, Sam wondered if he'd known then that their life in the county was coming to an end, that his father was fending off or surrendering to his failure. He must have known what was behind his father's grim expression or what caused his occasional manic abandon of things critical and important. When he would drop everything and drive quickly to the home of a friend and bang on the door or honk and pull the friend away from what necessary activity that kept him engaged to spend the afternoon into the late evening drinking or throwing horseshoes.

It wasn't until much later when Sam learned what they'd given up, that he began to resent his father. Maybe it had been the fact that he had been forced into close proximity to cousins he didn't know or like. Maybe it was that he was forced to share his bed with his older brother. Maybe it was because they'd gone from the wide-open scenes of Missouri, their house and outbuildings standing alone and a half-mile from the nearest structure, to a dirty white house with the electric wires hanging messily from the front and the neighboring homes seeming to lean against one another. Maybe it was because the life had drained out of his father's eyes soon after their arrival in Pennsylvania.

Gone were the manic episodes and the pleased look of exhaustion from a day spent in fruitful labor. Instead, he came home with a layer of grime, his face weathered and burnt from standing in close to the furnace all day, and took up position on the couch to watch television and drink beer. His uncle, in whose house they were living, who had been responsible for luring the family to Pennsylvania and away from the farm, and who had the same career in the steel mill, had the same look.

These things certainly wore on Sam the child, along with changing schools, forcing him to lose his high-ranking status in a small rural school to a school full of pale and bruised kids quick with a punch. It was a slow change in attitude until Sam hit about thirteen years. A period of escalating rebellion set it. Seeing some vulnerability in his father, the son set out to test the man's defenses. He wasn't ever successful because of his father's size. Life could hardly be more miserable for the child hitting puberty, so there was little his parents could do to punish him other than smack him around. And Sam had had--and given--enough of that at school to withstand quite a bit. This isn't to say it was pleasant for his mother to call down to Rook's, or whatever bar was in favor then, and tell his father that he needed to come home to discipline his boy.

When the war came it was easy for Sam to see what to do. His brother had by then began his career at the mill and it simply was not going to happen to him. While his father had been glad that the US Army was "killing all the gooks they could," the generally held belief was that Sam was going "to get his ass shot." He was, though, going to see the world, to see things his father and his brother could not imagine. He was going to get away.

It didn't feel like ambition. Escape, maybe. Later, though, Sam came to see it came out of wanting more. And when he returned and refused a mill job, opting instead to venture into the city each day to right the world's wrongs, he was trying for something different, maybe something more.

Was it ambition now that made him still wonder if he might want to become sheriff? Or was it, as his father would likely suspect, that Sam thought himself better than those around him? It was possible, wasn't it? Or was it something else that made him contemplate challenging a friend? Could he somehow make right an injustice? Could he somehow avenge Terry's death by taking Bill's job and becoming sheriff? Could he be more successful where others had clearly failed? He could be the man to correct what had gone wrong.

Terry had seen him as an achiever. She had admitted to him that she hadn't seen anyone so willing and eager to get things done. When he had volunteered an approach to handle a dispute between rival landowners which had an increasing level of violent activity, Terry had pulled him aside after leaving work.

"You think any of them would have thought of that, let alone offered to help get it done? Around here most people are willing to let them just shoot it out."

Sam had wondered if, with the wave of her hand that swung at the whole brick side of the courthouse and sheriff's office, she included Bill in that. He didn't have a humble enough response for her.

"Listen," she pulled the sleeve near his wrist. "We have a real opportunity to get some things done around here."

They were standing close on the sidewalk, the streetlight far away from them, upon the high main street. Terry's face was in shadow and her two eyes looking up him were glossy and dark.

"I don't know if you'd be interested, but you might like the idea. We have a real drug problem around here. Most of the crime around here comes from it—one way or another. We have to get a handle on it and I think you're the guy for it."

"You think?" He felt a thumping, rushing inside.

"Yeah. A kind of one-man task force. Line up the evidence we have against these meth cooks, make sure we have a case, and figure out how to get them."

It was a good idea, and she was right that it wouldn't get done otherwise. What he felt, though, wasn't dependent on the logic of her argument; it had more to do with the eyes looking up at him, praising him, seeing something in him that others had failed to see. It wasn't something he often felt. Not at home. Not in over twenty years on the force in Pittsburgh. Everything there was dependent on whose ass was getting kissed and what secrets you were willing to keep. Any advancement there really just meant more time behind a desk, more paperwork, and less real crime-fighting.

At home, he'd mined the well of admiration empty long, long ago. Toleration seemed like all he could ask for these days. Enough years of worrying about her husband's life had pushed her past a certain point.

Sam had wanted to somehow prolong that moment on the dark sidewalk outside the door to the sheriff's office, to somehow draw more praise out of Terry, to continue her looking at him as if he was the man to solve all her problems. "I'll do it. Absolutely."

With Terry's encouragement, he had leaped into it, building case files, taking work home with him, reading old reports on traffic stops, domestics, burglaries. He sorted out who was doing what and they began to bring them in. They'd begun to have success.

The trouble was that he became the sole source of information. In some ways, he was the only one working these cases and no one else knew or cared who these dealers were. If someone had talked to him the morning Terry was shot and killed, he could have told them that Jiles was a cook and a user and bat-shit crazy. He hadn't known what was happening and hadn't been able to warn them.

Stopping again to look at the Forest Service fence, nicer and tighter than any farmer's fence, the badge on each white sign warning all that what went on behind this boundary was none of anyone's business and the public was better off not knowing. Sam realized that as he had been called to action by Terry, the two men in suits nicer than could be bought within a fifty miles radius of Sheridan had also called him to action. He was being handed an opportunity to make a difference. He would be an idiot to pass on it.

Accepting it, though, meant an admission. It meant a sort of confession to a man he knew well, respected, and worked for. And somehow it was going to have to be okay with him.

A fenced-in dirt lot across the small street from the back of the courthouse was the impound lot. As Sam pulled in, he had noticed a tow-truck pulling in as well, hauling behind it a brown cargo can. Parker was back there guiding the truck's driver to a spot.

Over the noise of the hydraulic lowering of the van to the dirt and gravel, Sam shouted, "What you got there?"

"Bill brought in two deadheads today. Possession."

"Well, good." Turning away he noticed the Colorado plates.

Sometimes it was good to see that real things went on without him. At times, it seemed as if these guys wouldn't do anything but clean up car wrecks or go on loose dog calls if he weren't around. They had a responsibility to make progress, didn't they? To move forward instead of waiting for things to come to them? Really, this was why he had to talk to Bill.

Entering the door, Bill was standing by the dispatcher and he turned and spoke to Sam. "There should be a cell phone in the van. Look for somebody in there named Grainger. Ain't the kid's name but he says it's his old man. Give him a call, see if the pothead's telling the truth."

"Grainger?"

"Says he lives down near West Plains."

Sam turned away to be sure the crease between his eyebrows didn't show. "I'll check it out." He stepped back outside.

The fact was that he was pretty sure that he knew someone named Grainger down in that area. He found Parker just beginning to nose through the trash on the floorboards of the van. Sam didn't say a word as he retrieved the slim phone from the dash. He found the Missouri number in the phone and used it to make the call.

"Yello?" It sounded as if he had just caught him in the middle of something, as if he was surprised the phone rang, and surprised he answered it.

"Mr. Grainger?"

"That's who you got."

"Mr. Grainger, this is Sam Summers, Barnes County Sheriff's Department."

"Yes, sir." The voice turned serious and wary.

"You live near West Plains?"

"Yeah? What's this about?"

"You come up this way to buy a tractor last year?"

"S'it stolen?"

"No, no. It was me you bought it from."

"That right? What can I do for you today, then?"

"Looks like we've got your son up here?"

"What he do?"

"Drug possession."

"Can I come get him?"

"We just brought him in today. Won't be arraigned 'til the morning."

"Good then. A night in a cell might do him some good."

"I talked to Grainger." Sam stood against the frame of the door to Bill's office.

"So, it's true? He lives near West Plains?"

"I actually know the guy."

Bill put down the pen he was using to write his report and leaned back in his chair. "I thought for sure that kid was feeding me a line."

Sam watched Bill's eyes fade off like he was looking through the wall next to him. With his head turned, Bill revealed the scar on his neck. It looked like a knot of skin.

"Bill," Sam reached to pull the door closed, having to squeeze himself against the desk to let it pass, "there's something I got to say."

29

He'd wondered why the man was there, but Frank pulled on the door anyway. The resistance of it, unmoving when it should have given way, sent a panic through him. His heart suddenly began to beat against his chest like a rabbit's. He pulled on it again, believing he'd simply been wrong. It's the middle of the day; the liquor store should not be closed. Again, the door resisted him.

"Be right back, yeah right." The man on the sidewalk spoke.

Then Frank noticed the sign on the door, right in front of his face. A piece of paper, the message scrawled across it, hastily taped to the inside of the door, at a slight angle, made Frank feel like an idiot. His heart still beat rapidly.

"Don't know how long I been here, but this guy don't know what 'right back' mean."

Frank looked at the man then. He was an old man, easily in his eighties, thick black frames on his glasses, hair glowing white in the shade. Next to him, a worn cane sat on the sidewalk. A cigarette burned close to the knuckles of his shaking, primitively tattooed hand.

"Sign could've been there for days for all I know."

Frank knew it hadn't. He'd been there the day before. But he wasn't going to say that.

"Might as well have a seat here. Wait."

Frank sat, his legs going weak on his way down and nearly giving way. The concrete was cool under him, smelling of dirt.

"Hard enough for me to walk all the way down here with this leg. I ain't gonna stand around for no one."

They sat in the shade, but the other side of the street blazed white. Frank wondered if it would ever make sense for him to buy sunglasses, like some people.

"There's a bench over there, across the street, but it's too hot to be sitting in the sun on a day like this. You ever wonder why they ain't put a bench right here in front of the liquor store? There's folks'd never leave. 'This ain't Hemming,' they told me when I asked. Folks down there stand around all day. Just standing around the liquor store like it's the place to be. They ain't retired like me. I got a pension. I ain't got shit to do. Men there, young men, ought to be working, providing for their families, but they stand around there all day."

Frank began to think through excuses, something to give the man to explain why he was sitting in front of a liquor store in the middle of a weekday. He didn't say anything.

"Well, Jesus H. Christ, where the hell you been?" The man practically bellowed at another man walking towards them.

"Just calm down, Richard. Can't a man get lunch?"

"Not when another man's looking for a drink. Get your priorities straight. Help me up." He tapped Frank's foot with his cane.

Frank had to pull hard on the old man's thick hand. He'd obviously been a strong man once, but Frank was worried about hurting him. The man groaned and wheezed with the effort. His t-shirt read, "Real Old Navy." The word real added with iron-on transfer.

They hurried through their purchases, Canadian Mist for the veteran, Jim Beam for Frank, and were out on the sidewalk. Richard balanced himself and opened his bottle, a thick ring banging on the cap as he turned. Frank watched him drink and wipe his wet lips with the back of a shaking hand.

"Drink up. That sheriff or one of his henchmen show up, I'll handle him. Come on, drink up. I see it in your face that you're dying for a drink."

He was.

"That'll set things right, won't it?" Richard took a second drink.

"Yes," Frank said with hope and sincerity.

"Ain't nothin' wrong with a man wanting a drink now and again. There's enough of them getting themselves all sideways with drugs. Pardon my French, but that shit's everywhere. You wouldn't think that it'd be here, no you wouldn't, but I tell you I had a man in a bar try and push that stuff on me. Right there in that bar, off D in Vonn. Now,

I been around, you know. Seen enough of those guys strung out on stuff in the war. Eyes all poking out of their faces, jumpy. And they give these guys guns."

Frank had been listening closely, leaning towards his lecturer. In this innocuous conversation, he had heard something, a sort of salvation that went beyond the bottle in his hand. Possibility. If this offered an escape, at least to the extent that something illegal, something sold covertly in county bars, must offer a further escape.

"Jesus, man. You're staring. Have another drink."

He did, tilting the bottle to a severe angle, closing his eyes to the blue sky. The need in him was strong. The need for something drastic, some way to lash out at the world or at himself. If he could paint the whole world over, he would. If he could sleep a sweet, dreamless sleep, he would. Forever. But he was still aware of this world, aware of all that had happened. Any option to dramatically alter things was worth a try.

Escape had been a familiar theme in those days, those glorious days when Frank and Terry were together. When they were together as lovers. They would imagine that they were staying in fabulous hotels in faraway locales. When they were just learning each other in this new way, Terry learning that a lover could be different than her husband, now dead, and Frank having the luck to have a long attraction and desire be consummated and returned, they entered her bedroom as if it was a magnificent and well-appointed hotel room. To them, the blinds were closed against the hot Paris street and though they were weary from travel, having taken the train up from Venice, they were eager and hungry for each other.

They undressed each other with care and delicacy, ensuring every inch of skin received the attention it deserved. Their love-making began in these steps. Steps Frank knew had been forgotten in the years Terry spent with Bob. Frank was sure to make each experience seem new to her, as it was for him, to give her things that could not even be compared with the love she had seen over those years. And when they were in bed her pleasure was primary. Terry, though, never failed to show her appreciation or her pleasure. And in these times in their imaginary hotel rooms, they worked at each other harder than a day's worth of labor around the ranch. And afterward, in an expansive exasperation, they would lounge naked, damp and unashamed.

Leaving the old veteran standing on the shaded sidewalk with his bottle, Frank was pained by these thoughts, a constriction from his heart to his testicles. All of that was gone, all the pleasures that filled those regions. The tenderness with which she touched him, the contradiction of her foul mouth and hearty physical form with the gentleness of her lips, her fingers, and the kindness. She knew. She must have known of his inexperience, his inhibition. Though he looked at her without answering whenever she approached the topic. She showed him a kind of love that had always been missing, and now all of that was gone.

What could he do about it? What could he do to rid himself of these feelings? Could he bring her back? Could he join her? Could he somehow escape all of this?

He drank more from his bottle and headed his truck to a bar off D in Vonn.

30

If he just cut a large window in the wall, maybe he could get a cross-breeze, some relief from the heat. Harlan heard, in the whimper of the pitifully small air conditioning unit, the sentiment that left him looking for mercy from the heat, that had led him to strip off his clothes, except for his boxers, which he was nearly ready to rid himself of also, though he feared sticking to what he sat on, and feared what might stick to him.

He just needed one of those saws, reticulating saws. He'd stolen one a month or so before, a nice molded plastic case indicating value, from a shop, an out-building that sat closer to the road than the house. A nice place, he'd known it was likely to have nice things, things of value, things that could be sold. And the dogs penned on the other side of the house seemed to be barking all the time anyway. Any noises he made would likely be masked by the percussive shouts echoing in the dark night.

Harley had begun his thieving out of a need for money, but it had initially frightened him extremely. It only took a couple of these occasions before he came to enjoy the rush of fear. And as he had turned onto the road of his recent target and cut the lights on the car, waiting for his eyes to be able to make out the dirt road, his heart pleasantly, frighteningly, joyfully pounded in his chest. He parked the car some way down the road, letting it drop a little farther into the ditch than he'd intended. He jumped the fence and walked through the trees, trying his hardest to watch where he was going. He only fell once.

After cutting the lock with his trusty bolt cutters, he began to grope in the dark for things of weight and value. When he weighed down his two hands he went to the fence line, on the other side of which he'd laid out a tarp. He'd mucked his hands by handling oil cans and cobwebs, nicked his fingers on saw blades and nails. He had spent more time than he wanted. He was in, though, and he'd thought he'd better get everything he could. He put his hands on everything.

The tarp, when he returned to it, his hands holding a hammer and two boxes of nails, was burdened by so many items, so much weight that he'd had to struggle to get it moving, pulling at two grommeted corners. And when he did, the sound was enormous, like, to Harley, the sound of an ocean liner through waves. He was not to be deterred, though.

It was still quite a bit of work on the other side and now he was in a hurry. He didn't want to be standing next to an open trunk with stolen goods in his hands when headlights suddenly illuminated the night. He tossed things in the trunk, into the open passenger door. A drill, a length of hose, a circular saw, even some stout saucer-shaped air compressor, and a reticulating saw.

He started the car, stepped on the gas, the front tires turned, but the car didn't move. High-centered, the car only jumped slightly each time he pressed on the pedal, the wheel wells being blasted by gravel. Forward and back, forward and back, rocking his body with the car, banging the steering wheel. The car would not budge. He left the car in neutral and got out.

There was joy in the getaway. Harley had been stalled at the peak of the event's excitement and that ramping of adrenaline and emotion spilled over into anger. He kicked the car, solid kicks with the bottom of his shoes that dented the thing. Then he tried to push the car from the front, from behind. Finally, he opened the trunk and began to take things out, starting with the weighty air compressor.

He stood behind the shield of the trunk, looking for something else to remove to lessen the load when he heard a distant hum. He cocked his head to listen, to try to identify the sound. He leaned his head around the trunk to see, in the dark, a light bouncing down the dirt road towards him.

Harley grabbed a length of pipe which he had stolen from the shed and went towards the approaching light and sound. At a clip. A man atop the four-wheeler, a flashlight held awkwardly under his arm, was slowing and just about to offer help when Harley swung the pipe. The vehicle rolled empty-saddled into the ditch and the man lay on the dirt.

Harley hurried, without breaking into a run, back to his car and, with the trunk still open and tires spitting, it leaped from the ditch and past the man bleeding into the gravel.

Among the stolen goods in Harley's house he looked for something to use, a circular saw maybe, to begin his renovations. A knock on the door startled him and he dropped, without thinking, to the floor. Crawling to his gun.

Lifting back the flag as a window shade, Harley saw the familiar Camaro. CeeCee.

She came in with her white-blond hair pulled back, blue eyes surrounded by dark circles and carrying an infant carrier. A pair of baby feet, fat from milk, protruded from a blanket. CeeCee wore shorts that covered little more than one usually likes to keep covered, exposing legs that were long and pale, slightly sunburned above the knees. Her arms, too, were bare and the sight of all that skin suddenly made Harley aware of his skin, bare, except his shorts.

As she sat down the baby and went past him, they might have said greetings, but Harley had glimpsed a tattoo on the small of CeeCee's back, a design of curves and sharp points, red and black, and could think of little else. She sat on his couch, dumped the contents of a small cosmetics bag on the coffee table. A needle, a spoon, cotton balls. She lighted a cigarette with a Zippo lighter and said, "You gonna help me out?"

She was pushing and he didn't like it, but, yes, he would. He lit his cigarette and grabbed a green chewing tobacco container from the kitchen counter. Sitting next to her, he opened the can to expose several tiny plastic bags of meth. He tossed one at her. Watching it fall between her legs, watching as she reached there to retrieve it.

"Fuck yeah," she exclaimed as she withdrew the needle from her arm. "You?" She held up the needle to him.

"Do it for me." He leaned back on the couch and she prepared it for him, feeling the loose waistband of his boxers on his thin bare stomach, feeling skin radiating heat, a thin layer of damp. She leaned an elbow on his thigh as she injected him. The rush hit him like being dunked in cold water and he seized her arm at the wrist, took away the syringe and pressed her thin yellow fingers against the only clothed part of his body.

After leaving his job at White Castle, he left the neighborhood, sleeping on the couches of acquaintances in the university district until he was able to get his own place. No place nor job lasted all that long but he had a steady rotation of friends, college students, and it was in this area that he'd been just before abandoning his life in St. Louis to run to Barnes County.

He was in one of his phases where he was out of work and drinking too much, each night looking for something to do, some way to explode himself into every star-filled night. His chest, then, felt too big for his bones. It struggled inside him like a bagged cat. Each night was some attempt to set if free. And often he felt like he'd been set free, as if he had become a celestial being, drifting above and beaming light. He was fearless, reckless, then. No consequences, no thought of the next morning, he spoke his mind, acted his will.

Under this influence, and the influence of a half-consumed $2.99 twelve-pack, he earnestly explained to friends, this group that changed with the seasons and semesters, why certain of them were unfriendly, what others said behind their backs, and who did what that he or she didn't want the others to know.

On a particular evening, feeling like some oracle, he'd had to be extricated from a conversation-turned-altercation with a particular pretty boy who wore his hair like a girl's after explaining to him that most of them didn't like him expressly because of a smirk he wore through all circumstances, even when being told this, and that, though the girl Harley had been working on earlier that week had gone to bed with the smirking pretty boy, she could do better. The eventful night had been a regretful compromise. The smirk didn't disguise the anger when he came at Harley with fists drawn, but it did encourage Harley to confess that he really was so pretty that he was willing to let him blow him.

Being separated and moved to another room by gripping hands and kind words, he found himself sitting on a couch next to a well-maintained girl, all style and magazine beauty and otherwise vapid. Harley had seen her around quite a bit and knew her to be generally resentful that she'd been shipped off from the east coast to this midwestern college. For this, she resented her parents and all of those around and beneath her. She had, though, been subject to the wiles of a tall anthropology major with an understanding smile, a sensitivity to human nature, and curls, one lock of which fell purposefully carelessly down his thoughtful brow. He was like this with every girl he met and those susceptible believed the attention and caring look were meant to display some emotion particular to them.

He, the warm-eyed anthropology major, was as hollow as she, Whitney, this girl seated next to Harley, and they would make a great match, all clothing catalog, mall store beauty, her and Mr. Sensitive. She had sacrificed herself to him and though she termed it this way, she had seen her way to offer herself up for sacrifice to more than a few so obviously beneath her, so Harley was aware.

He began to explain that he knew of her offering herself to the tall man and she feigned embarrassment, obviously not concerned that he was aware of her affairs, though she did look to those around her, other students standing, seated on the coffee table and the arm of the sofa.

Noticing her concern, he told her that he had information for her that should be shared in private.

"Um, I don't think so."

"So, where is Glen tonight?"

"He's finishing up a research paper."

"And where was he Tuesday night?"'

"At the library late. But he came by afterward."

"Eww."

"What?"

Harley took her by the hand then. She did not resist, just trailed behind him, finishing the mixed drink in her red plastic cup. He led her to the end of a darkened hall, knowing that pulling her into a room right now might draw attention. Looking at her, he saw that her eyes swam in her head and she leaned against the wall in a sort of exhaustion.

He explained to her in his usual directness and lack of tact that he sure hoped she hadn't slept with him Tuesday night because Glen had not been at the library that evening but had, in fact, been behind the closed bedroom door across the hall with some freshman.

Whitney seemed to know better than to doubt Harley, seeming to have known that she would regret volunteering herself. Her eyes grew large with tears and she banged an open hand on the hollow core door of the bedroom. "Here?"

"That's right," and Harley opened the door, grateful to find no one within.

Whitney practically fell forward into the room and let herself drop to the bed.

He'd seen then the way the bed covers had been tossed around, the empty red cups on the nightstand, Whitney's vulnerable position, her hair tossed about like the sheets, and he shut the door with his foot and approached her.

He had taken her resistance to be the normal playful antagonism that all the college girls he'd been with had exhibited. Her tears were the result of her sadness. The pounding against his chest was out of pleasure.

After this night, he was treated like a man with a hair lip. The people he knew would not look at him, no one came to his house to smoke weed, no one acknowledged him in the bars. He had not, then, realized what had turned him into a leper, what made those who sat together in a booth across the bar from him tilt their heads in whispers. He sat at the bar, his glances to them turning steadily to looks of disgust. They were sneering, ridiculing and a hatred built up in him and spilled over. The group snuggled in their booth, the numbers and faces changing, others pulled up chairs, leaned nearby. When eyes would look up at him he would return a mildly voiced, "Fuck you."

They were better than him, younger, their families paying for their college, for the binge drinking, for growing drug habits. He was the outsider, always had been. He was a hanger-on and letch. And they all saw him for what he was. He was a nobody and a nobody he would stay.

Fuck you. You don't know what makes up life. You live in your sheltered lives on daddy's money, learning what they want you to learn out of books deliberately crafted to make you sure you never think for yourselves, never question. I am not one of you. I have set myself apart, thumbing my nose to your conformities, your careers, your futures. You keep your dirty future, enjoy your unlived lives. I want nothing to do with your world.

He left his tab unpaid, raised a finger to the room as he walked out. On the street he, with calm and deliberation, set fire to a car belonging to one of the group, pouring a small portion of the small bottle of whiskey he'd just purchased across the windshield and hood and striking a match to it. He turned down a side street and was in his apartment before he heard sirens.

At times, he felt chased out of town, at others he was driven by a need to eschew the norms, to live apart from normal society. Either or both served to motivate Harley and before leaving he'd earned enough to find his way out.

As he did what he did to CeeCee, tossing her about on the couch, testing her form, her limbs, he felt no guiltier than he had when leaving Whitney lying curled and naked, in tears. Indeed, Harley felt a righteousness, a need, a duty to punish, to give CeeCee what she deserved, to show her something previously unseen, to leave her feeling sorry for who she was and what she'd done. She hollered, she screamed out, waking her baby, but she made no move to stop him. And her submission drove him on, willing him to punish her further and more deeply.

31

Annette readied herself for bed, hearing Rachel stirring and banging about elsewhere in the house. It turned her skin to prickles. Reminding her of when she was newly married and the sound elsewhere in the house was the sound of her husband, a man she'd sworn herself to, a man that would soon be making his way to her to do things to her, things she would never grow used to. Only once would she be grateful for these things, when they provided a child and an extended period of freedom from these activities.

She would not say that she was sorry she married him. It was an option given to her. But when her mother needed constant care, she was more than willing to move up the hill and leave him alone in their old house. Taking their child along with her. And maybe it drove him to drink more, or maybe without her looks of disapproval, he was less apt to hide it.

She was aware that she was relieved at his death. It was fitting, appropriate. On occasion, though, she found herself feeling faint, her heart positively palpitating and she felt he was near, very near, whispering in her ear, his cold breath on her neck, blaming her. These notions came late at night when she was overtired and they were easy to dismiss. Yet when a light quit working, her keys went missing, a houseplant suddenly went dead, she was quick to blame Ralph.

Maybe he wouldn't show himself directly to her, but he proved himself to be around. She had, on more than one occasion, awaken to banging noises radiating up the hill and her tired eyes believed she saw light in the barn. And now she saw the curtains had moved in the old house. Soon, soon he really would make his way up the hill to confront her where she slept.

Unless she were to confront him.

32

Not even three weeks into summer, Logan's freedom had disappeared. Just as he was foreseeing a summer spent languishing in beds and backseats, under trees and behind barns with Rachel, Logan began working at the diner. His father didn't really give him a choice about it. He wanted to argue, to refuse, but without then being presented with them he knew that other options would be worse. He bussed tables and washed dishes. He couldn't say it was fun, but he found it interesting. He had never thought what this kind of work would be like. He'd not once given a thought to who might be washing his plate when he finished or even a thought to who was preparing it. There was a whole method, a complete language around it. It amused him to think that he was living in a new world. Indeed, among the white walls, stainless steel, where even the brightest lights wouldn't stop it from seeming dark and dingy, it was easy for him to believe that he was living as an adult in some faraway city.

The diner had two cooks, one a large black man who laughed while teaching him to mop but could whistle "Dock of the Bay" like he'd never heard. The other was a younger man with a thin straggly mustache and hair too long splaying over his ears. Logan knew that they mocked him, but it was more for amusement, as opposed to maliciousness. And Logan found them amusing as well.

He'd been working for three days, and in a sort of agony that he'd gone the previous two days without Rachel. She'd already come to occupy a place in his heart, a place that seemed to hollow out in her absence. On this day, though, she was coming to town to meet him when his shift ended.

The lunch rush was ending and Logan was beginning to clean up, wiping down tables, mopping out the line and taking out the garbage. He was in the alley, standing on the grease-stained concrete, swinging a garbage bag high into the open dumpster when David, the cook with the thin mustache, came out and lit a cigarette.

"Fucking hot one."

The sun at nearly three in the afternoon flared down into the alley and the two of them squinted in the light and heat.

"Come on."

Logan followed the ill-fitting checkered pants of the cook across the alley where a small car sat in the shade.

"Get in."

Why he was inclined to follow he wasn't sure. He was in a learning mode and simply complied.

The car was rank with BO and mold. The fabric of the ceiling hung in tatters, the vinyl of the seats was cracked and stuffing exposed. A cheap after-market stereo sat loosely in the spot where the manufacturer's stereo had been. The ashtray below it was overloaded. Logan had to brush trash and kick cans aside to sit in the passenger seat and as he did, David rifled through the cigarette butts to find a half-smoked joint.

He fired it up, took a drag and passed it to Logan without ever questioning his interest. Logan didn't feel it was in his power to refuse. To decline would have meant acceptance to standards he didn't want to define and contain him. He simply imitated the move he had just seen, intending fully to hold the smoke in his lungs, but it overwhelmed and he hacked until David handed him the joint again.

Returning to finish his job, he felt glossy, like he was walking in someone else's body. Each action was distant from him. When David shouted back that there was some "hot young freak" here to see him, Logan didn't really believe it was her. The whole idea was alien. The idea that a girl was there to see him. That this girl, this beauty had seen fit to spend time with him, to do things with him.

He hustled as best he could to finish his tasks, but his hands were not his, his legs were not his. He became aware that he was seeing with eyes, that he was looking at the world through these two portals, as if he were seated somewhere within, watching what passed without. It seemed to Logan familiar, as if he might now be realizing how he went about his living in the world. He was an observer, studying the world, watching, even, his own actions. Even when he felt something, even when he strolled around with his heart in some form of twisted agony over some imagined betrayal by some tart named Dot Baxter, he was performing, acting out a studied routine. Had he, even then, ever felt, ever actually experienced anything?

Rachel sat at the near-end of the counter when Logan emerged from the swinging door, and her existence stunned. Again, she proved to be something actual, not something imagined. She took one look at him, grabbed his arm, pulled him next to her and whispered in his ear, "You're high."

Once he'd pulled away and regained himself after her hot breath in his ear, he looked around with feigned innocence, also looking past her to see if his state might be noticed by anyone else there. Anyone who might tell his father.

She held out her empty hand to him, her palm felt soft, wrinkled, and real. Tender.

"Oh, not me."

"Well?"

He took her by the hand then and led her out the door and around the corner to the alley. The ratty little car was gone, though, and he was thrown into a deep feeling of disappointment. He'd wanted to do something for her without really thinking about what it was. "He's gone." He'd been given the chance to do something for her. To do something. To engage. But he'd missed his window. And without really trying, he had failed.

He walked, then, into the shade where the car had been. Rachel, leading with her hips, came to him. There against the brick, hidden in the town's center, two blocks from his father's office, from the house built by the man who stole his mother, they pressed their clothed bodies together, their tongues wetly engaged.

Logan wanted again to be alone with her, stomach-tightened, skin bare and tingling, the ache filling his marrow. He thought of their methods of escape and he thought about his stolen car stashed among trees less than a mile from where they were, his palm around the softness of her hind-end, through the frustrating mediator of her pants. The thought then of the freedom to move around the countryside at will led him to the memory of directions given. Given to a destination that could very well provide what it was she was looking for and thus restore his power and allow him a success.

She'd thought he was leading her to his house, or so she informed him when they walked through the dark grass where foot-tall oaks grew in the shade of what had been a driveway. His house wouldn't have been a bad idea except, of course, that his father would find out. He would somehow smell her in the house, know by the shifted position of some barely noticed object that he had brought a girl into the house and took her to his bed.

Originally, he had some trouble coming up with a way to explain the gold Taurus. Telling a girl you just met that you've stolen a car might not be the best way to endear yourself to her, but Logan had reason to believe that common thievery might not be repulsive to someone like Rachel.

The disbelief was in her eyes, even as he retrieved the key from under the mat, but it was a smile that came next.

He'd come to take pride in her smile, especially when he had been its source. Logan could not see that smile now without recalling the way it spread across her face in an earnest innocence. It was not pretense or performance. It was joy brought on by a primal act of intimacy. And he only imagined that his grin at the time might have been bigger. It felt like it occupied his entire face.

It had happened without much effort, without much concern or anticipation. It had happened during their rendezvous at the steadily collapsing house before Logan had a chance to build up the possibility of the event. Before he could agonize and his anxiousness prevents him from any sort of action.

Rachel had come to him naturally, her hands on him as if they had long wanted the sensation of his bare skin as if their drawing together was an act determined in advance by a nature with a plan. Rain washed the dust off trees in a similar fashion. Waves crashed in and flowed out by the same plan. And his response could not be contained. He did not have the option of hiding his desire for her. And his wanting of her only made her that much more eager.

With this hunger they tangled their pale bodies in the shadowed dusk of one of the old house's bedrooms, wrestling on top of a musty white quilt.

He'd had no time to question her experience in this sort of action, though later it became clear to him that it was unlikely that she would volunteer herself in such a fashion if she hadn't done as much before. He wouldn't permit himself much thought in this direction because it turned his stomach some, and he was eager to do it again and didn't want these sorts of thoughts crowding his mind.

When he drove the car towards the narrow trailer, Logan realized that his previous state had shifted and had gone from his awareness of all things large and small back to his normal anxious awareness, and he was uncomfortable with his plan. He wanted to do something for Rachel, to help her smile return, but he didn't know this guy except that he'd offered drugs, hit on Angie and made fun of him. It was, though, his goal now to experience life, to not remain an observer. Rachel had tossed him into the world and he found himself engaged, an actor instead of only being acted upon. He was now actually doing something.

It took a while for Logan's knock against the aluminum door to elicit any response, but a sudden bark, a burst of man's voice startled him. "What you want?"

Logan looked back to Rachel who hung behind, her hand stuffed in her back pockets, pushing her breasts under a tight t-shirt forward. "Uh, you selling anything."

"This ain't Wal-Mart, kid."

"You said if we were ever looking for something to come by."

"Did I?"

"Down at The Bend."

Logan had thought the man had withdrawn until the door suddenly whipped open, swinging quickly outward at him. "Get in here, then."

The trailer was dark and littered with things, all sorts of things. Boxes and objects stacked against the walls, on the couch. Logan could make out, as his eyes adjusted to the dark, a TV lying on its face, stacked over with clothes on their hangers, a garden hose, a child's bike, jumper cables, a box of empty blister packs, a microwave, a turkey fryer.

The man, Harley, as he introduced himself to Rachel, standing too close to her, was shirtless, in jeans too large for his thin waist, too short for his long legs, with dark stains on the front of each leg. His eyes were harried and red, his long and stringy hair disheveled and tangled and, to Logan, he looked like a man who had not slept in some time and might just as well have forgotten what sleep was. His long fingers, also dotted like his jeans, were pale and in constant motion. Logan wanted to pull Rachel back from him to a safe distance.

"How much?"

"Huh?" Logan was wishing Rachel would do the talking, but she was mutely letting him take the lead.

"You just need an eighth? Let's get it done."

"I don't know." Logan stammered. He didn't know what the hell he was doing and he was no longer interested in doing it, whatever it was.

"Shit, kid." Harley waved his arms. "Don't waste my fucking time. Maybe your girlfriend here knows what she's looking for." He approached her where they stood together, awkwardly pressed back against a stack of junk. "Let me give you a taste." And he hustled out of sight.

They looked at each other but Rachel didn't seem to exhibit the same sort of anxiety that Logan felt. And that made him more anxious.

Harley returned in a flash, with a trio of white lines on a CD case. Logan recognized it as some piece of heavy metal hair band trash that he wouldn't use as a coaster. But then he realized what was happening, that he was being offered methamphetamines, that this white-trash freak was wanting to sell them crank, that he wasn't going to stop it all from happening. Indeed, looking at Rachel revealed an attractive girl with a gleam in her eye. He was not going to stand in the way of her getting what she wanted.

33

When he finally got that little goth rocker and his hot little tart out the door, Harley began to breathe easier. Or more quickly, really. The line he'd done with them had set him off, got him wanting more. He'd been in some sort of state before the knock on the door. He had been lying on the couch, staring through squinting eyes at the ceiling, running his fingertips over his bare torso, just lightly enough to make the skin tingle. He'd probably been like that for hours. It kept his mind from revealing anything concrete. It flitted around, or it did, until those kids showed up and now he was eager for a second line, or maybe straight in his vein this time. And now his mind was working again, the door to his memory opened.

Nothing seemed to make sense. Surely he could be making up what he saw. What his mind was playing back to him could simply be his imagination. Visions of desires. Fantasies, he saw. It was what he thought about doing, not what he had done. It was too vicious, too brutal for him. He would never have done it. These sorts of things had filled dozing hours, when anger might not allow sleep, but could he have done it?

He saw the splash of blood, but what he remembered, what came to him now in tactile sensation, was the pain from the gnashing of teeth when he pulled the trigger. With each shot, he squeezed teeth, a pain firing through his jaw and up into his skull. He wielded the gun without consideration. It was a reaction, like a spasm, not unlike vomiting. It came up quickly, deep from within and exploding outward. Seeing the fat man there, he rushed to him, the fury suddenly drowning him. He was nearly on top of him before the little gun popped in his hand. The slob probably fell more out of fear and shock than serious injury.

Harley saw himself straddling the fat man, legs wide over all of him when he fired into his mass again.

A man had been with him, a man in an obvious state, who seemed initially unaware of what was happening. He was just beginning to turn to escape when Harley turned the gun casually to him and fired twice.

He'd felt about him then a swirling commotion. He sensed a communal need to flee and he accepted it. The tiny, shiny gun in his back pocket, he'd run through the trees to his car. The area, this scenic river bend, darkening in dusk, was full of people like him, running from a danger unknown and incomprehensible.

And somehow he'd made it home, a manic and wild ride that his car probably suffered from, and inside, stripped of his shirt, it had all floated away. Maybe it was because he'd done a hit so strong that his eyes swirled in his head and moving about made him feel like his feet would not stay on the ground. Eventually, he found himself on the couch in some sort of delirious state.

He felt then like he was everywhere at once, like all time had run together. At once he was again twelve years old, sitting in a parked car with a puppy in his lap. The love for this new dog was overwhelming, so strong he could barely contain it. The paws in the lap of his jeans had given him an erection. The fur behind the pup's ears was an unknown sort of soft. The dog twitched and licked. Harlan squeezed the animal against his chest as if he could take him into his heart. The dog then yelped, snapped at him, and jumped away. There alone in the car, Harlan cried.

At the same time, he was ten, sitting in what he called "his" tree. A tree-like plant grew up and outward forming a sort of shelter along the bank of a narrow river that ran through his suburb. A soiled condom lay discarded not far from him on the dark, cold and damp earth. A group of baseball players in their close-fitting pants, striped shirts, caps and cleats tearing up the tender ground, came his way and Harlan was without means of escape. His inferiority was obvious. Victim was written across his thin chest, in his avoiding eyes. They stood around the condom making lewd jokes, seeing him and directing their comments his way. One called him over and he complied. He knew only that the words were intended to hurt, so they did. When they directed him to pick up the condom, he refused. They then shouted and pushed and he tightened his face to hold back tears. One of them punched him in the nose, a sensation that dropped him, made him see red, and drew tears like an afternoon storm. They ran off laughing.

He was also sixteen, wandering alleys of a commercial district at night for something to do. Hidden areas he felt these were. He was an adventurer in some form. He climbed up stacks of pallets, jumped from electrical boxes. A ladder that came down the side of a building was an encouragement. Because it stopped eight feet from the ground, teasing him, he had to defeat their attempt to stop him from climbing up. Dragging two pallets from further down the building, the scraping sound like an unending crash of a wave, Harlan then sat them against the cinder block, one at an angle, the other standing on top. And he climbed right up.

It was a unique perspective and he felt like he'd stolen something or was reading someone's diary. The roof of the long stretch of building was covered in gravel, small rocks dredged from some dry riverbed. He was peering through skylights into the back rooms and warehouses of stores when he heard the radio. It was the crackling communication of law enforcement. He froze. He identified the distance and proceeded with soft, slow steps to the building's edge. A police car sat where Harlan had made his way up. A searchlight scanned the roofline and he dove backward. He darted for the far end of the building, no longer concerned about the sound. He hid behind an air conditioning unit and listened for what he could hear besides his breathing. Here he stayed, listening, peeking around the corner for hours until he decided to make a break for it and get home. He went to the edge and peered over, saw nothing, crawled over, hanging by his fingers before dropping to the ground, running on a pained ankle down a slope and into a concrete culvert that passed under a street.

And he was also, sometime in his twenties, passing through a hotel's lobby, where he pulled a lamp from a table, cord springing from the outlet, and walked out the side door with it. He was darting for the bathroom in a swanky downtown bar, not quite making his destination before spewing across the tile floor. He was engaged with a woman in a bus stop shelter. He was walking, holding the hand of a four-year-old child of a woman he also held hands with, while his insides felt as if someone had turned up the internal temperature as if microwaves were exciting and cooking the molecules inside him. He was driving a car when the oil light flashed on and smoke billowed from under the hood, the car stopped in the right lane of an overpass and he walked away from it. He was preparing to dial another number from a list when the supervisor called a break, and he got up from his tiny carrel and walked out of the building and away.

And now he was here, having completed a small sale, awakened from his experience-like remembrances to think about what he had done.

His first concern was whether or not anyone would know it was him. He'd shot the two guys that could ID him and who knew if they even lived. In the panic that followed, no one likely knew he was the one responsible. But still, he had to worry, didn't he? The police could show up anytime. He needed to prepare, to do something to protect himself. Tripwires in the woods. With grenades attached. He chuckled at himself. That would be nice, but he was not that resourceful. Maybe a bigger gun was really what he needed. Jimmy had somewhere found a bigger gun after Harley had lifted the shiny gun from the top of the man's television set one night. And he'd been prepared when the police came looking for him.

Something was twisting him. It wasn't the fear, it was a worse sort of recognition that made him pull at his hair, scratch at his forearms. He had become something. Someone. He'd practically become the man that just months ago had gone on a shooting spree while looking to kill him. And now he was shooting strangers. A fat man rival dealer and his customer. Did he think this was Detroit? Like he was some bad-ass gang member? No, he was a jerk-off who didn't know what the hell he was doing. But now he was bad-ass, wasn't he? Maybe the right people would know.

Still, he needed to be careful.

34

It was pain that woke him. A searing sort of pain that he somehow knew had been steadily rising, increasing intensity until it stirred him to consciousness, slowly. Initially, the pain seemed centered in his left arm, but as he came to realize the pain, to recognize it, the sensation swarmed him.

Frank had not yet opened his eyes and he was not interested. To do that would mean he would have to recognize where he was and to think about how he got there. He had learned lately that it was best to put that sort of thing off as long as possible. He began, though, to moan before he realized it was him making that dreadful sound and listening to it also made him listen to other sounds. Footsteps in a hallway, the hum of equipment.

He tried to turn, to shift, to put off the waking if possible, but his body did not respond as easily as it should. The pain in his arm also appeared in his leg. And he knew he was not going to slip back into sleep. He knew the pain was going to get worse.

Reluctantly, he opened an eye to see a room awash with light. He saw, at first, a television high on a cabinet, a mute, neutral wallpaper behind it. The giveaway was a track on the acoustic ceiling tiles that held a curtain. Frank recognized then the hard, thin mattress under him, the rough sheets pulled high up on his chest. He was in the hospital.

That explained the pain. Something had happened. But he couldn't recall anything. Maybe it was an accident. That was likely. Then he deserved it.

A woman in blue, short, came bustling in, pushing aside the curtain. Frank stared at her. She seemed to him like the first person he'd seen in years. Her movements, the lines and structures of her face, the flow of her short hair. She might not have been beautiful, but she was beautiful, an artwork, a living, breathing miracle.

"You're awake." She spoke.

"Yes." His throat was dry and cracked.

"How's the pain?" Her eyes voiced her concern.

He nodded, trying to find the words to explain the pain, trying to understand what it was he felt. His eyes were wet.

"Let's see if I can get you a little morphine." She patted his forearm.

Frank tried to think of how such a drug might make him feel. Might he then just slip away, put all of this pain and whatever had happened into a trash bag tossed off a high bridge, allowing him to escape to a world where his body, his consciousness didn't feel like burnt paper.

It was, though, this desire for escape, this desire to transform the world from something brutal and painful and ugly into something possible and significant, that had likely led to his current circumstance. Maybe it had been something coincidental, a tornado or fire or something, but more than likely it had come from drinking too much, getting kicked out of another bar, or another fight, or driving in a state below consciousness.

The woman, the nurse, returned and she was more beautiful than before, a perfect specimen of human existence. The lines around her eyes, the discolorations on her cheeks, the fullness of her lips, all described her as someone human, someone who was living a life that had its trials and chores, and likely some joy.

"This'll get you feeling better." And she put the needle into the IV in the back of his hand.

Things suddenly became cool. An icy tincture in his head, bathing his brain.

Things had come off the rails for him, hadn't they? It was what he'd wanted, to release himself from the world that had wronged him, stolen Terry from him. And if the world wasn't going to take him, then Frank would do what he could to not be present in this world any longer; he would close a curtain to it, live disengaged, in a delirium from one minute to the next. It became hard to maintain. Eventually, he had to come down. Eventually, all that he'd ingested from the time he woke would catch up and he would find himself asleep, sometimes in awkward places.

A white-walled church the size of a one-room schoolhouse, beams and battens exposed and washed white, in which he wandered in the pre-dawn, to rest while his eyes could not stay open without force, in the period between their closing. He'd woken to the sight of the white boards of the sloped ceiling, the gaps between the boards like pinstripes, woken to voices around him, booming in the room.

There is a state when the transition from sleep to full wakefulness is mixed with an ongoing mania when one cannot be sure that what is being seen, or heard, exists in any reasonable way. It took many moments of Frank's listening to the voices, sounds but not words, the ceiling's stripes swaying in his eyes, for him to realize that they were indeed real.

He righted himself quickly. Too quickly. He'd no sooner slid upright on the handmade pew than his stomach lurched and a roomful of black faces pitched and swirled. What came out of him came from the depths of him and with such force that he thought it would split him in two, that his whole insides would be expelled in each convulsion. As his body squeezed and loosened, again and again, Frank was aware of eyes on him, white eyes in dark faces in a white room, a cross hung solemnly, modestly. The eyes on him did not belong only to those in the room.

When his body surrendered and slumped into the mess he'd made on the floorboards, hands were at his feet, voices now raised, and he was dragged from the church, painfully down two steps and into the sun-drenched grass outside, where he curled away from the light.

He had needed some way to not let these things catch up with him, he needed some sort of perpetual motion. He'd had offers, concerned strangers, seeing him slumped beleaguered over his drink, offers for a substance that would lift him up, his head and his spirits. He'd declined again and again, rejecting the generosity of strangers, avoiding anything that might awaken him, take him out of his continued delirium.

Eventually, though, he surrendered, realizing that fear of anything at this point was ridiculous. He would take all offers. A fat man had cut a line for him on a grimy toilet tank and handed him a hollow pen body. He took to it like this was how he'd always spent his life, as if he had not once been a hard-working young man descended from hard-working and rebellious Cherokee. It was flame and ice in one; strings that held him floating, just above the earth's surface. He felt the flow of existence like the river, air as thick and buoyant as the water.

The sensation lasted for what felt like days before it faltered. He was deposited like a stone on the river's bottom and felt suffocated by the water, abandoned by this good feeling. He crashed hard but, unlike other tragedies in his life, he knew the remedy. He couldn't though, take his chances of running into the fat guy again in the same bar. Which bar he couldn't even remember. There was one place in the county where people went to search out things they couldn't locate elsewhere.

When he arrived at The Bend, Frank was in a desperate state. He'd been drinking heavily, more quickly and furiously than ever. The sweetly bitter biting taste of the whiskey did not deter him from drinking as much as possible to dull him, to transform him. The trees of The Bend tilted back and forth, a metronome ticking off the seconds before his collapse. He stumbled this way and that, accosting strangers, unable to vocalize his need. He thought he would collapse and be swallowed by the soft soil. Or else he might walk right out onto the flowing river, and slide slowly underneath.

A glowing orb floating among the dark beams of the trees fixated Frank. He was drawn to it, like a siren's call. As he drew closer, the form filled excessively to become the fat man. Frank floundered in his pockets for dollar bills which felt increasingly useless but might, this once, provide something that would transport him, transform him, allow him to transcend this existence, to go beyond it to some something further, greater, larger, better. And it was desperately necessary.

The smile on the fat man's face told Frank that he saw his need and was eager to assist. And then there was a sound, a sharp clap that seemed to come from all directions. Frank could not understand it, had not completely registered it when the glowing orb, large as it was, fell to the ground. Another form, thin and manic, a long-haired wood sprite, the frantically bent and knotted branches of the trees alive, mounted the fat man, like a demon. And a second clap followed.

Frank had turned then to run. He'd sought transformation, an escape from earth, but the world he was moving to was filled with hellish creatures who were able to deliver deathly blows with a spark of sound that filled everything. And two subsequent sounds felled him.

35

Sam had been at home, seated in his easy chair, Natalie on the couch next to him, the TV blasting a show featuring some famous forensic pathologist when the phone rang. With a creak of swinging metal, Sam lowered his elevated legs and made his way to the phone sitting on the kitchen counter.

They'd been having another one of their virtually speechless evenings. Commenting on the program was permitted, but any other commentary, about their activities, opinions, or even the weather, was forbidden. It wasn't as if they would fight. They didn't need to. They knew each other too well. Each knew the look of gentle scorn, embarrassment, shame, and frustration. Every move of an eyebrow, a cheek, each breath, mute acknowledgment, told more and was more effective than any raised voice could be. Sometime in the last several months, Natalie had begun to disapprove of everything he did. Everything about him. He refused to allow this to change a thing.

"Sam. There's been a shooting at The Bend." The voice on the other end was Bill. Breathless and requesting assistance.

"When?"

"About twenty minutes ago. At least two shot."

"And the shooter?"

"No one knows. Yet."

"I'm on my way."

"Alright, then. See you there."

Sam turned then to hurry and change into his uniform, but then he thought of Natalie. He would have to tell her. And she would give him that look, and probably say something. Maybe it was a good thing that she was worried. A good sign, at least. But it wasn't simply worry. It was that she still worried when she knew she shouldn't have to anymore. She resented the fact that he was working. They were to have been retired. To be enjoying life, raising cattle, and finally living some.

They were both getting older quickly and the time for enjoyment was running out. Sam was aware of this. He was aware that his continuing to work was stealing time from Natalie and, really, from himself. And somehow it was putting off what it was they had come back to Barnes County to do: to rectify his father's mistakes. And, sure, he owned a farm now, but he wasn't a farmer. He was still a cop, just in a different locale. It wasn't a steel mill, but he wasn't ready to leave it earlier. At least he could say that he wasn't so frustrated, worn out and generally unsatisfied with his job that he spent his evenings drinking beer until sleep overtook him.

"There's been a shooting at The Bend," he told Natalie and nearly winced and how he had mimicked Bill.

"Oh, God. They catch the guy?"

"No."

"You're going to go?"

"I have to."

"Of course." She had answered with enough lightness to nearly disguise her disapproval. Still, he kissed her cheek when he left.

The scene at The Bend was chaotic. Lights of many colors flashed back and forth through the trees, throwing shadows this way and that like zombie creatures, all shadow, wandering aimlessly near the river. The water itself shimmered, gurgling pleasantly as if it held a secret and the opposite cliff above, a band of white limestone in dark green, was as bright as a drive-in movie screen.

Sam was aware that he would normally be sleeping at this time. He felt it in his head, but the pulse of light, the speed he used to arrive, and the anticipation to learn and sort out what had happened made his blood pump with great force.

His flashlight trained on the ground a few feet in front of him, Sam made his way quickly to what looked like the center of activity. He nodded to other deputies taking witness statements from men too drunk or drugged to probably tell them anything of value.

He was spotted by Bill who raised his head from where he'd been looking down at paramedics hunched together over the ground. He looked grateful for Sam's arrival.

"They still working one?"

"Sam."

"Is it only one?"

"They took one away already."

"And only the two?"

"Sam, the other one was Frank Redbird."

"Wait, what?"

"Terry's Frank."

"Shit."

"One in the chest and one in the leg."

"He gonna make it?"

"He wasn't conscious."

"The shooter?"

"Can't be anywhere near here now."

"Witnesses?"

"Nothing worth anything."

"Do we know the other victim?"

"No ID, but I'm sure we know him."

After a flashlight inspection down into the huddle of EMTs, Sam was pretty sure he knew the man. A guy called Round Randy. A dealer.

"Did you check his pockets?" He turned to Bill.

Bill looked back at him stupidly and Sam felt himself grow angry.

"If no one's cleaned him out already, he'll have something on him." And Sam squeezed into the scrum to retrieve a wad of cash and several small plastic bags. He held up the cache to Bill. "This was why he was shot."

"Then why does he still have it?"

"Well," Sam paused, wanting to give a smart answer without delay, but he needed that minute to think. He scanned the dark, then answered, "It wasn't a robbery. It must have been the competition."

"Geez. So much for the free market."

They spent the next several hours debriefing deputies, demanding they write reports on scene before details slipped away like the miles they would cover on the way back to the department, and scouring the ground for a dropped or discarded weapon, or any evidence of the shooter. As Sam did this, though, his mind alternated between two particular avenues. The first was contemplation of who might have wanted to take out Round Randy. The other was his frustration with Bill.

He hadn't been giving it serious consideration, he believed, but he'd never stopped thinking about the possibility of his running for sheriff. And it wasn't all his fault.

He had been at the hardware store, looking for a particular bolt and frustrated by it. Sam hated to go out for one single part. It was part of the reason his workbench in the shop was laden with jars and coffee cans filled with every spare part he ever had. Nothing was tossed out. You just never knew when the occasion might call for that exact piece. He had spent nearly an hour sifting through these screws, nuts, nails, bolts, pins, and the like. His hands were grimy with dust and grease from the exercise. And still, he'd had to drive the twenty minutes to Sheridan for the one part that would repair his brush hog so that maybe he might get around to mowing down the three acres up by the house before it looked like the place was vacant and being reclaimed by the land.

Sam was in this state, scanning the bins in the store's dim light when a voice spoke to him. Immediately he didn't want to turn around or acknowledge that he'd heard a thing, but as he prepared to face whoever it was, the voice spoke again.

"Deputy Summers." The call belonged to Pastor Toujours.

"Good Afternoon." Sam wiped his hand on his leg before thrusting it forward.

"Afternoon. How are you?"

They weren't exactly on personal terms. They had only known each other professionally. Sam had received the call when the pastor reported that a member of his congregation had been molesting his neighbor's boys. The man had come to the pastor after being beaten to a grotesque red and purple swollen state by his neighbor, who had only given him a reprieve so that he could get a gun. The pastor had told Sam that his decision had been simple. Some in his position might have felt a responsibility to the confessor, but the man had committed a horrible sin and already destroyed his life. And to prevent another man, the neighbor, from ruining his life he had only one call to make. Sam found his reasoning admirable.

"Good, thank you."

"I heard that you're going to be running for sheriff."

"Sorry?"

"Might do you some good with the folks around here if you start attending one of the many local churches."

"I don't think— "

"We all love Sheriff Wallis, God bless him. He's been through an ordeal. There are just some that might want a man in a different position to be our sheriff come the fall."

The Pastor was a tall man with a commanding way about him. In another time, another place, he would have made a great general. He made Sam feel like had no choice but to obey.

"I appreciate that, I do, but---"

"Our congregation could be of great assistance to you."

"Thank you. I don't think, though, that I'm likely to try to take Bill's job."

"I understand your felicity, deputy. But, sometimes we have a greater calling than mere brotherhood."

The meeting might not have bothered Sam had his mind been made up, had his decision against the opportunity been firm. But it was an opportunity, a chance at a sort of ascension normally denied to men in his family. His father would fume at the idea, with his beer and heat-scorched face. It wasn't though, the right sort of comeuppance he sought. The idea was to succeed where his father had failed. To resurrect the Summers farm. Already, though, he was sacrificing that dream some by having his job at the sheriff's Department.

Maybe some part of him was afraid of the challenge. Full devotion to a cattle ranch was a risk. If he was all-in there were only two possible outcomes. Now, at least, he knew that it was stalled by his own doing, not some failure that mimicked his father's. And what would success mean? What goddamn good was it going to do to succeed where his father had failed? Would the old man actually give a shit? He'd probably still call Sam an idiot for even trying. So, what would come from a successful ranch? Some years of happiness, then what? What would become of the place when they were too old to do the work it required? Sure, they could hire their own Frank Redbird, but what would be the point? It wasn't like there was anyone to whom they could leave it.

Bringing children into this world had never seemed a reasonable thing to Sam and Natalie. She had come from a pack of siblings, each with their own sets of troubles, who began birthing their own troublemakers as soon as nature permitted. She'd described it to Sam like being from a family of farm cats in desperate need of neutering. He wasn't always sure he believed her, though. For some years Natalie had had a sort of longing in her eyes. Anytime he pressed her about the discomfort she held in her small face, she dismissed him. The hot flashes came, and the look settled into the long lines around her lips.

For Sam, the issue was too mixed up to ever put into words. His experiences had given him the idea that some certain darkness was held contained in the center of everyone's soul. And he'd seen how it had surfaced in even the most honorable of people. It was a sort of evil that could just take over a person. Seeing that, even the possibility of it, in his own child, reflective eyes that bore traces of his heritage would be too much to bear.

His brother's kids had also given him some perspective. Sam had been a witness to bad parenting, to children out of control and a destructive situation. The allegations against him only sealed it for him. A man was just one accusation away from a prison term. His brother's failings as a parent came, he believed, from a single source. Their father had not given them the best example of how to be a father. Sam had no fatherly role models, no decent example of good parenting. So, there was every chance that he might be a father to his children the same way his father was a parent to them. With violence and neglect, ridicule and fear.

Every child deserved more. Few ever got it. He'd seen kids living in squalid conditions, feces on their faces, neglected, left to fend for themselves for the length of a day. There was no reason to question the direction of things if only you'd seen the way the current generation was being raised. No wonder things were changing even in this isolated county in the center of the country. No interstate even goes through Barnes County, yet the things that have infiltrated the big city slums have made their way here. And the older generation, what are they going to do about it? Not a thing. Not even put a finger in the dike. Just stand helplessly as the water spills over them.

So, maybe it was up to him. Someone has to do what they can to protect these people.

He was contemplating what would be required of him to run for office as he slowed the car in front of Harlan Lustig's trailer. He was headed home to get some sleep after spending the whole of the night and most of the next day at The Bend when he saw a new car parked in front of the small trailer. A gold Taurus. This one was new to him. If he wasn't in such a need for sleep he might see what he could do to see the license plate. But his mind was heavy and he needed to get home. And he was trying to settle on which of the area's characters might be responsible for the night's crimes.

36

His hands smelled of syrup and were puffy and damp. A cut on the side of his first finger was deep and split open, but no blood filled the fresh wound, cauterized by the hot water. The afternoon was so hot on Logan that he felt like splaying himself on the sun-drenched sidewalk to sleep. Home seemed so far away from the diner.

Maybe this feeling had finally caught up with him. The previous, chemically assisted feeling had entirely disappeared. It had seemed like days without sleep. Certainly a day's worth of experience. Who would have thought his life would change in such a fashion? On this afternoon was he not a new Logan? A young man with a different destiny? How could he possibly still be the sheriff's son? The town freak? That old Logan certainly would not have been up all night on drugs, not have had lengthy, languorous sex. That old Logan could never claim a girl as his own.

Logan and Rachel had left that junk-filled trailer and returned to the abandoned house, pulling open the windows, pulling off their clothes and lying on top of the old dusty bed while a breeze, light and smelling of oak, played with the curtains. A sort of inactivity seemed, initially, as the only way to experience the drug, to notice the blood pulsing in every capillary, the tingling that came in waves. When Logan closed his eyes, sparks danced in the dark. Tactile sensation, though, was more enthralling.

The touch of Rachel's bare thigh through the tips of his fingers felt like he'd touched something he was unworthy to touch, like once, at maybe seven years old, alone in an empty chapel he had dipped his fingers into holy water. It coated the tips of his fingers like a magic-imbued oil.

And the feeling when she touched him was a feeling beyond feelings. It was a sensation that he didn't think that bodies were normally permitted to feel. No other pleasant experience compared. And when, in this state, they had sex, he thought that he must have died, literally, to feel such a thing. Feelings like this didn't exist in the real world. It was so rich that he was surely going to explode, his cells, each and every one, a hundred-thousand stars shooting off, trembling into the nothingness.

This feeling—these feelings were fleeting. Replaced by other feelings, each unique and brand new, but steadily diminishing in some indefinable aspect. And before he knew it the room grew dusky, his stomach shrank inside him as he knew he was going to have to go home. With pledges and declarations, he left her and returned to his own darkened house.

That night was a long one, the old house silent and empty, except for Logan in his bed, prepared for his father to arrive home at any moment. And the whole time his mind raced, his skin crawled while he lay in his bed, one bare leg kicked out from under the bedclothes to catch the bit of cool air that blew in the open window. Is air conditioning too much to ask for around here?

Why was he always shortchanged? He saw his world as paper-thin, lighted brightly, hotly; the whole thing, his home, his school, the long grasses ripe with swinging seeds, was close to bursting into flame. It was a hollow world where he was as valuable and desired as dust. He was meant for a different reality, he believed. One where merit and individuality were prized over conformity and silence. Where all physical expressions were those of love, not violence. Where, maybe, he wouldn't be left to raise himself. Or at least where might be left alone.

He wanted a cigarette. A drink. More drugs. Anything to make him feel differently. Something to make him different from the Logan he had been just a few weeks before. Some sort of transcendence, maybe. He deserved to be delivered to a new reality. Something beyond this one that held him trapped and pinned to the bed like someone prepared for shock treatments.

Things had changed, though. Things were different. A girl, a live being of soft flesh, living eyes and smiles, had made herself a part of him. She was like a doctor who, with care and intellect, treated the illness from which he had suffered most of his life, and now Logan was cured and able to see the world anew.

Rachel was, he knew, something precious. A temporal anomaly, she would someday be gone, like she had never existed at all. It was a fact hard to face. How was it possible that at the end of the summer she would return to St. Louis and he would return to that vile high school? And he would have nothing to show for it. No one would believe him, even if there was someone to tell. He would have to be different. How, after sex with Rachel, would he not be different? To think of it now made him tingle, his heart contract with the unlikelihood of it all. It was improbable, her coming to him. Like it had been planned. Set up. Maybe, his mind flashing to somewhere dark, it was all some trick to humiliate him.

Logan wished he could call her and be reassured. It was the middle of the night. What if his father came home to catch him on the phone? What if Rachel's phone was on, the ringer turned up, and sitting somewhere to wake up Mrs. Headrick? What if, though, she was on the phone, talking to some boy back in St. Louis, or someone in town? What if she weren't home at all, but out with some other kid, some Bo Newell? The thought hurt him physically. His eyes swelled, his blood heated. He tossed himself over, pressing his hot face into his cool pillow, but he didn't feel better. Not for the rest of the night.

And maybe he had slept some, but he never noticed. Nor did he hear his father come home. Because he didn't. Again. When the red numbers of the clocked mutated to declare the time as five in the morning, he got up and found himself again alone in the house. Frustrated that his father had not bothered to come home or call and sorry that he had missed an opportunity to defy the rules with impunity and possibly, clandestinely, spend the night with Rachel.

And when Rachel was not there when his shift ended, when he called her from the phone at work and it went straight to voicemail, he didn't know what to do with himself. Not in this mood, a doubt slipping in like a splinter under his fingernail. Not with his body feeling he'd been flattened by a cartoon steamroller and he had to shake himself into a semblance of his previous form. So, he went to see his father at work.

Logan had gotten to know the sheriff's office when he was young, but he never grew very comfortable with it. Some of it had to do with the macho display of the deputies, with their mustaches and biceps. And the idea of those men behind those doors, imprisoned. It made him uneasy. They likely deserved it and Logan believed in justice, but even as they shouted obscenities at him, he empathized.

Entering, he was struck by a smell unique to this place, a combination of cigarette smoke and the cleansers they used to clean the cells, which never completely masked the smell of urine. The scent was captured in the acoustic ceiling tiles, the fake wood paneling that rose only chest-high on the walls, and in the files of paperwork and reports.

A sassy, bulbous woman sat behind the dispatcher's desk and waved him to pass while voicing coded inanities into a microphone. The radio thinly squawked back similar nonsense. In an office at the end of the hall, two men chuckled loudly, one pounding the other in the arm. The primitive triviality made Logan involuntarily roll his eyes.

His father's office was halfway down the narrow hall, and he found the door open only a few inches. Logan paused to be sure he wouldn't be interrupting a phone call or the dressing down of a delinquent deputy. With his fingertips he pushed the door open to see his father's boots resting on the desk, his head reclined in the chair, closed eyes staring up at the blaring fluorescents, lips dry and parted. He looked like the men seen sleeping and sunning themselves in their pen outside the old folks' home on Ninth. Maybe that was where he belonged.

Logan stood there helpless. What could he do? From his experience waking a sleeping person was a prescription for trouble. And his father? It could prove fatal. He couldn't, though, turn around and walk out. What sense would that make? He didn't feel good and he was envious of his father for sleeping.

"So, this is where you sleep now?"

The sheriff's eyes cracked open, a tongue dampened his dry lips. Then he sat up. Just enough to see his visitor. "What's that?"

"Nothin'."

Bill ran a hand through his wisp of dusty hair and dropped his feet to the floor. "What are you up to?"

He looked like shit. Then again, they both probably did. "Heading home."

"Oh, yeah. Got stuck on something last night."

"And the night before?"

"Is that right?"

"Two nights."

"A couple of guys got shot down at The Bend."

"Hmm."

"Ain't a safe place."

They sat there in silence. Logan wished he hadn't bothered to stop by. He could be home asleep.

"How's the job?"

"Huh?" Any question from his father was best answered with this, allowing time to compose a response appropriate for the audience.

"Things going well at the diner?"

"Oh, sure. I'm waiting for my check, though."

"It'll come and it'll feel worthwhile, then."

"I suppose."

"Get used to it." He leaned back in his chair, feet back up on the desk again.

Logan stared at him, not quite pleased with the thought that even at his father's age he might be waiting for a paycheck to make his life and work feel worthwhile.

"Here," his father sat up quickly, retrieved his wallet, and with long, thick-knuckled fingers pulled a twenty from his wallet. "In case I don't make it home for dinner, you can go get yourself something to eat."

He took the bill from the sheriff's outstretched hand and backed out the door. Did every interaction with his father have to be as unpleasant as that? Couldn't they ever feel comfortable with one another? Logan knew that he should be happy; he was more or less living on his own. Some kids would envy him. It was what he wanted, what he thought he needed since the time he was twelve. But who would have ever thought it would feel as empty as this? Logan saw his house as some gray cave, some great industrial facility that was once full of activity and color but had since been abandoned and stripped of everything but the dusty hollows where machinery had once sat.

One absent spot of color, a whirring buzzing machine emitting scents and sounds, was Logan's mother. She could always be counted on for laughter, even if it was awkward and out of place. She could laugh at the evening news. And when she passed she left a scent trail, all lavender, heliotrope, and patchouli, her lips red, hair in tight sprayed curls. At the end, she became an extreme version of the woman she had been, the saturation turned up, and then she was gone. Draining the house of color, smell, and life.

And where was Rachel to come to occupy some space? Today, he was ready to ignore the rules and take her to his room. His father, in that state, wouldn't notice anything. To take her into his room would be like letting her inside his interior, allowing her to step inside and look around. Did his room express him? Did it represent him? No, it couldn't. Maybe if the walls were painted black. But even then, would it display how vibrantly he felt about things? Could it show what was hidden by the black, by his disgust with the world, with his marginalization? Could it show his want for more, more than his life would currently permit?

What would she think? What would she make of him if she knew the way he vibrated under his skin? And what would she think about how quickly it shifted to anger? What if she could see how he fantasized about taking a gun to each and every kid at school who had ever wronged him? Fantasies complete with jets of blood, pleas for forgiveness, and screams of pain. What would she think if she knew that on days, days not unlike this day, he felt drained and wanted to lay himself across the dining room table and wait for God to just take the rest of his life from him? Begging for death.

When he entered the house, as devoid of life as ever, he went directly to the phone and dialed the number he now knew by heart, hoping that Rachel might come and save him from his quickly disintegrating mood. When the phone finally went to voicemail, he collapsed to the kitchen floor and let the tears come.

37

If he slowed down for a minute he would realize that he couldn't keep up this pace, and he felt it chasing him, like a big black dog nipping at his heels. For safety, though, he had to work at night, avoiding detection in a barn long abandoned; the only animals it held being birds among the rafters, spiders in webs at the joints, and a dervish of a man spinning around his mad scientist's lab. So, naturally, these late-night labors required some chemical assistance, a little lighter fluid on the coals. Then in the morning's dusk, the world's half-awake state, Harley made his way home. But an intense heat still smoldered inside. Sometimes he would collapse into sleep, other times he would lay among the junk that covered his bed, scratching at sores, at the tracks the needle had left in his arm.

Sometimes, in this state, he schemed his takeover of the world. He imagined many things. He thought of himself as some Mexican drug lord, with all the cops on his payroll, feared by all and living a life of leisure and luxury. Other times, though, he imagined working harder and harder, amassing as much funds as possible to pay for another escape, to somewhere that wouldn't require this of him, somewhere he might be able to sleep like a normal person, or at least sleep at all. He could be many things, he knew. Maybe he would find a new city, a larger city, where he could be more anonymous, where he could maybe go to college. He saw himself as the eager student, front row seat, a red "A" emblazoned across his paper. He would study economics. Forget doing someone's taxes, like his father. He would formulate a new economic theory. He would find reasonable ways for helping all prosper, where the corporations didn't succeed by helping to keep people down, where one didn't get by on the backs of others.

Other times, though, his rambling thoughts were more fact-based. Or fear-based. It wasn't just his imminent collapse that was chasing him. The law was out there too. Likely watching his trailer as he fidgeted in his bed. He needed weapons, trip-lines with explosives in the woods surrounding him. Maybe his big black dog would keep the fools back. Maybe a gate so no one could even dare approach his door. They were watching him, he knew. He saw the glances at him in town, the mirrors and cameras on him when he strolled through the Country Mart. He heard the cars slow as they drove by his house, the small planes that flew overhead. He was going to need security. Cameras, alarms, a militia.

But thinking about what could happen, what he might do, didn't alleviate the fear. The consideration of possibilities only made what was likely seem more so. They were still coming for him. He'd shot two men. He'd felt the gun in his hand, the small explosions. He'd seen two men drop to the ground, yet it didn't seem real. It didn't seem like anything he could have done. It was easy to think he didn't. But did he kill them? Did he really stop one or two lives with that girly gun? If either of them died, the law would be after him with a vengeance, anger in their eyes. They wasted no time coming after Jimmy. Yet two nights had passed and no one had been to his door. Maybe they knew better now. Maybe they wouldn't dare approach the door, lest the bullets come flying. Instead, they might simply wait for him. They could be out there now, camped out just down the road waiting for him to leave.

He needed a course of action; he couldn't just wait for them. He would have to move, find somewhere else to be. He was too vulnerable here. And what if it wasn't the inept sheriff's Department coming after him? What if that fat bastard was still alive? He could have his own militia, come shoot the place full of holes with a machine gun. If he knew who he was, where he was. It was imperative that he got the hell out.

He leaped out of bed with more energy than he knew he had. He rummaged through some things before locating a duffle bag, stolen. He filled it with clothes, a fast food bag that held the uncounted cash he'd been hoarding, the tobacco tin full of bindles, and a couple of larger bundles that he retrieved from the framing of the couch. He then grabbed his cell phone and his keys, then stopped.

What was he thinking? If they really were waiting for him just down the road, he couldn't just drive out of here. He could call someone. He looked down at his cell phone. It was full of idiots and friends, no more loyal to him than to the law. There wasn't a one of them who could be trusted. A little pressure by the cops or anyone else and they'd give him up. He was going to have to walk.

He thought of himself walking around the back of the trailer, hopping over the fence and taking off through the forest. He had no idea how far away the next road might be or how he would possibly cover all the miles between here and the barn. He sighed.

As he did, the sound continued after he had stopped. The sound wasn't him at all. It was a car pulling up. They wouldn't dare. He hustled down the small hall, prepared to toss himself out the back bedroom window. Peeling back the foil that covered a window to the front, he saw not a cop car, or anything nearly as threatening. It was a plush Oldsmobile. Someone was lost. Or it was a trap.

He threw open the opposite window and heaved the bag out. As far towards the fence as he could. His gun the only thing left in his hands, he looked out the front again.

It was not an old lady walking toward his door. It was that hot little goth girl. If it was a trap, it was a cruel one. A risk he was willing to take. At the front door, he listened for the first foot on the step then ripped open the door, grabbed the fist that had been extended to knock, pulled the girl quickly in, and shut the door.

She lay on the floor in a tired state of shock. She obviously didn't know what to think. She looked at him as if she expected some more violent act. He studied her expectant fear.

"What're you doing here?"

"More."

He blinked. He should have recognized that look in her eyes. She'd had a taste that set her off. A door had opened to a world she was not about to leave. Well, of course, he was willing to help. Especially her.

"I'll make you a deal."

She backed up on her elbows, a look of resignation settling in.

"Go back out to your car, start 'er up, make sure the doors are all unlocked."

She looked at him, then down at his hand.

The gun hung there like another appendage. "Go on. I'll be there in a minute."

Without words, she walked out either actually or artfully angry. And Harley went to the bedroom, he scanned it as another man might look around a hotel room which he is leaving for the last time. Then he went feet first out the back window.

He hit the ground and stayed down, making military style for the bag. As it lay in the grass in front of him, he thought of its consolidated value. It contained cash and drugs with tangible street value, but the bag in his possession also had a value counted in years of a prison sentence. For this reason, he kept low to the ground as he took the bag back around to the front of the trailer, towards the car.

The fear he felt was something new. It wasn't the intangible fear of paranoia, with which he was familiar, but it had its antecedents.

In those years after leaving home, jaded by the actions during his time at White Castle, he'd fallen into a sort of meaningless state. He didn't know what to make of life and so it meant little. He'd fallen in with a guy named Ramón. He was of mixed heritage so that his skin was a shade of brown strived for by sunbathers, a sheen to it like breath on glass. He was shorter than Harley, a wrestler's physique, and had a bushy head of hair, dense and dark. Harley found him surprisingly charismatic. He had no other reason for liking or hanging around with the guy.

They spent much of their time wandering the downtown St. Louis streets, wandering into bars and drinking until they were cut off. It was aimless and pointless and, thus, as fruitless as life itself. They were trolling for women. That's what they said. It really meant they would, from their barstool perches, stare at the most attractive women in the place, and do nothing. When these women, or the men they were with, didn't care for the attention, this sometimes became a problem. Ramón, it turned out, was quick with a fist.

Quite a few nights found them among a crowd sprawled out in the street, fists swinging. Harley was not much of a fighter. Thin and weak, his fists didn't pack much punch, but he also wasn't afraid and this made him dangerous. His bravado was aided by his companion whose punch could knock down the most prepared man.

Closing time was always trouble. Preparing to go home empty-handed left some men agitated. Earlier in the evening Ramón and Harley had been talking to a pair of blondes. They knew the women were out of their league, but it had been early in the evening, and the level of scamming hadn't yet been cranked up. When the women were still there at closing time, it was time for some sort of action.

About the same time, the bartender called last call, a couple of guys sat themselves down at the table with the blondes. Ramón and Harley glared and stared, drank their hastily ordered last drinks. These other men were trying hard but were distracted by the staring pair at the bar. Finally, one of them lifted a middle finger and Ramón and Harley erupted with laughter.

The waitress began rushing people out the door and these two men came past the bar next to the women. Ramón and Harley interceded.

They stepped up to the women, who greeted them with familiarity, which further set off their new companions.

"Fuck off, man." One of the men made a move to push Ramón back, but he struck at the advancing arm with a quickness and force that put fury into the guy's eyes.

"You got a problem?"

"Looks like you're the one with the problem, asshole." Harley stretched himself tall.

"Outside!" The waitress shouted, pushing them as a bundle out the narrow front door.

On the sidewalk, Ramón began the provocation, "You want to start something?"

"Stop it," one of the blondes shouted at them both, her friend pulling at her hand.

The foul-mouthed aggressor with the middle-finger pushed her aside and came forward at Ramón who wasted no time striking him in the jaw. And the two collapsed on each other.

The sidekick looked at Harley and put his arms out as if to say, "You want a piece of me?" Harley came quickly at him with hands down, and the guy swung. Harley dodged, swept the guy's ankles, and together they fell to the pavement.

The fight had barely gotten underway when there was a sudden, short squawk of a police car's siren. The crowd dispersed in a flash, Harley and Ramón ran down an alley, into another street, around a corner and down another alley. They hid there, catching their breath until they could walk nonchalantly into the street.

Ramón and Harley were starting to stand tall again to walk out onto the sidewalk when they saw a figure walking on the opposite side of the street. A tall guy, his shirt was half untucked, his collar twisted, and hair in disarray. It was Ramón's opponent and he was walking alone.

Ramón pushed Harley against the wall and peered around the corner before waving for Harley to follow. He copied Ramón as they ran low and quiet across the amber-lighted street, crouching along the cars parked at the curb. The figure they were stalking then produced car keys from his pocket and turned into a darkened parking lot. It was late and many of the cars had already been driven home, but they managed to make their way to the lee side of the remaining cars, out of sight, nearer the whole time.

When it was apparent that the man was headed for a particular SUV, they darted around the adjacent car. In the few moments that they waited, Harley saw the grin in Ramón's dark eyes, his breathing silent and shallow. He looked at Harley, slugged him in the shoulder, then popped up from the front of the car.

The man who had been so vocal before didn't seem to know what to say as he stared at the two of them there in the dark between shadowed cars, but when his open lips made a move to form some sort of objection, Ramón's fist sailed through the night to stop it. He stumbled backward and then fell forward, attempting to right himself. In this crouched stance, the man received repeated blows to the back of his neck, head, and shoulders.

Harley wanted a piece of him too. He was biting down on his tongue, his muscles jumping. Ramón bounced back, giving the man a minute to see if he might be able to fight properly. He did regain himself and stood upright, fists down. His stance of preparedness was no match for someone as edgy and fast as Harley, who had slipped past Ramón and brought a fist around in a wide swing that connected with the side of the guy's head. He fell against the side of his car and to the blacktop.

Harley was ready to declare victory, seeing the heavy-breathing man there on the ground, slowing trying to sit up. Ramón, though, wasn't ready to just leave him there. Ramón was like an animal after wounded prey. He came at the guy, pulled him up by the hair and punched him in the face, kicked him in the head, in the legs, and when the guy fell completely to the ground, Ramón kicked at his torso, stomped on a hand.

Harley was drunk, worked up with violence, and shocked by what he saw, but he could not move, couldn't remove himself, or attempt to stop Ramón. He could only watch as the violence against a victim this passive continued. He heard bones break, cries of pain, sounds that made him wince involuntarily. Ramón's shoes and fists were colored with blood.

When they finally ran from the scene, the man's breath was gurgling through the blood in his throat.

Harlan didn't answer his phone for more than a month after this and found new places to hang out.

The anticipation he felt as he crept alongside the Oldsmobile was similar. He could nearly feel the violence coming.

He slid himself across the backseat and directed the girl to drive. He stayed down but told her to tell him when she saw any other vehicles. No patrol cars were waiting just down the road. No cops their entire trip. He peeked up only to tell her where to turn and, at each turn, she asked him where they were going. After the fifth time of not bothering to respond, he finally told her to "shut the fuck up."

He told her to squeeze the car between the trees on the shadowed north side of the barn, and he hustled her into the barn even though she stalled to look at the abandoned house across the yard and a house farther up the hill. It looked much closer in this daylight. In the shade of the darkened barn, Harley felt better.

His companion, though, was agitated. She looked around at his set-up like it was a torture chamber. She looked like she was getting more than she asked for. And she looked like she'd better get what she came for or else she was liable to split at the seams, stuffing coming out at the joints of her arms and around her neck.

The eagerness in her face, though her eyes were dark and heavy, her lips down-turned and purple, excited him. She was desirous. Not necessarily for him, but wanting none the less. He studied her again.

She pulled green, damp dollar bills from her pocket.

"Now, you don't think a girl like you needs cash, do you?"

Her arms dropped some.

"A girl like you could get through life without hardly lifting a finger. You'll never have to pay for your own drink, never buy your own dinner. Your company might not always be to your liking, and things might not go the way you like, but you'll be taken care of."

She looked on the edge of tears.

"Don't you worry. I'll take care of you, dear. Have yourself a seat and I'll get you a treat." He laughed. "Seat—treat." He turned and walked across the trampled hay to one of a line of tables, tossed down his bag, and rummaged through it for his gear.

Harley recognized the small high that precedes the actual hit. Endorphins kicking in like Pavlov's dog. He acknowledged the drug's hold on him and couldn't bring himself to care.

Going back to the girl he saw the same sort of anticipation in her face in her bouncing leg and twitching fingers. He pulled over a battered kitchen chair to where she sat, pulled her hand out and ran his fingers on the plumpy flesh of her forearm, enjoying the soft extra flesh.

When the drug hit her, her eyes rolled in her head and she lolled backward. Goosebumps dotted her flesh in his hand.

"Oh, shit. Shit. Shit."

"Ain't bad, huh? Harley makes some good shit."

"Oh, my God."

"Enjoy it, dear."

"Woo."

He laughed at her.

She turned her dark, dilated eyes to him, and he stared back. He wanted her to know that what she thought was true.

He pulled his chair closer to her and she shuddered.

38

Bill couldn't shake being tired. It hung over him like he was a man in chains. It didn't help that he hadn't been home, hadn't actually laid in his bed for days. When he fell asleep at his desk, though, he fell far. Whenever he awoke his face felt bruised, his mind confused. It wasn't just fatigue or a lack of sleep. Bill felt defeated.

Another shooting in the county. He felt as if he was being overrun like advance troops had overtaken his position and he had been forced to retreat. It might as well have been him who had been shot. First, a pair of murders and his deputy killed, and now two more folks had been shot. At least they were alive. The fat man and Frank. And did he have any idea who had done it? Did he know at all where to turn? No.

The truth was that he didn't much care. He could care and he could try, but where would it lead him? He didn't feel likely to find out who it was and there was absolutely no evidence to convict. And would it stop the next one? Wouldn't someone else just be shot in another few months? What could he do to stop it?

These weren't thoughts he liked but sitting still in his office, there were his only thoughts. He felt susceptible to his emotions. Like Logan.

Logan was an emotional kid. Always had been. Two years old and thunder would make him cry. Nine years old and he'd cry if no one talked to him for a few minutes. And the kids at school pestered him. Seeing his vulnerability. At least the kid had the guts to rebel. To run around with his hair like that, dressed like he was going to some weirdo funeral. That was the only reason he let him go on looking like that. Because he was making his way, despite being picked on for it.

And God bless the kid for putting up with him. Lord knows he could be getting a little more attention, but Bill didn't think it was his fault. He blamed it on Logan's whore of a mother. She's the one who should be around for him. She's the one who should be taking care of him, but she had moved off to Texas County to live with her gigolo. It was bad enough that she didn't love Bill and was willing to walk away from a twenty-year marriage, but to walk away from her fifteen-year-old son too? Whore.

She didn't call or contact them. Never even offered him a divorce. Just abandoned and embarrassed him. And now Bill had abandoned him as well. Left him alone to fend for himself. Welcome to the world, buddy. Things don't always go your way and sometimes the only one looking out for you is you. Maybe it would toughen him up, anyway.

Bill stood up then, straightened his belt. He would go see Frank. See how he was doing and see what he knows.

Frank looked worse than Bill felt. Bandages and tubes, machines beeping, eyes like drying grapes. It had been a while since Bill had seen him. Maybe since Terry's funeral, and there weren't no one looked good that day.

The patient didn't seem to notice the sheriff standing at the foot of the hospital bed, though Frank didn't look like he was asleep. His head was turned to the window with its shades drawn.

"Afternoon, Frank."

He turned his head, blinking. "Sheriff."

"They say you'll be alright."

"They say."

"How you feeling?"

"Like I been shot. Twice. Worse."

"Sorry 'bout it all, Frank." He choked on the words that came out like a confession. Bill was amazed by the truth of the statement.

Frank had turned his head back to the window.

"Listen," Bill walked around to the side of the bed, between Frank and the window. "I know you already talked to one of my guys, but I need you to tell me everything about what happened."

"Was that guy even out of school?"

Bill laughed. "Hey, I take who I can get."

"I can't tell you much."

"I know. I know." He gave him a minute. "Why were you there?"

"Ah, Bill…." He moved like he was going to shrug his shoulder, but winced severely and grabbed at his bandage.

"Frank, I'm after the guy that shot you. Not you. I know things've been hard for you. And sometimes we don't always do the right things by ourselves when we don't know where to go. What to do. No offense, but I ain't worried 'bout what you been up to."

"I don't know what's going on, Bill."

Bill didn't know Frank as anything more than Terry's hired man. He'd been around, always in the background. He knew that he was earnest and hard working. And he didn't know why he would fall so hard. It seemed obvious, though, that the guy had been into trouble. Trouble enough to get shot.

When Bill looked back at him, Frank was crying. His eyes looking like they'd been doused with water.

"I just wanted a way out. Something . . . something different."

"So, you were buying drugs?"

"I was going to. It wasn't like I'd done it before. But I couldn't drink enough to make it all stop."

"From who? Who were you there to meet?"

"I don't really remember, Bill. I don't remember much. For a long time now."

"How'd you know the guy? You met him somewhere before?"

"I'm sure I met him in some bar. Where else have I been?"

"Why The Bend, then. Why'd you go there?"

"Shit, Bill."

"You don't know who you was there to see? Was it him that shot you? Or someone else?"

"I don't know."

"Did you see him shoot the fat guy?"

Frank was sobbing, trying his best to curl up in his bed despite the bandages and wires.

Bill studied him, frustrated that the guy couldn't hold it together. What on earth was so devastating that it was worth bawling like this? Sure, Terry died, but was that enough to send the guy over the edge? So far that he can't remember a thing?

He let up for a minute, trying to understand how Frank could be feeling. Looking over the mess of sheets, the thinnest worn-out blanket, Bill tried to see himself in the same dark pit that Frank occupied. He saw the darkness, the cold, the isolation, but this pit was something to get out of. Not something to wallow in. If you fall down in the mud do you just roll around in it instead of getting up and cleaning yourself off?

Bill thought then of sleep, of sleeping in his office as if he'd been afraid to go outside, afraid to go home, to face Logan or the rest of the world because of the circumstances, the pit in which he had fallen. Maybe he'd been wallowing. Maybe he had just been lying in the mud.

He sat on the bed, shifting the angle of his holster that poked into the mattress. "Frank." Bill looked at Frank, who had stopped his sobbing and lay there now with his eyes closed. "You're still alive. You still have a life to live. When Jimmy Jiles shot Terry, God took her—not you. When this guy at The Bend, whoever he was, shot you, God spared you. Someone still wants you here, buddy. And you're gonna use up this life drinking and doing drugs? Laying here crying? We have things to do in our lives. And right now, Frank, you need to tell me who in the world shot you."

Frank's eyes looked at him like the eyes of a driver who saw a deer standing up ahead in the road. He obviously didn't know how to react.

"You remember something, don't you? Anything."

"Sure. I was looking for that guy. The fat guy. He must have told me that he hung out there--."

"Selling drugs."

"Sure. And if he weren't there, I'm sure someone else would be."

"And so you found him."

"I saw him. I remember going to him and then he fell. I guess he was shot."

"What did you do?"

"Nothing. I don't think I realized it."

"Well, what happened?"

"There was some guy. Some skinny guy. I don't know. He looked strange, moved around like a bug, all legs and arms."

"Like he was hopped up?"

"I guess."

"And what'd he do?"

"He shot him again."

"And you're standing there."

"I ran then."

"And he shot you."

"I guess."

"You didn't know the guy? Hadn't seen him before, in a bar or somewhere?"

"No. I don't think so."

"You remember anything else about him? Tattoos? What he was wearing?"

"It was a blur."

"Anything."

Trying to remember pained Frank. "I'm pretty sure his hair was long."

"Long, like a little long? Or long like a woman's?"

"Long like a woman."

"Good, Frank. That's good. I knew you'd remember something."

"Sorry."

"No, no. You did good."

Bill wanted to point out what good a little coherence can do. He wanted to drive home that Frank had better snap out of this and start living his life. But maybe it would be enough for him to know that he had helped, that his living was going to make a difference.

He stood. "That'll help, Frank." He turned and headed to the door, talking over his shoulder. "You get some rest and get yourself healed and I'll let you know what we find out. We'll find this guy. Thanks," he said as he stepped out the door.

39

Sam and Natalie's dining room table resembled a war room, or maybe the board room of a company in crisis. Folders lay on top of one another, pages overlapping, stacks of binders, copies of case files. It was all laid out on the table, all of his work as a one-man drug task force. Somewhere here was a clue that would lead Sam to whoever had done the shooting at The Bend. He stood in front of all this, his thick arms folded over one another, his muscles involuntarily flexed.

He had been through every conceivable target, and while at times it seemed like the county was full of meth-fueled lunatics, he couldn't find one of them that he believed might have done it. He'd watched and studied each of them, interviewed them and their associates. He knew them, what they did, what they thought. The truth was that they were all on notice and not a one of them was quite so reckless as to be out putting bullets into the competition and their customers.

The binders contained copies of closed case files going back five years. He'd made copies of every case he thought relevant, every case where drugs might have been involved, and cost the department a fortune in toner to get it done. He hadn't been through them all and while that fact taunted him as he stared at the table, he didn't believe they were relevant to today's objective. Somewhere in the open folders before him was what he was looking for.

If Jiles was still around, still active, he'd be the likely suspect. A history of violence, irrational reactions. And a .22. Jiles, though, had been moved up to the state prison. No trial. Thankfully.

Natalie appeared at the doorway, ice clinking in her glass of tea.

He tried to give her a look that might explain his confusion, but the look came out like a blank stare.

"Anything I can do to help?"

"Any of your friends crazy enough to do this?"

She chuckled.

He put his fingers on the open file of Round Ralph, considering for a moment that he'd missed a line of inquest. Maybe it had been a woman. Someone he'd been involved with. But that wasn't the case. Sam was pretty sure that Ralph wasn't much interested in women and was more likely getting enough action from buyers, men desperate enough for drugs to compromise themselves.

"You'll figure it out," she told him.

"I have to." He said this and continued staring at the table.

"You have any leads?"

He looked at her closely to read her intentions. "I know the sort of person who did it, but I don't know anyone who fits the bill."

"Then it's no one you know."

"Hmm." He began quickly closing all the folders, haphazardly, maybe angrily.

"I didn't mean anything."

"I know. But if it's no one I know, then why am I looking at all this shit?"

"It's just--," Natalie looked behind her, back into the kitchen. "Your instincts are usually more right than all of these details. All this is probably more distracting than anything."

She was probably right. He was trying to make someone fit the bill when no one did. Natalie was a smart one. It was one of the reasons he'd married her, one of the reasons he loved her today. Even though things weren't great.

She also knew him. She trusted him, knowing his nature more than he did sometimes. Maybe this was part of her current frustration. She knew him so well that she formed certain expectations as to who he was and how he might act under certain conditions. Natalie knew this idea of picking up where his father left off was important to him. She had known how driven he was to show his father that it could be done. So, then she was surprised that he would put this goal on hold in order to go back to being a cop. It had to be frustrating.

She didn't know what he was thinking, didn't know his fear. Of course, he'd never really had to explain himself to her. Even when things went bad for them in Pennsylvania, Natalie seemed to know exactly what he would do and how he felt.

When she had greeted him standing in the arched doorway, eyes alive with tears over the accusations being leveled against him by his own brother, she had never expressed an ounce of doubt. She had never focused an accusatory eye on him. She also knew that they had entered a state that wouldn't pass with time. It was something from which they were going to have to extricate themselves.

He had stood on his narrow front porch, him in his Pittsburgh PD uniform, two officers in their Ambridge PD uniforms, and answered their questions, reading both their guilt and their assumption of his guilt in their eyes. He'd had a hard time keeping his anger in check. He felt like striking at them for even entertaining the idea that he might molest his own niece.

They left him, unable to take him in with merely this accusation, and he went back inside, the adrenaline quickly draining from him and leaving him feeling empty and bruised.

He was deflated, singed by his new circumstance, and Natalie could have offered sympathy, she could have come to him, draped him in her long mud-colored hair, and maybe he would have cried. Maybe it would have been a release. But it wouldn't make him feel better. And Natalie knew it. Sam required action.

She would have packed all of their things and been ready to go when he came back if that had been possible. Instead, she had been on the phone.

She held the cordless phone in her hand when he walked into the kitchen. His belt and its supplies clanged a reverberating, tinny echo in the hard room as he sat them down on the table. "You're off Tuesday and Wednesday?" she asked.

Sam opened a cabinet, looked at its contents. "Yep."

"I made us an appointment with a realtor in Barnes County for Tuesday."

"Did you?" He swung the cabinet door closed but still held the handle.

"She said there was quite a bit available."

His mind began to spin through the details. How much land would they need? How much would they get for the Ambridge house? What would their budget be? He had pondered these things before, scribbling numbers, adding figures on paper napkins in restaurants. It was something guaranteed to make for good dinner conversation between them. Now, though, he needed more details.

He pulled a notepad out of another cabinet and tossed it on the table. "You have the last bank statement?"

"Sure, I'll get it for you."

The doctors found no evidence of trauma and her story never held, so no charges were ever brought. This never stopped his brother from appearing at his door drunk, the crickets in full night chorus, to bang, throw things and shout at the house. Curses and threats of violence. Sam did not speak to him. Or his father. But there was no hiding the for-sale sign.

They had already moved and were beginning to establish themselves on their new farm, running new fences, clearing brush, to establish decent pasture land, when the truth came to light. Natalie, who had still been talking clandestinely to her sister-in-law, told him that a boy down the street from Sam's brother, a skinny, silent sort of kid just entering adolescence, had been hauled off for repeatedly molesting a pair of twin sisters. They all knew of the kid. His father had been found dead in an alley in McKees Rocks. Rumor had it that he'd been caught offering money to boys for action around the baseball park.

Sam had felt relief in the information. He felt that at least in some way his name had been cleared. And he was glad for his niece, and likely his nephew, wouldn't be the subject of their abuse any longer.

Looking again over his mess of files, Sam thought of the way their perpetrator had been someone on the edges, a suspicious sort, someone he knew of but didn't suspect. Though they should have. Maybe that was the case here. Maybe it wasn't someone who should automatically be suspect, but someone ancillary, someone who didn't necessarily seem the type, didn't seem guilty enough for this sort of action, who might be just as likely.

He didn't need to look at the files again. His mind scanned these sorts of characters and he settled on one person who should have been obvious all along. "Harlan Lustig."

40

The music couldn't get loud enough. The drums beat against his chest, the guitar solos pierced his skull. And Logan still wanted it louder. Every half-step, that shift that begged for tears, ripped at him. The drums pulsed, and yet there was hollowness in the sound as if it occupied a large dark space. And he wanted more of it.

He had tried to sleep. Unable to reach Rachel, he had fallen into some sort of sleep-like stupor, but it clearly was not sleep. It offered none of the peace he sought. He was not able to escape a thing as he drifted from consciousness. Sliding from reality only allowed his imagination to take control of the facts. He saw her with her throat slashed lying at the bottom of a sinkhole. He saw her, bottom up, offering herself to the whole of the football team. He saw her snickering with her friends in St. Louis about this lame country kid with a small dick.

The only way to shut any of it off had been to get off the couch, go up to his room, and crank up the stereo. With his cheap speakers rattling on his desk, he pulled pictures from magazines and put them on the wall, seeking to paper the walls with photos of bands and musicians. Seeking to define himself through what appeared. He wanted his room to portray him, and the strange anguish he felt at this moment.

Every so often he went to the phone, dialed the ingrained number, waited for the switch to voicemail, and hung up. When he finally heard the delayed ring, he didn't exactly know what to do. He felt like hanging up again, not feeling in the mood to talk to her and not wanting his anger to dissipate, for his mood, so suited to the throbs and minor key of the music, to be altered. He stepped out into the hall.

A ring, mechanical and grating was cut short, and there was a hollow sound of rushing air, someone breathing.

"Hello?"

"Hello?"

"Rachel?"

"Huh?" Again, the whistling air, rapid breathing.

"It's Logan."

"Oh. Yeah. Hey." Her voice was, maybe, distracted.

"Where are you?"

"Home. Yeah, at home."

"You sure?"

She laughed. "How are you?"

"Where have you been?"

"Good. Wait, what?"

"Where have you been? I've been trying to call since I got off."

"Oh…."

He waited but she did not finish her response.

"Is it not a good time to talk?"

"It's alright, it's alright."

"Rachel?"

"Logan."

"Are you drunk or high, or what?"

"Oh…." He thought he heard her lips moving, but no sound came out. "Yeah, a little."

"Shit, Rach. What about me?"

"Yeah, sorry."

"Couldn't you wait for me?"

"I said I was sorry." Though the words sounded mean to Logan, her voice turned.

"I was just thinking we'd get together again."

The breathing again. Short gasps. Sobs?

"Rach?"

She was crying.

"Are you alright?"

Sniffles.

"What's wrong?" He didn't know if he felt sympathy, anger or plain curiosity.

"I'm sorry."

"What?"

"I…I…."

"Are you going to make me guess here? Because I've been imagining some pretty awful things all afternoon."

Rachel cried louder on the other end.

He was surprised at his anger, but he could not understand a reason to contain it.

"I went to that guy." A question, a statement, an apology.

"What?"

"For more."

"That fricking white trash meth dealer?"

"I just thought I'd get a little more."

"Without me?" He was still mad at her, mad at his exclusion, angry at the way it appeared she was letting him down. Just as he had imagined.

She didn't answer, though, and the digital whistle of her phone gave him a moment to think.

"Wait, what happened?"

"Oh...."

"What happened?"

"I can't say." The words came between sobs.

"Did he...?" He couldn't say it. To say it would be to imagine it. To imagine it might make it real.

"He...."

"That son of a bitch!"

"It's my fault, Logan. It's my fault."

"If he even touched you, it's not your fault."

"I didn't know what to do. He had a gun."

"A gun?" Logan saw for a moment his father's gun safe, the rifles and shotguns in their velvet notches. The pistols on the shelf above.

"He made me drive him. He thought the cops were looking for him." Her voice had calmed a little. Still shaky, but settled some, and Logan didn't want to stop her. "And do you know where he made me drive? Do you? Our house. Our abandoned house. But not the house. The barn. He's got a whole meth lab there in the barn. Think about that. The whole time, right there in the barn."

What was he supposed to say? What was he supposed to do?

"And then," tears again, "I was scared. And jonesing. I think, really bad. I don't know. I don't know why. I don't know. And so he gave me some. In the arm. I didn't know what to do. How to stop him. And then, I don't know." Crying harder now? "Logan. He was just there. And I was somewhere else. I couldn't stop him. I didn't even tell him to stop. I couldn't."

They each said nothing. The phone hissing their tears. Logan cried along with her, for her, for his inability to protect her. He felt like his hands had been cut off. Like whatever it is he wanted to do, he was simply incapable. It was surely something horrible for Rachel, but it burned Logan because it had happened to his girlfriend and there was nothing he could do to stop it. He was somewhere off to the side, a bystander, an observant party to the tragedies and injustices of life, and he could not stop the action before him.

Logan thought then of his father. Cuckolded and abandoned, and submissive the whole time. His father had let it happen, never lifted a finger to stop her, to right the wrongs, to correct the injustices. Well, he would not be his father. He would not just sit on his hands, helpless to the contingencies of the world. He would teach his father a lesson. He would fix things.

41

Across the Missouri plains, a storm had formed. A line of clouds built high and angry as they crossed from Kansas, over Springfield, headed east, pushing hot wind in front of it. Annette heard this wind pushing the house, mistakenly placed on the high ridge where every storm battered against its windows, while she looked down on the old sheltered house down the hill. She moved through the house, her feet shuffling from one room to the next, while she tidied up.

Everything had a place. A dirty house made her restless, while cleanliness made her feel at ease. Something Ralph never understood. And something her sole granddaughter didn't appear to understand. The girl was up there in her room (a pit, that room), sobbing. The girl was all drama. She knew it before inviting her down. But Annette was not going to entertain her. Walked all over her mother, that girl did, but now she was here and she could sit up there and bawl her eyes out and it wouldn't make a lick of difference. Let her see that the world doesn't revolve around sixteen-year-old girls. There are other lives to be led, work to be done, houses to be cleaned.

The crying, vibrating like it was through the home's frame, a chorus with the wind and darkening sky outside, rattled Annette. She had been sitting calmly in her old chair, the yellow chenille worn thin and soft, looking for a recipe for preparing kidneys that she knew she had, though it wasn't with her recipes and wasn't in the orange cookbook with the missing spine. Maybe it was in the one that the Junior League put together. But she couldn't sit there and have any peace with the house being torn apart from inside and out.

She wasn't cleaning, though. She was standing now at the back door, looking through the panel of glass, watching the wind whip the trees that lined the creek, and the ones around the old house and barn. The wind caught each of the big leaves, pushing them and their hundred-year-old trees with its will. And the old house, its white planks peeling, window frames no longer true, sat still above the movement. A graying apparition in the violent air.

He was there. She felt him there. Just down there. Ralph banging around that house like he'd never left. Drinking himself into some rage that caused him to storm from one room to the next, shouting curses at her. But she wasn't there. No, she was up the hill with her daughter and her mother. The women together and the lone man down the hill.

She'd still been his wife. She changed his sheets, laundered his clothes, even picked up, throwing out the empty bottles. She did these things when he wasn't around. And maybe she could have made him dinners, but he could have been a man enough to come up the hill and join the women for dinner. But he didn't.

He could come up here now. Even if Ralph, spirit, apparition, ghost, zombie, whatever, was down there in that house this second, he might curse her name, haunt her dreams, raise the hair on her neck and bring sweat to her face as she slept, but he wasn't about to cross the pasture to see her. Maybe, maybe, she was just going to go down the hill and tell him to finally go away.

42

Large raindrops smacked against the windshield of the cruiser and the wipers with their stalled heartbeat rhythm turned in their arcs to briefly clear them away before the whole process repeated. It was a strong rain, one that made quick puddles in the street, streams out of gutters, and turned everyone out of sorts. Thunder cracked overhead and people on the Sheridan streets were running for cover.

Bill drove while Sam sat in the passenger seat, in his hand a paper on which several car descriptions, license plates and, if known, the owner's name. It was a list of the cars seen outside Harlan Lustig's place and they were determined to find one of the cars, one of the owners, to see if they could find out where Lustig was cooking.

When Bill had emerged from the county's little single-story hospital where he had visited Frank Redbird, he immediately got on the radio to look for Sam. Bill didn't particularly want to have to turn to Sam, but he would likely have an idea of who they were looking for just from Frank's description.

It confirmed Sam's suspicion and they knew they had their suspect.

Sam was just then slowing his car in front of Lustig's trailer.

"Now don't be a damn fool and go storming in there."

"Not at all. I just want to see if he's around."

Lustig's car was there, but under darkening skies, no lights were on inside. So, the two met up to try and find a lead.

Bill turned the cruiser in a large arc into the parking lot of the Country Mart. It was as good a place as any to find folks who weren't big on being in one place for very long.

In the first row of cars a woman, white-blond hair, an infant carrier, a cigarette dangling from her mouth, was splashing down the blacktop.

"Her," Sam's voice boomed louder than necessary. "CeeCee Dawkins."

Bill cut off her approach to the store. He rolled down his window an inch and told her, "Get in."

She brought into the car the smell of a wet ashtray. CeeCee's breathing was rapid.

"How's your mother," Bill asked her when he parked the car.

"Good. She's going to Branson this weekend with her quilt club, though I don't know that she wants to spend that much time with them. Four of 'em to a room, I guess."

Bill exchanged a glance with Sam, who was giving him the lead. Though he was obviously eager to begin interrogating.

"And how's your boy?"

"Oh, fantastic! Still can't call me mama, but with his cry, I guess he doesn't need to."

"Harley?" Sam looked at her directly and forcefully. Bill felt a little sorry for her.

"Huh?" She looked at Bill.

"You're buddy, Harley. Where is he?"

"How the hell should I know?"

"Miss Dawkins."

"Sorry, Sheriff. I barely know the guy."

"We know you buy drugs from him, so there's no need to hide anything." Sam.

"You don't know anything."

"And how's your boy again?"

CeeCee looked at the child sleeping in his car seat. She rocked him a little.

"Where's he cook?" Bill.

"He said something about a barn."

"Great. Where?"

"I dunno. Ain't been there."

"What else he tell you?"

"It's some old abandoned place. Empty house. All overgrown."

"And that's where he cooks."

"I don't know. But, hey, you didn't hear anything from me."

"Of course." Bill.

"Anything else?" Sam.

"Just that I don't know that guy's got it all together."

"Probably right." Sam.

"Alright. Don't go near him again."

"No, no." She pulled the car seat to her and prepared to exit the cruiser.

"Wait a second." Sam reached his hand to grab hold of the child carrier's handle. "You got his number?"

CeeCee looked at the child, at Bill. "Yeah."

"Call him. Tell him you want to score." Sam.

"Score?"

"You know."

CeeCee did as directed, the nervousness in her voice sounding little different than the normal worked-up voice of a meth addict looking for a fix. When she learned that he wasn't at home, she gave both Sam and Bill a look. As if she knew what they were up to, that they were going to catch him, and that it was more or less her fault. That she would have to accept the blame.

Bill felt bad for her again. It didn't matter to him that she was a meth addict or that she was neglecting her child. Her face showed a defeated sort of guilt. It was worse for her than it probably would have been if they had busted her for possession. Even though there is probably enough evidence in her purse to haul her away. To get her child taken away.

He didn't like this feeling. He was not generally a sympathetic man. Sometimes this didn't help him in his role. He was nice. People would say he was kind. But if someone was in a bind he didn't much care about the extenuating circumstances. Couldn't put himself in someone else's shoes. Terry was better at that.

Once they had received a call for an attempted robbery, in the south of the county. It was a convenience store outside a patch of houses called Alta. Of course, the assailant was long gone, but he didn't get away with any cash. The owner-operator had raised an aluminum bat at the kid and he left in a hurry. They had a decent enough description for Terry to have a good idea of who he was.

About a mile outside Alta, a piece of shadowed property was populated with one house and three trailers. A chain-linked section in the front yard appeared to act as a holding pen for children, containing at this moment two shirtless boys, four or five-years-old, flinging colored plastic toys at each other.

Terry drove while Bill sat as a passenger. She pulled the car slowly into the yard. Their rolled-down windows brought in the sound of the crunching gravel. She stopped the car on the grass next to one of the trailers, within sight of a lanky character taking a leak against a chicken coop.

"Fletcher." Terry stood up out of the car.

Bill saw the boy turn, crew cut and wide-set blue eyes that darted from inside a freckled face, searching for a way out. He was probably barely fourteen, but his spare form made him light on his feet, and Bill had to put himself into motion quickly to cut off his escape. When Bill was close enough to the running teenager, he threw a leg out into the kid's whirring limbs and he somersaulted into the grass. And before he could scramble to his feet, Bill seized an arm, squeezed it and yanked the boy upward. The bones of his upper arm were there under Bill's fingers as he dragged him to the car. He could squeeze, he could twist, he could cause an injury from which it would take the boy weeks to recover.

"Now, what reason would you have to run, young Mr. Fletcher?" Terry asked.

"You guys are the cops." The kid squinted into the sun to see them.

"Been down to Alta today?"

"Why would I go down there?"

"To hold up the store."

He smiled at them.

"You gonna deny it, John?"

"I didn't say nothin'."

"You didn't even wear a mask. Sunglasses. Anything. You think there's another kid around here looks like you?"

Bill, in his supporting role, took the handcuffs from his belt and let them dangle. "I guess we better take him down there. Get an ID."

"It wasn't like I got anything." The boy's voice had gone up in pitch.

"Still a crime, John."

His eyes squeezed, trying not to cry.

"Why'd you do it?"

"I broke David's PlayStation and my mom ain't gonna buy a new one and I gotta get him one or he said he's gonna break my nose and he will."

"Sounds like you're in trouble." Bill was sarcastic. As if he was concerned.

"He's your cousin; he's gonna break your nose?"

"He broke his brother's leg, threw him out the back of the truck."

"You're in trouble, buddy." Bill chuckled a little as the kid began to sniffle.

"Well, listen," Terry pulled the kid up from where he leaned against the car. "I want you to tell your momma what you did today."

John Fletcher hollered in protest.

"You tell her what you did today or I'll come back here and haul you in. I'm gonna call her tonight," Terry looked at Bill, "and you better have told her or I'm gonna have to tell her that I'm coming down to arrest you and take you to jail."

Standing straight now, the boy looked at his feet.

"You didn't even have a gun, did you?" Bill asked.

The boy put his hand under his shirt, faking the look of a gun.

"You gonna do what I say?"

He nodded.

"Don't make a promise you can't live up to."

"I swear."

"You screw this up and I'll make it hard on you." She pushed him out of the way and opened the door.

"Don't wait until after dinner because I call and you ain't told her, I'm coming for you."

It wasn't how he would have done it. Let the kid stew in jail awhile. But Terry always had a little more compassion than him. And maybe she would have felt bad for CeeCee, too. Or maybe he was just getting soft.

Then again, he hadn't been easy on Frank although that poor kid probably needed it more than anyone. Could have shown a little heart. Guy lost the only woman he knew best, next to his momma. It was bad enough for Bill to have lost Terry. At least he didn't depend on her for a living. For his whole existence. But he did rely on her, didn't he? Wasn't that why things were this turned around now? Why he didn't know what to do about anything? Because she wasn't around. Why he had turned to Sam?

Sam was a good man, really knew what he was doing. The whole county's better off now that he's working for the department. Certainly, Bill's lucky to have him around. But did he have to rely on him the same way he had leaned on Terry? Did he really need someone else to prop him up? Maybe he really wasn't that good. Maybe he didn't really deserve to be sheriff. Or maybe he'd just done it so long that he knew better than to work himself to death. Maybe he had done it so long that he couldn't care about things as much as Terry or Sam. Maybe Sam would make a better sheriff.

Sitting next to Sam in his car, the thought ate at Bill. It wasn't like the guy wasn't qualified, but what did he know about Barnes County? Did he know who was who? Did he know the history of all the families? Did he know what it was like before he came back? Oh, sure he'd seen it as a kid, but his family up and left. He wasn't about to let this guy weasel in and take his job. Sure, things ain't been great but he was not about to just fold up shop and go home, spend the rest of his days sitting around that dark house.

It's funny how someone your own age can seem so much older, Sam thought as he rode shotgun in Bill's cruiser, the rain hammering the roof. The directions to the location of Lustig's lab were scrawled in his thin, scratchy handwriting on yellow paper in his lap. It was possibly his excitement that made him feel youthful. The sense of anxiety and anticipation made him nervous. And they were speeding to the site now. They weren't going in with guns blazing, though Sam felt his bravado so tuned up that it was what he desired. Surveillance was key, though. He and Bill agreed. Watch for a little bit, make sure he's there and alone. But was the man next to him excited at all?

Maybe that was the problem. If the sheriff doesn't even get riled at the prospect of capturing a man that tried to kill a couple of people, how the hell is he supposed to provide for the safety of the county's residents. Sam saw himself for a minute standing atop a bandstand, red, white, and blue banners decorating its edges, a crowd before him, listening eagerly as he explained with words earnest and wise that he was better suited to the role of county sheriff than the man who had served in that position for the last twenty years. It wasn't his nature, Sam thought, talking in front of people, shaking hands and kissing babies, but if he was the best man for the job than it was his responsibility.

He could do it, he thought. Lead a team of deputies, establish a stronger sense of order, set new priorities, petition the state or the federal government for assistance with the meth problem. If he wasn't too old. Maybe he didn't have the patience for it either. Maybe he didn't believe in the goodness of people. How could he then try and do the best for people who were selfish and generally ill-intentioned to begin with? Would he have the energy or the patience for it? And would Natalie be willing to put up with any of it?

Ah, there was the real question. It didn't matter what he wanted to do. He was only one vote in a two-vote democracy. To pass anything required not only a majority vote but also a unanimous vote. He was pushing his luck already, he knew. She was unhappy and making him unhappy, and any greater commitment was going to make things worse. It would have to be worth it.

He might have resented her for resenting him. Her disdain had lasted so long that it seemed a permanent fixture, a permanent facet to her expression. It hardly made him want to leave his police work to come spend his days at home, working on their ranch. It was likely what kept him working so hard, especially when he was given more attention and respect there. At least that used to be the situation before Terry died.

Terry's smile was always bright and eager. No one would call her excessively chipper or cheerful, but she was always extremely nice. At least to Sam. Before her death, her murder, he had wondered if she liked him. Liked him, in that way. He came, though, to doubt that, believing instead that he must have felt some sort of attraction to her. It was the only way he could have ever thought that she had some sort of thing for him.

It was all ridiculous, he knew. In conscious states, he had it all in perspective. He knew where his energies were focused, knew what made sense. In the back of his mind, though, and at those moments when sleep advanced or withdrew, he found himself thinking of her. Thinking of her smile, her treatment of him, the jokes she told, how when expletives spilled from her mouth they sounded not vile but nearly elegant. He never thought of touching, never a consideration of consummation. He didn't have to. What filled his chest, what lingered with him after spending time in her company, in actuality or imagination, left him feeling bold, energized with sleepy eyes.

Her death stripped this from him. She was suddenly gone and thoughts of her made him aware of the void she left in him. Work became merely work, and home became even less pleasant. Natalie never made any attempt to console him. She certainly didn't know of his need for consolation. Terry's death only confirmed to Natalie the dangers of the job and the lack of need Sam had for the work.

It wasn't truly her fault. But what was he to do about it? He didn't feel ready to abandon his work, abandon the county to the leadership of the current sheriff. What would happen to all of his work? Wouldn't all the dealers and meth-heads just flourish? Who was going to do anything about them? What did it have to do with him, Natalie would argue. It was not his responsibility. Not anymore. He had put in his time. Dedicated and risked his life to make the world a better place. Now it was time to live simply, to spend his time on the land, with the earnest simplicity of animals and the seasons. Not with the vilest people God produced. Not with those who lacked regard for decency, for the lives of others.

She had a point. It was the excitement that ran through him as they hurried to apprehend a man suspected of attempted murder that she didn't know, that she couldn't understand.

Without even surveying the scene, Sam imagined the ways of overtaking their suspect, bursting through the grayed boards of an old barn door, overwhelming him, shoving him face-first to the ground, the end of his pistol pressed against the base of the perp's head. Sam dropped all other contemplation, any consideration of Bill, of ascending to sheriff, of Terry, of Natalie, and focused on how the next hour might play out.

44

The sheets around him were scratchy and stiff and his awareness of them was, he felt, too acute. Frank was too aware of their coarse fibers, the way the top sheet did not fall over him but instead lay on him like paper. Despite the medication for pain, his body was very apparent to him under the sheets. He had been shot in the shoulder and the leg.

Lucky, the doctor told him he was, but Frank couldn't understand what that meant. Things could have been worse was the implication. And that didn't make any sense.

Each of his wounds felt to him hot and heavy. Two steaming stones pressing on him, keeping him fixed to the bed. These wounds, though, were only part of his sensation of being. He was equally aware of his hands, how they were cold and dry, the skin catching on the blanket on which they lay. His head, too, was pressed into a pillow that seemed made of plastic.

He thought he might cry again. Each time the nurse came in, briskly moving, checking the IV, the monitor, looking more alive, more vibrant than he imagined people could be, he would cry when she spoke to him. Her kindness, merely asking him how he was feeling, brought tears before he could respond.

He didn't know what to do with it when she spoke to him. Her concern seemed misplaced, mistaken. She should not feel for him. It had been difficult enough when Bill talked to him. Frank did not feel kindness from Bill; instead, he felt shame before him. What had happened was a product of his own making. He had tried to be earnest, nice himself. This was the sheriff, though, the most upright citizen around, who had himself suffered at Terry's loss, and Frank could not help thinking of what he'd been up to, how he'd been living his life, and the emptiness, the utter misery he felt.

Bill had offered some sort of sympathy, some attempt at understanding. As if he was trying to perk him up, to lift him out of the mud. No, like he was telling him he should pick himself up out of the mud. Lot of help that might do. Frank was still concerned with one thing Bill had said: "God spared you."

Did he? Who is to say? What gave him the right? And why on earth should he? Frank wasn't one to think about these sorts of things. He'd come to learn that in life you have to make your own way. He couldn't believe that there was someone upstairs pulling strings, making things happen. If that were the case, what would be the point of anything? If everything was decided by outside forces, no one would have to take responsibility. Not for their own actions. Not for anything.

And if he did believe all of this, it wouldn't mean anything good at all. He would see God's sparing him as innately cruel. And how could he believe in a cruel God? If anything, he believed in a benevolent God or gods. Gods that made the earth, the moon, the stars, the plants, and the animals. And sometimes gods could be vengeful. He knew God to believe in justice. He, or they, could create storms, plagues, pests, vermin, and maybe we, or someone, deserved it.

Frank didn't want to believe that any God had chosen to take Terry, whether to punish him or to be cruel. He had tried to live a hard-working, simple life. He had stayed away from what others would call sin. He had, though, lust in his heart. Lusted after another man's wife.

Bob Stegman's death had not been an easy thing for Frank. He had turned from a strong, fear-making man to a bed-ridden child. It was a shock and it had untethered Frank. And what was worse about it all was seeing Terry lose her tough veneer. It made her tougher, really, but he also saw through the cracks, saw how she hurt inside. As strong as his feelings might have been for Terry, there was no celebrating that Bob had died.

Bill's statement implied that he should be grateful that he hadn't died. Frank wasn't quite sure that he was happy that he had been spared. Wouldn't that have been the easy way? Wouldn't his death have released him from this earth and allowed him to float among the stars? And wouldn't that be better?

Frank was no longer sure that death would mean deliverance. Thinking again about being shot, about the chance that either bullet strayed any distance to sever an artery or pierce his heart, made him feel as if he'd stepped off the edge of a high rocky ridge. This fear was a stronger emotion than the misery that had engulfed him for these many months.

The nurse breezed into his room again. She brought with her the scent of lilac, of juniper, of things alive and vibrant, things absorbing and expiring. Frank studied her as she pushed buttons on the machines, held for a moment in her hand the paper tape that fed out from the machine like a long pale tongue. Her eyes were blue, like clear skies, and around them, stretching into her pale skin were thin wrinkles, creases of flesh. These lines had come with age, from smiling, from staring into the sun. The skin of her face was pale, covered lightly with make-up that dulled the textures, the fluctuations in flesh tones, the maps of capillaries that ran over her cheekbones. The natural color of her lips, a strong red, drew a strong contrast with her pale skin. And he could make out a few light-colored hairs above her lip.

The tears came back. Her presence seemed to make his core shake, like a jolt of electricity. She appeared to him more real than anything he'd ever seen. More real, more alive. And Frank didn't know what to do with that fact. It made him aware of a clarity, an achievable life that he'd never come across. It meant life, real life, was possible. Here before him was an example. And he saw her, saw this life, more clearly than he'd seen anything. Ever. Or, at least, as long as his mind could recall.

45

The gun safe was in an unused bedroom of the house and all Logan had been required to do was turn the heavy handle and, with a solid clunk of metal, he had access to any weapon he needed. Reaching, he contemplated taking the whole arsenal, but the contemplation required conscious thought, leaving the immediacy of his impulse. He grabbed a pistol from the shelf, shoved in a full clip as he'd seen his father do a million times.

He had run, then, in the beginning of the downpour to the hidden car, keeping his mind narrowed on his intent. The car slipped and slid in the rain, but he wheeled it into the driveway of the old house at an angle. He leaped from the car and for only a moment he looked at the house, the disintegrating shelter which had served as a refuge for him and Rachel. It was a place of education and romance and in the pouring rain it looked only like a house on verge of collapse, something deliberately left in the open to weather the elements, to be reclaimed by the earth.

The barn was in worse shape. Surrounded by vehicles and implements turning steadily to rust, the barn itself was being actively overtaken, vines had climbed its north side and hung over the eaves on the nearside. A tree had grown up against the large barn door, the doors themselves beginning to shift and buckle inward over time. A path through weeds led to a door to which Logan ran.

He rammed his shoulder into the door and it gave easily. Logan practically fell into the room, both arms swinging the gun around looking for a target. He turned to a voice shouting "Whoa" and a pair of long, bare arms flailing and fired once. It came easily, with no great effort, but before he intended it and he missed his target.

"Christ, kid!" The drug dealer, Harley, his bony arms crossed defensively over his chest, stood in the middle of a room built for milking cows. A trough lined one side and a ditch in the concrete on the other to catch their defecation. It was filled, though, with junk as his trailer had been. Stolen goods. And his lab. A smell that coated and burnt his nostrils.

"Don't shoot that fucking thing again!"

"Shut up!"

"Now, wait a minute. You come in here with guns blazing like you're looking to kill someone and I'm supposed to be calm. Get out."

"Shut up."

"Now, did you come here to rob me? Huh? We can make some arrangements. I'm not making any promises. I can't say I won't track you down and kill you while you sleep, but you want to walk out of here with some dope, we can make that happen."

"I don't want any of your drugs."

"You weren't exactly complaining when you came by with your hot little girlfriend, but if it's cash you want--oh, wait." A smile lit up the guy's face and his dirty hands scratched a week-old growth of beard. "That's why you're here."

"Shut up."

"Shit, did she tell you about that? Aw, man. Not a smart girl. Why is it chicks can't keep their mouths shut?"

"You fucker!"

"Oh, wait a minute. Don't you go blaming me for what happened. She didn't exactly come to me waving cash, you know what I mean. She knew what it was going to cost her."

"You raped her."

"Should I consult my lawyer? No. I don't believe she ever said no or made any attempt to protest. My lawyer says that constitutes consent."

"Bullshit! You took advantage—raped her. Because she wanted drugs."

"You know anything about the free-market, kid? She came to me for something I had to sell and she was willing to pay the price. Shit, with her I would have been willing to negotiate. But I tell you what. She'll be back."

"That's not true."

"Oh, it is. She might have been all ashamed and sad for you, but when she gets that itch again and there's no cash in her pocket, she'll still come back. And I'll be happy to have her."

"You son of a bitch, you fucking son of a bitch. It's not right." Logan began to explode with all the injustices suffered, all of the things that were wrong with the world, unjust wars, genocide, lynchings, torture, cruelty, racism, sexism, and more.

"That's the way it goes, kid."

"You think that's how life is supposed to be just because people like you make it that way. It's supposed to be good. Life is supposed to be good but people turn it to shit. You think you got some right to pick on other people, to take advantage of girls, to make everyone live by your rules."

"Hey, I have no doubt that people treat you like shit. That's just how things are."

"No. It's not true. You pick on people because it makes you feel better, because you think you become a bigger, stronger person because of it. And if you didn't you'd be tiny and insignificant. Like the rest of us."

"I don't know who you think I am, kid. But I ain't one of them."

"Yes, you are. An asshole like all of them."

"Wait a fucking minute, kid. You think I'm here because the world treated me better than it did you? Holy shit are you wrong."

"You think you got some right to rape teenage girls."

"Hey, I just know how the world is. Fuck man, I'm just following the rules of the game."

"They're your rules."

"Don't blame me because people pick on you 'cos you look like a freak. And it ain't my fault that your girl was willing to trade pussy for drugs."

Logan felt himself grow flush, his skin hot like fresh-laid tar. It was just wrong. The world was wrong. Things were wrong and he was going to change things. "No, I'm changing the fucking rules. Changing the rules. No more. It's no longer okay for fucking ballplayers to run the school, to beat up other kids without having to pay for it."

"Alright then."

"And it's not okay to trade drugs for sex. Because it might get you shot."

Harley put his arms over himself in an 'X'. "Slow down, man."

Logan felt then that it was up to him to set things right. To correct some of the wrongs on his own. His father may be sheriff, but he sure as hell wasn't here to protect him, to enforce the laws, to even look out for his safety. And his mother? Well, at least this guy would learn not to take some other guy's girl. At least somebody was going to learn a lesson. It was up to him to do it.

He raised the gun again to shoot, but the bare-chested lanky form darted and Logan spun and fired the gun.

46

The sound of the gun made him feel cold and bare. A little defenseless. As if he'd never put clothes on again after the girl left. He dove to the ground, away from the bullets that followed. Bursting. Tiny powerful explosions that held in that sound all their potential, the ability to take lives, to puncture skin, organs, ripping wide holes through living tissues. It was also like a sharp concussion, an aluminum bat against his head. The sounds, repeating, were more than the movement of airwaves, a wide band of frequencies exploding from the gun, also riding the waves was something that felt to Harley like reality. Not so much like it turned a switch in him and he suddenly saw everything how it really was. More like a sensation of a separate distinct existence from the one in which he was entrenched. He saw things like through a hole in a curtain.

He saw in each sound a world where things weren't gritty, where his hands didn't smell of chemicals, and old cigarettes, his teeth didn't hurt, where when the sun shone bright but didn't hurt his eyes, where the day itself didn't feel like some burden that pressed itself upon him in each waking moment. Somewhere, at some time, his life had been like that. As a child had he ever seen the potential in life? Had he ever looked at the full world, the big empty sky and thought that it was all open to him? Or had he always felt in those moments guilt over such notions? Life was based on hard facts, on numbers on a page, by a calculation on a calculator, with its final equals sign putting it all down to a definitive answer. How could he, at the beginning of a wide-open summer day, think of all the mysteries and adventures the day could hold? There was always a lot waiting for him.

He had rejected order and replaced it, though, with another order.

Drinking and taking drugs took him close to that idea of a sky so blue that it begged to be soared though. Indeed, at times at the height of some intoxicated evenings, it felt as if he was up there with the geese, gliding among the wisps of clouds. Icarus, he fell hard. There was always a morning after and all that came with it, questioning what he had done, the slow filter of memories, a pain that he knew was fundamental.

And all of it had brought him here to be crawling on the concrete floor, among the hay and dirt and grease and manure, while some equally burdened teenager aimed a gun at him—trying to kill him. The kid looked awfully pained and awfully determined. His eyes may have been filled with tears, but his eyebrows pointed together in anger, and his lips were twisted with purpose. Harley felt bad for him. Surely, he understood some of what he was going through. This kid had an anger, though, that Harley had never been able to manufacture. He wanted a way to calm the kid, to steal his anger, to leave him only with his sadness. He couldn't think then of any words that could get through the tears, the rushing of blood in his head, the successive explosions of the gun in his head.

He might have said something about how fucked up the world was, about how, yeah, it'll never treat you right. About how women make it seem better, but only for a little bit before they turn it all around on you and make things worse for you. About how that damned idea of love ain't nothing but a ruse. They get you to believe in it, and you're convinced, but man, there ain't nothing there. Not inside, not outside. Yeah, kid, it's all rigged against you, but what you gonna do about it? You gonna swing that gun on everything that screws you over? On the bird that shits on you, on the car that cuts you off, the cop who pulls you over, the book you paid for and wasted two weeks reading only to realize there was no goddamn ending and no goddamn point to the whole thing, on the clouds making it rain when you're stuck walking, on the TV when the newscaster tells you some other shitty piece of news like how the President thinks God granted him the right snoop through your drawers when your sleeping and your thoughts while you're on the shitter?

No, kid, you're better off realizing now that it is one shitty place and things are rigged against the folks who actually give a shit, but you figure all that out and you've got a leg up. You learn the rules, what you can get away with, and you'll do better than those guys that just roll along. And, really, that's most folks.

He might have said these things, but who was he to say anything? Like he had it all figured out. He was the one being shot at now. The one who somebody was out to kill when he killed three others, including a cop. The one who shot two guys, just like a day ago, and didn't even know if they were alive or dead. The one who didn't think it mattered either way.

There was, then, on the table where his gear was all laid out, glass jugs, hoses, a cookstove, propane tank, an explosion. A fluid flame fell over him on the ground, splashing around him, over him, like raindrops lit up by the sun. He screamed. He was screaming. A second, larger explosion followed. Everything, he felt, was consumed by flame.

47

"Either he's there and we can finally have this out, he can finally explain it all to me, and I can tell the man that I'm sorry things turned out the way they did. I really am. Or else he's not there. There's no ghost in the old house and I can put it all to rest. And sleep again." Annette had explained this to Rachel even though her granddaughter seemed barely to be paying attention. Barely seemed to be awake anyway.

Either way, she pulled the girl up out of bed and told her she had to walk her down to the old house. Rachel had been resistant but Annette told the ungrateful girl to do as she was told. And she did.

They were nearly to the house, Annette gripping Rachel's soft elbow when she heard the noises. Gunshots. He's there, she thought. Shooting himself. Over and over. Her companion and guide didn't even seem to notice, which confirmed for Annette that Ralph was here for her only. Surviving somehow on the guilt that lived in her still.

Tears were in her eyes and the walking had been difficult. She was winded and tired, the hem of her dress wet, the large high boots chaffed her calves. When the explosion came it nearly made her fall to the ground. As she watched boards and flames shoot out from the barn, she thought this was it. Ralph had opened the gates of Hell to drag her back with him. The flames leaped like talons, like outstretched hands, like the souls of the damned, including her husband, reaching for her, to take her in, to make her one of them.

"I'm sorry, Ralph." She sat on the wet grass. "Sorry. I couldn't. I couldn't be with you. I know it was wrong to leave you here all alone, abandon you as if you weren't my husband, as if you weren't the father of our only child. But Ralph. You were a drunk, Ralph. Always drunk.

And you were not nice and you were not kind. And Mama needed me. You knew that. I couldn't leave her all alone. She was sick and she needed me. And you were here all by yourself. I know why you did what you did. I understand; I do. But was it my fault, Ralph? Was it? If it was, if it really was my fault, then take me. I'm ready. Sorry, Rachel. Tell your mother I love her. I guess it's my time."

Her granddaughter was trying with desperation to pull Annette to her feet. "We've got to get back, Grandma. Come on. Don't talk crazy. Let's get back before something else explodes."

Annette let herself be lifted up. "You see it?"

"Let's get back."

"It's real."

"Grandma, the barn's on fire," Rachel shouted. "We've gotta get back."

"It's on fire." She smiled. "He's not here for me, hon. He's not. The devil himself is here to take your Grandpa back with him. To take him away."

48

Bill and Sam had just been walking low along the fence-line trees across the road from the abandoned farm when the gunshots began. Bill had whispered loudly as he could into his radio to send every damn person they had. In an awful hurry. Something was going down and they weren't going to let anyone get away, and they weren't going to get any deputies shot.

He waited patiently for Sam to finish with the binoculars before he studied the scene. He couldn't make out anything in the barn, didn't recognize the car that sat in front, and didn't see anything that would prohibit them from getting closer.

He waved 'come on' to Sam and jumped the fence and ran at an angle across the road and to the shelter of the side of the old house.

The rain had stopped but everything was soaked, including his pant legs. He noticed this as he tried to catch his breath, at the same time as he noticed the ache in his knees from the impact of the activity. There was rarely a time that he wasn't aware of a steady ache, but now a bone-aching throb radiated up from his knees to his hips.

Sam, by his side now, moved with comparative ease.

Bill was just beginning to drift into contemplative thoughts when there was a small explosion from within the barn. He was just grabbing at his radio to call for fire help when there was a second explosion that shot a hole in the old boards and balls of smoke and flame out of every hole, crack, and crevice.

And nearly simultaneously the door burst open and a figure came running out. Bill drew his gun and advanced on the person.

"Drop the gun. Drop the gun!" Bill had his own gun raised, watching a gun in the person's hand, waiting for any movement in that hand. Ready to fire.

"Drop the gun," he demanded again when the figure stopped. Bill looked up to the face, preparing to assess the potential for a standoff. What he saw initially made no sense. He saw the rain-drenched face of his child, his hair worn long in the front, laying down wet to his chin. But it couldn't be. It had to be some manifestation of his mind, something suddenly making him aware of his neglected son. Some image that conjures a subconscious connection.

The image did not fade. The figure before him, beyond the sight of his gun, was his pistol-carrying son.

"Logan."

The boy shook, but he didn't drop the gun. His eyes were wide, shifting from his father's face to the gun pointed at him. The eyes were his mother's eyes, his own eyes, the eyes that had once looked at him with admiration, with love. They weren't just eyes, not just someone's eyes, but they were eyes that were his, a part of him.

"I need you to put it down. Logan, the gun. Drop it to the ground."

Logan twisted his wrist and looked down at the gun as if he hadn't noticed that he held it. And then it was as if he was considering something. Something.

Bill rushed him then, tackling him into the grass. The gun fell out of Logan's hand.

On the ground, he looked the boy in the eye. With a look that said it would all be okay. No matter what, it would all be okay.

49

Sam pushed Bill and his son away, looking back at the barn and steeling himself for what might be necessary. There was another person in the burning barn. The flames were bright against a sky still dark. He would risk his life to save a man, a criminal, an attempted murderer. He would.

Taking off his jacket, to put it to his mouth and nose to protect himself from the smoke, Sam couldn't help thinking about death. He could die. Sure, it could happen every day. An accident. A shooting. It was always a risk. An elevated one, to be sure, because of his profession, but he usually felt nothing more than an occasional spike in the level of danger. Here he was, though, putting himself at risk, stepping into it and it made him think about his death.

Sam had seen people die. Stepped over the dying body of his friend. And he knew that however horrible it might be, it would eventually be over. And suffering would cease. The question was about what he was going to leave behind. Natalie would be furious. Oh, would she. She'd probably go out and shoot every one of those cows to spite him. For all she'd done, her sacrifices, for putting up with him continuing to work despite his pledges and promises, it really would be wrong for Sam to get himself killed.

It would mean his plan failed, that his attempt to make up for his father's failures would have failed as well. He had been unwilling to go all in, to push all of his chips across the table. He had been attempting to have it both ways, to keep the security of a job he knew and understood while also run a farm on the side. And if he died today by storming into a blazing barn, he would have failed both. And he would have failed Natalie.

He had made a commitment to her and he had been failing to keep it. It was wrong. Sam tried to envision Natalie without him and he saw her storming around the house, eyes wet and hot, sadness and anger together. And he knew it was only a portrayal. It wasn't real empathy because he didn't know what that sort of loss was like. He had lost Terry and that had been bad. Bad in its own way. He had lost a friend, someone he worked with every day, someone he knew well, he was close to. And it had been hard. But her loss was something different than losing a good friend. It was losing someone who treated him the way she did. Someone who made him feel the way she did. Someone who looked at him with some sort of intimate admiration. And it was maybe this that he missed more. It had been losing this that had pained him and he felt guilty for it.

These thoughts had pounded at him as the flames reached at him, blasted him and his anxiety peaked. The time had come, though, and with his left hand holding the bundle of cloth to his face, he hurried to the open door.

Before he could enter he was confronted by the image of a man on fire, a figure in flame that stumbled out of the dark. From behind the flames that ran up the man's chest, he saw two eyes looking at him in an empty sort of fear. They were the eyes he'd seen not so long ago staring out in fear from under a trailer. It was their suspect, Harlan Lustig.

In the eyes, Sam saw a man who knew he had made all the wrong decisions. He'd been presented with choices, a whole string of them that led him to this exact moment, to be burning up in a chemical fire. The eyes acknowledged his mistakes, they displayed to Sam a recognition of the poor choices in his past. And the distorted eyes, eyes through flame, begged for a second chance.

Sam knew there wasn't a time for fooling around. It was the time to make the right choice, to do what was to be done, to quit wasting time. He was done putting things off, done staying with what was safe, with what appealed to his pride. It was time to stand by what he had said, what he had committed to do.

Sam leaped on him, pressing the jacket to Harlan's face, then shoving him headfirst into the wet grass. He kicked at him to get him to roll. And soon the flames were extinguished.

50

In the heat of a late August afternoon, the sun blazed down on the whole of Barnes County. The shadows at noon on this Sunday were just a little longer than they had been just for a month or so earlier and the corn hung heavy on their stalks, waiting for harvest, the cows were heavy with pregnant bellies. The hay in the fields awaited a cutting, lay on the ground awaiting bailing, or was strewn across fields in large round bales. And the pastures were empty of men, the kitchens of the area were busy with people preparing and eating lunch, the roads were busy with folks coming from church, and the diner in Sheridan was packed full of people giddy with their day of rest, with school starting, with the sense of harvest, with the coming changing of seasons.

Annette sat in a back booth with a view of the restaurant's patrons and the general sentiment held by all of them was nearly bursting within her. Things just felt so right for her that she could barely stand it. She had to look down at her plate of wet yolks and a half-eaten slice of toast to hide her wet eyes from her friend.

"So, your daughter made it back to St. Louis okay?"

"As far as I know."

"Think her daughter's going to be any better?"

"I did for her what I could. Got her away from her friends. Poor thing spent the last two months by my side nearly every minute."

"Maybe the fire had an effect on her."

"Mm-hmm. Maybe. It was a shock. For everyone." Without a doubt. Fire cleanses, sometimes.

"I heard that guy burnt off most of the skin on his body."

"Survived, though. Wound up in some special hospital in New York set up to treat people that burned up."

"And all that time, right there."

"Making drugs in my barn. All that time."

"At least he won't be around here anymore."

"You can say that again."

A hand reached in to grab her plate. "Can I take that for you, ma'am?"

It was the sheriff's son. "Yes, please." New haircut sure made him look better.

"And that deputy up and quit?"

"Who?"

"The one over there with his wife."

"That's right."

"I thought I heard that he was going to run for sheriff."

"Maybe he decided it was too dangerous around here."

"Seeing someone with their skin all burning up might do it."

They laughed together. Sheriff Wallis stood at the counter, shaking a man's hand. He was a good man. Just the sort of man they needed around here.

"Who's that man with the sheriff?" Annette asked.

"Frank Redbird. The one that worked on the Stegman place."

"The one that was shot?"

"Yes."

"Oh my, has he looked better."

"I guess the family finally settled with him and he got to keep the ranch."

"He was such a loyal man."

"Good for him."

It was one of the moments for Annette when everything seemed just right. It was fleeting, she knew. By the end of the day, there would likely be some horrible news of some sort, but for right now everything seemed in perfect order. Rachel had gone home to her mother and the specter of Ralph was gone forever and she had her life to herself. And everyone around her seemed happy, every face in the place seemed to hold a smile. For now. And that was enough.

ACKNOWLEDGEMENTS

Thank you to my family for always asking, "Are you writing?"

Thank you to the men and women of the Dent County, Missouri, Sheriff's Department.

Damon Garr spent his early years among the back roads of rural Missouri before growing up in Colorado, where he received an MFA from Colorado State University. He lives now outside Pittsburgh. *Barnes County* is his first novel.